BILLY HOUSTON

FALL FROM GRACE

By
GREG HOLMAN

Also by Greg Holman

BILLY HOUSTON
RAGS TO RICHES

CHAPTER 1

THERE WAS A knock on the dressing room door. Without pausing for an invitation, Larry ducked his head through the opening. "Billy, you're on in ten minutes—and there are two guys out here who say they're old friends of yours from Santa Monica."

"Show them in," I said, a big smile beaming across my face as my two best mates, Pat Gabriel and Chook Burns, walked in.

"Billy! How are you doing?" Pat asked, as he embraced me warmly, patting me on the back.

"Billy—it's great to see you, man. You're looking good! So much better than last time," Chook Burns added, smiling.

"Yeah guys, I'm feeling good. Really good. Fancy you guys coming all the way up to Seattle to hear me speak this evening?" Tears formed in my eyes, as I was overcome with emotion at seeing my two best mates for the first time in six weeks.

"We didn't get to hear you speak in New York last week—so there was no way we were going to miss your one and only appearance on the west coast," said Chook.

"I appreciate it, guys. We'll catch up after my talk. You're going to hear some shit tonight! Stuff I haven't even told you before."

"Billy," Larry strode into the dressing room, "you've got five minutes to go. We have to get down to the stage." He fussily adjusted my jacket and gave my hair one last brush.

"I'll see you guys backstage in a few hours," I called to my friends, as Larry escorted me past them, out of the dressing room, and down the corridor to the side of the stage.

"Full house tonight, Billy," Larry hissed into my ear as he led me towards the stage. "Close to a thousand people. Not as big as New York last week—but still impressive for your second speaking gig."

I said nothing, staring at the stage as we approached it.

"Go get 'em, Billy. Go get 'em, man," Larry had a big smile on his face as he placed his hand on my back—and gave me a gentle shove toward the stage.

• • •

"HI! MY NAME is Billy Houston, and this is my story."

I stood on the stage, looking out at the audience sitting in semi-darkness all around me.

"This is story that those close to me call *Billy Houston's Fall from Grace*." I spoke to the faceless listeners, barely visible with auditorium lights dimmed. "Six years ago, I had the world at my feet. I listed my company, Future Wealth, on the New York Stock Exchange for $480 million. A company I'd started eight years earlier with my best mate, Pat Gabriel—who's actually travelled all the way up from Santa Monica to hear me speak tonight."

I gestured blindly to the audience, where I believed Larry would find seats for my two friends.

"So, a big welcome to you, Pat! And to my other best mate, Chook Burns."

There was a polite ripple of applause—plus, I imagine, red cheeks from my two mates, who I'd suddenly made the center of attention. But not for long—because I continued addressing the audience:

"Ladies and gentlemen—excuse the language, but I fucked things up *badly* over the past five years. Well, in particular, the last twelve months. I lost the fortune I made—every single cent—although perhaps *lost* isn't the right word to use."

"I *gave away* my fortune because of what happened to me, and those very close to me. I know it's an old cliché, but money *can* be the root of all evil. In my case—it was. I got involved with some very dubious people—people on the dark side."

"I also lost a couple of people who were very close to me. I turned to alcohol to drown my sorrows, and I wallowed away in a personal cesspool. If it wasn't for an old work colleague, who I hadn't even seen for fifteen years, I'd probably be dead now. And the point of

3

telling you this story is that, if it can happen to me, it can happen to anyone."

"So, this is my story—and, unfortunately, it's not all pleasant. The story starts in Bangkok. Over the next three hours, I'm going to take you on my journey from there, to China, out across to Hong Kong, Cambodia, and then back to the United States of America."

"I forgot to also mention that on this journey, I was on the road to becoming an alcoholic. Some people who witnessed my behavior would say I already *was* an alcoholic. For some time, my brain depended on alcohol to function. I couldn't get through the day without alcohol. I'll come to that part a bit later in my story."

I searched for a tissue as I spoke, to wipe away the tears rolling down my cheeks. I was almost over-whelmed with emotion.

"I'll start my story three years ago—when I happened to meet up with that bloke sitting over there," I pointed vaguely in the direction of where I assumed Pat Gabriel was sitting, "at a rooftop bar called the Sky Bar, in central Bangkok."

CHAPTER 2

"WOW! YOU'RE LOOKING good, Billy. The gym is paying off!" Pat grabbed my left bicep, giving it a squeeze as he gazed around the Sky Bar. "What a cool bar, Billy. Unbelievable place."

It really was. The Sky Bar was where they'd filmed part of *The Hangover: Part Two*. We were sixty-three floors above, overlooking the city of Bangkok.

"It's called the Sky Bar for a reason—the incredible views."

I pointed toward the furthest east-facing wall, where there was a spare table and chairs.

"Let's grab a seat over there, away from the crowd."

"You're looking so good, Billy," Pat repeated, as I led him towards the table.

I chuckled, patting him on the shoulder.

"Eighteen months ago, Pat, I started using the exercise programs my team developed, and started going to the gym three times a week." I snorted. "For a bloke who's never set foot in a gym before, it was a life-changing experience. I mean, I've always run, walked and surfed—but at the gym, I did weights and muscle strengthening." I flexed my bicep in an exaggerated gesture. "For a bloke approaching fifty-three, I reckon I'm looking okay."

It had been more than twelve months since Pat and I had last seen each other in the flesh. There'd been the odd phone call, but Pat was always busy as the Chairman of Future Wealth in America—a business that was going from strength to strength.

Me? I was busy taking the world of fitness, diet and gym apparel to Southeast Asia—an untapped market of over 600 million people, with one of the highest uptakes of new Internet connections on the planet. The digital revolution had only recently hit the region, so eighteen months earlier I'd seen the opportunity to combine all these newly-adopted mobile apps with the fitness revolution I believed would start to sweep across Southeast Asia. With the enormous growth of wealth within the expanding middle class, I saw the opportunity to make some *serious* money.

And that's something I'm good at, and love to do. You see, I'm a serial entrepreneur. My specialty in the past had been the world of taxation and financial services in America, where I'd make a truckload of money. Now I saw the opportunity to make much, much more.

But first, the reunion with my old friend.

We'd reached the table now, and as we sat down, I growled: "Fucking *really* good to see you, Pat. Still can't believe you're here in the flesh."

I took a swig from what would no doubt be the first of many cold Tiger beers that night, as I planned to take Pat out on the town and show him the nightlife that Bangkok was famous for.

Ah, Bangkok—a city I'd come to thoroughly enjoy. I was now spending half my time living in Bangkok, with the other half spent at my house on the beach in Choeng Mon, a small township on the island of Koh Samui, located in the gulf of Thailand.

"So," Pat sipped his own beer. "Tell me all about this latest business venture of yours, Billy."

"You should have invested when I gave the opportunity! Back when I called you eighteen months ago, from Koh Samui."

"I remember that phone call, Billy. You called me on my cell, and you'd forgotten the time difference between LA and Koh Samui. It was after midnight in LA—and I remember your words clearly. You said: '*I've worked out the secret of building a beautiful, seamless business. You need a lot of people paying you a small sum of money each week, which is automatically deducted from their bank account and deposited into yours*'. Do you remember my reply, Billy?"

"Nah, not really."

"I said: *So, you're going to illegally hack into people's bank accounts, Billy? That's fraud and I have no intention of going to jail.*"

Pat was laughing as he uttered those words.

"Yeah, I remember now—but I've achieved it, Pat. I've built the perfect, seamless business. I literally have *millions* of people paying me a small sum of money each week, which is directly deposited into my bank accounts in Thailand and Malaysia."

"Billy, I never doubted your ability to build the business. The reason I declined to invest was because I thought if *I* didn't go along with your business idea, then you wouldn't proceed at all." Pat stared at his beer bottle thoughtfully. "Our businesses in the past have always been businesses we've built together."

"I don't understand, Pat. Why wouldn't you want me to successfully build another business? It's what I do! I'm a business builder. It's my life!"

"Billy, I saw how Future Wealth nearly killed you. All that travel across America, living in hotel rooms Monday to Friday, recruiting advisers. The crap we had to put up with those two corporate cowboys, Tom Carroll and Steve Roberts. Your brain was *fried*, Billy. I wanted you to stop chasing business success. The happiest I saw you was when you'd retired to Koh Samui and started your relationship with Chimlin— that Thai woman from Bangkok—who'd fly down each weekend to Koh Samui to be with you. You'd *finally* appeared to have found inner peace in yourself. I felt happy for you, Billy—and I was hoping for your sake that the relationship would last."

"Three failed marriages and the break up with Chimlin made me realize I'm no good at this relationship stuff, Pat."

"I think it's because you're a workaholic, Billy. You get tunnel vision and become so absorbed in building the business that you forget about the woman in your life. I admit your enterprise—your vision and drive has made both of us very wealthy, along with the fifty staff at Future Wealth who we gifted shares to. For that, I'll forever be grateful to you."

"I've known you for nearly forty years, Pat—from when I arrived at Santa Monica High School as a fourteen-year-old Australian schoolboy. Mate, we've shared many highs and lows together—but you still don't understand me, Pat. I *need* to be building businesses. If I stop building businesses, it'll mean I drop dead from boredom."

"Billy, you have many great traits—but you have two inherent flaws. The first flaw is that you're a workaholic. The second flaw is you always accept what people tell you as the truth. Oh, I'll admit we both stuffed up with Carrol, Roberts, and their cohorts—and we very nearly lost Future Wealth before the listing on Wall Street. But in Southeast Asia, you're a million miles away from home. It's a different culture and a different way of life. I've always been concerned you'd end up trusting the wrong people here in Southeast Asia and come a cropper. You're in a different jurisdiction here, with different laws, where it may be harder to right a wrong. In America, we were lucky the authorities picked things up and penalized Carroll and his cohorts. But here, Billy, it's like a jungle—where the likes of you and I don't understand the lay of the land."

"But Pat, I've done it. I've *been* successful. In the space of eighteen months, I've built a fitness, diet, and yoga business in Thailand and Malaysia. Next month, we launch in Vietnam and Singapore, followed by the

Philippines shortly after. And then the big one—China. I've *done it*, Pat, and it's been far easier and quicker than I expected."

"Well, tell me all about it, Billy. We've got all night. Another cold Tiger?" Pat called the Thai waiter over to our table. I could see tonight was going to be a big night on the drink for both of us. I had to remind myself we were both in our early fifties and couldn't party like we'd used to when we'd been in our twenties.

"Well, this is how it started," I told Pat as we waited for our fresh beers. "I met Cheyenne Holly in Choeng Mon nearly two years ago. She was backpacking around Thailand at the time. She's an Australian with a master's degree in sports science. She worked in the fitness industry as a trainer in Sydney's eastern suburbs, looking after the fitness needs of the rich and famous. She's also a qualified yoga instructor and went to India for six months to attend some famous, ancient yoga school there to further enhance her yoga skills. Cheyenne is an extremely gifted and motivated individual. I got Cheyenne on board to design the fitness and yoga apps. I could sense she had wanderlust, backpacking around the globe as a 26-year-old. I told her if she stayed with my business for three years, I'd gift her five percent of the company shares - set her traveling up for life."

"A bit like that surf company you set up, Billy— where you gifted all the key people shares, on the basis they worked for below market salary."

"Similar in that sense, Pat—but also very different. That business failed, mate. This one is a roaring success."

I opened my cell phone to our fitness apps, branded '21st Century Fitness'.

"Look at this, Pat," I showed him the apps, and explained: "While Cheyenne was designing the fitness and yoga programs, she also recruited two young, attractive Thai fitness instructors as the face of the mobile apps. One male and one female."

Pat's eyes widened. "Wow! Stunning, Billy."

"I don't mean the Thai girl, Pat! Look at what they're doing with the exercise programs. Simple, clear and easy for anyone to follow. There are three program levels: Startup, Intermediate and Advanced. We also have three yoga programs—with a male and female Thai instructor. The range of instructors has now expanded to include English, American, German and French-speaking instructors to deal with the large expat community in Thailand. In Malaysia, we have Malaysian instructors and we've also recruited local instructors in both Vietnam and Singapore for our impending launch in those countries."

"Never a dull moment with you, Billy. As I expected, the finished product is up there with the best of its kind in the world. The programs look great—but how did you get people to sign up?"

For a second, I was so into my spiel that I didn't answer.

"We've also moved into diet. We have a whole range of pre-packaged vitamins and food supplements under our brand." Then Pat's question clicked, and I repeated it to myself: "But how did I get people to sign up?"

I turned to him, leaning closer:

"For that, I've got an American expat living in Bangkok named Johnny Kean. The guy is a social media guru; an expert in Facebook, Twitter, Instagram, LinkedIn and all the rest of them. As you know, my IT skills are non-existent, but I've always been a big believer that if you surround yourself with experts in their chosen fields—providing you have the right strategy in place—you can build a very, very successful business. You know, Pat, with Facebook, we can drill right down into the demographics of each Facebook user. We've done loads of research on the characteristics of our users. With Facebook paid advertising, we can select a target market of say, females aged between 28 and 55 years of age, who live in Bangkok, and who've listed an interest in yoga on their Facebook profile. These people will receive an advertisement from our company about our revolutionary yoga app on their Facebook feed. Look here," I showed Pat one of our advertisements from Facebook on my phone.

"As you can see, Pat—we've got great images, and not too many words. I just click here where it says, '*Want more Info*' and I'm taken to our website landing page. Click here where it says '*Try out for free for 14 days*' and, once bank account details are provided through PayPal, we start deducting 20 cents every week after the initial fourteen-day trial period—unless they opt out."

I grinned.

"Believe me, Pat, ninety-nine percent of people *don't* opt out. People are lazy. Whether they use the product or not, after a few weeks it's too much hassle for them to go to the trouble of stopping the payment.

For a lot of people, what's twenty cents coming from the bank account each week—whether they continue to use the app or not? Or, they can download our app from the Apple store. All nice and simple, with a minimum of clicks required."

"So, how many users do you have so far?"

"In Thailand and Malaysia, we have over one million users across our fitness and yoga apps."

"Wow! My simple math tells me that's about $200,000 per week." Pat shook his head with a look of disbelief. "Wait, that *can't* be right."

"It *is* right, Pat. We have over $10 million of revenue every year. We'll double that again when we add Singapore, Vietnam, and the Philippines. The big one in the next two years will be China. The numbers we'll be doing there will blow your mind. On top of that, we also have the revenue from our dietary range and the gymnasiums."

"Gymnasiums? How do you get revenue from the gyms?"

"We charge a license fee for every gymnasium that uses our product—and we train their instructors on using the 21st Century Fitness programs. We currently have over two thousand instructors across Thailand and Malaysia using our programs."

"You're fucking incredible, Billy. Fucking incredible!"

"Don't call me crazy, Pat, but I'm also about to branch into our own fitness clothing label."

"Billy, tell me you're joking, man. Our last little clothing venture in the States—the Huntington Beach Surf Company—cost you over four million bucks, and me a little over two million. We both said we'd *never* get involved in clothing again."

"This is different, Pat. I've already got the people lined up to buy the clothing. Everything is branded 21st Century. I have 21st Century Fitness apps, 21st Century Yoga, 21st Century Food Supplements and the soon-to-be 21st Century Fitness Clothing. It's a sure winner, Pat. Most people using our fitness, yoga and dietary apps will buy our fitness clothing."

"Who are the key people driving the day-to-day operations, Billy? Not you, I hope. I don't want to see you get burnt out again, man."

"I made a conscious decision that after the initial six months, I didn't want to be involved in the day-to-day operations. Of course, I wanted to be involved in the strategy at a board level—but I needed someone with experience in the fitness world, with business nous to run the company. I've hired an English guy named Martin Spinkle to run the show. He was the CEO of a major group with gyms in the UK and Southeast Asia. He's been with me for twelve months—although between you and me, I'm not quite sure he's the right person to be leading the business. A bit up himself, and a bit cocky. He can be a bit of a bully—and can be pretty arrogant. At times, he reminds me of the late Steve Roberts."

"Um—if he has similar characteristics to Roberts, that's not good. We both know what a complete wanker he was."

"Agree, Pat. Here's to the late Steve Roberts—a complete fuckwit." We raised our glasses in agreement.

I continued: "Of course, as you know, I've got Dane Turnbull on the company board. I plan to undertake a listing of the business in the next three years, once we conquer the Chinese market. Not sure yet which stock exchange in Southeast Asia we'll list the business on. That's Dane's gig—to determine the right exchange. With his Wall Street background, and those years of experience working in Hong Kong, he adds a lot of expertise to our impending IPO on one of the exchanges."

"Yep, Dane's a great man, Billy. Once we sacked Carroll from the board of Future Wealth, he was instrumental in getting the institutional support from Wall Street for our company. It's been great having him on the Future Wealth board. Obviously, he doesn't tell me or the other Future Wealth board members anything about what he's doing with your business—other than flying across to Bangkok every second month for your board meetings."

"Yep, when I approached him about joining me on the 21st Century board, he didn't see any conflict by being on both my board and that of Future Wealth. His biggest concern was his availability—given he had to attend your monthly board meetings in the States *and* mine in Bangkok. I told him I'd always schedule my board meetings so they didn't clash with the Future Wealth dates. He was also a bit concerned about travelling between New York and Bangkok each month, so I agreed for him to only attend every second board meeting in person. We Skype him in for the alternate meetings—and that works really well."

I leaned back in my seat. "Unfortunately, Cheyenne resigned after twelve months working for me. She got the travel bug once again. Cheyenne did tell me about one of her lecturers at Sydney University, who she'd kept in contact with. She'd taught Cheyenne during her master's degree. Her name's Mandy Jones. I knew Cheyenne had kept in regular contact with Mandy, sharing all the great things we'd been doing at 21st Century Fitness. What I didn't know was that Cheyenne had secretly been coaching Mandy to become her ideal replacement in the company."

I explained: "Cheyenne didn't want to leave the business without having someone ready to assume her role—and she told me that Mandy was actually far more qualified in sports science than she was. Mandy has three young kids under 12 years of age, and the family has been coming to Thailand for years on holidays. Her husband looks after the kids full-time as a stay-at-home-dad, and they've always harbored an ambition to one day live and work in Thailand. So, Mandy jumped at the chance to join the company— and she, along with the husband and kids, love living in Bangkok now."

Pat continued to look impressed— but I wasn't finished yet!

"I've also got Johnny Kean running a team of social marketing experts who are crucial for our entry into Singapore, Vietnam, Indonesia, Philippines, and eventually the Chinese market. They're the means of enabling our business to sign up consumers in all these different countries. It's amazing what those guys can do on the various social media platforms. If I'd known this stuff back when we were running Future Wealth, we'd have doubled the size of the business."

I paused to have a mouthful of the beer sitting in front of me.

"Yep, it's the way of the future—all this social media marketing," Pat nodded. "You remember when we first started The Tax Refund Shop twenty years ago? It was all about newspaper advertising back then. The bigger the ads in the paper, the more phone calls our Tax Refund shops received."

"Tell me about it, Pat!" I scoffed. "Change is inevitable in every walk of life—from how we shop, how we travel, education... Everything. You can't stop change. I'm a big believer in success being determined by how well you adapt to change. If you fight change, or bury your head in the sand and ignore it, you'll be overrun by your competitors."

"Totally agree, Billy. I went to a talk at Stanford University a few weeks ago on AI, or whatever they call artificial intelligence. For the kids in schools across America today, eighty percent of the jobs they'll be doing haven't even been invented yet."

"Yep, I've been reading up on AI, Pat. Some people even suggest there may be AI human beings already among us—machines that look like and think like human beings, and we can't even tell the difference."

"Scary stuff, Billy."

Pat leaned closer.

"But tell me more about this fitness empire you're building here in Southeast Asia. Who else is helping you shape this business?"

"I've also got a couple of influencers on board. I pay them a monthly retainer."

"What the fuck are influencers, Billy? Some special Thai thing?"

"No, Pat." I laughed. "They're all the rage in digital marketing. They're people with millions of followers on social media—whether it be Facebook, Snapchat, Twitter, Instagram, or YouTube. Influencers have millions of people following everything they do. They use my products and drive traffic to my website and apps. They're who help generate new sign-ups for 21st Century Fitness. We use influencers in all our target countries. They're excellent value for money. You should be using influencers in the States with your business, Pat."

"Influencers, hey? I'll make a note of that." Pat sipped his beer. "I knew if I came here I'd take back some great ideas I could use for Future Wealth."

I continued explaining the business to him.

"Our head of Corporate Sales is Peggy Lane, an American woman residing in Bangkok who has extensive sales experience in the fitness world. There are another twenty or so local Thai people working in the business, too—in accounting, administration, IT, and support roles."

Pat narrowed his eyes. "So, my back-of-the-envelope calculations tell me that with revenue of over $10 million, this business is highly profitable, Billy."

"It is, Pat. Revenue, with the gyms included, is closer to fifteen million—with costs of less than $10 million. I own all the shares, with a few key employees set to receive shares equal to forty percent of the company once we list. That includes Cheyenne Holly. She was crucial in getting this business set up—so even though I'd stipulated she had to stay on for three years, given she'd worked so hard to find her ideal replacement in Mandy Jones, I've let her keep her five percent. She'll receive that when we finally list on the market."

"Sounds very much like Future Wealth—where we set aside twenty percent of the company for staff before we listed on Wall Street."

"Exactly the same model. I want my key executives to treat this business as their own—to put in the hard yards over the next few years, and then reap the ultimate gain by virtue of the shares they'll receive when we go public. That model worked so well for us when we listed Future Wealth on Wall Street two years ago."

Pat nodded. "It certainly did. I was actually crunching some numbers last week on Future Wealth, in preparation for our mid-year executive retreat. Of those fifty staff who received shares when we listed, forty-six are still working for the company. One unfortunately passed away, and three left to raise families. The shares have increased by thirty-seven percent since listing. They've all done well."

The Thai barmaid stepped over, and I nodded at her: "Two more Tigers, please."

Turning back to my friend, I asked: "Are you still happily married?"

Pat nodded.

"I sure am, Billy. Life is great. I'm happily married, with three beautiful kids. I enjoy my role as chairman of Future Wealth, the business is humming along nicely, there's not much stress—and the team are a dream to work with."

"Well, as they say, Pat, what happens on tour stays on tour. We'll finish these drinks and I'll take you on a tour of the nightlife here in Bangkok. It's a bit different to Santa Monica, believe me." I winked at Pat. "You like watching ping pong?"

With a wide beaming smile, Pat replied: "I'm happily married, Billy—and want to stay that way!"

"Young Pat!" I feigned taking offense. "We'll have a fun night! Nothing untoward, trust me."

"As long as we don't wake up tomorrow morning like those guys did in the first *Hangover* movie."

"Nothing like that, Pat—plus, I wouldn't even know where to find a tiger in Bangkok. Unless, of course, we went via the Bangkok zoo in the early hours." I threw him a grin.

"Onwards and upwards, Billy. Show me the sights of Bangkok. So good to be catching up with you. Just *so* good."

CHAPTER 3

IT WAS SATURDAY morning—my third day back at my house in Choeng Mon. I'd taken a few days away from the office in Bangkok, where I'd spent the previous two weeks planning for the launch of our products in Singapore, Vietnam, and the Philippines.

I was thoroughly enjoying my daily ritual in Choeng Mon, which consisted of a morning walk up and down Choeng Mon beach, followed by a paddle in the bay on my stand-up paddleboard. I was contemplating how to deal with the news my chairman, Dane Turnbull, had delivered the day before. Dane had phoned me from New York to update me on the call he'd received from the CEO of 21st Century Fitness, Martin Spinkle.

"Billy, sorry to disturb you—I know you're taking a few days off in Koh Samui. I wouldn't have called if I didn't think it was important."

"Not a worry at all, Dane. I shouldn't be saying this, but I enjoyed being hands on the last few weeks—what with steering the launch of our fitness and yoga apps into the other Asian markets. What's up?"

"I got a call from Martin Spinkle earlier today. I wasn't going to phone you until you were back on board in the Bangkok office next week, but I've stewed on it for the last few hours and decided: Stuff it, I'll call you now."

"What did Martin want?"

"He told me, on a confidential basis, that he believes Mandy Jones is planning to set up a fitness app in direct competition with ours—with Cheyenne Holly, no less. He wanted permission to undertake some investigative work—to confirm what he believes they're both up to. I immediately told him he needed to meet with you and I to elaborate further before he did anything like that."

There was a pause, before Dane added:

"Martin said he didn't want you to know anything about all this until he had concrete evidence. He said you were too close to Mandy and wouldn't believe anything adverse about her."

"He's quite right there—I wouldn't believe such fucking garbage." My tone was rather heated.

"I'm just the messenger here, Billy," Dane responded. "I don't believe it either—but I thought I should tell you."

"The truth be told, Dane, I've got my doubts about Spinkle's long-term future in our company. He has several of the traits of the late CEO of Future

Wealth, Steve Robert's—and we all know what a disaster he turned out to be."

Dane chuckled politely. I continued:

"Oh, I don't doubt Martin's ability to achieve the financial results we want for our business—I'm just concerned he might destroy the culture of the business as he does it, just like Roberts did at Future Wealth. We might find all our key executives leave the company regardless of the shares they'll get if they stay when we list on the stock exchange."

I lowered my voice as I spoke into the receiver:

"Dane, Spinkle approached me six weeks ago about wanting to employ his wife in the business—to run the administration team. He also wanted to appoint his previous right-hand man, a guy called Gary Turpin. Guess what role he wanted Gary Turpin to fill?"

I didn't give Dane a chance to answer.

"He wanted Turpin to run the sports science side of the business—to directly oversee Mandy and her team. Now, I mean, his wife *does* have many years of experience in administration, and I know Turpin has many years of experience in the fitness industry as Martin's previous side kick—but I said 'no' to both appointments. Mandy already does a fantastic job—we couldn't ask for a better person running that side of the business. She requires little, if any, management, her team loves her, and she thinks outside the box. More than that—she gets things done."

"I agree."

"Besides, Mandy and Cheyenne both love this company. They both stand to receive five percent of the shares once we list. With an anticipated listing value

23

just north of $500 million, they'd each stand to receive shares worth $25 million. Why would they jeopardize that? If they set up in competition to us, they'd never receive their shares! Ultimately, I have the right to veto any shares issued if one of the key executives leaves our company before we list on the stock exchange."

I paused, my brain racing.

"You know, Spinkle wouldn't even know Cheyenne is entitled to receive shares—given she finished before her three-year qualifying period. It was my decision, and my decision alone, to still give her those shares."

Dane was silent as I continued talking.

"Cheyenne and I have a legally-binding agreement, which was my suggestion. It basically says that she'll receive five percent of the company shares subject to just a few exclusions—for example, if she was ever to badmouth our company, or set up any type of similar business anywhere in the world; whether it be fitness, yoga apps, dietary supplements, or fitness clothing. If she did that, she'd be disqualified from receiving those shares."

21st Century Fitness was less than three years away from listing on the stock exchange.

"Cheyenne and Mandy both know what I did with Future Wealth, and what a success it was. It was a business Pat and I started eight years earlier, from scratch—and eventually we listed it on Wall Street at a value of $485 million. Those two *know* I'm an implementer. They *know* I successfully build businesses. So, does Spinkle really think they're going to start a business from scratch and make it worth more than fifty

million within three years? Mate, he's dreaming—
absolutely dreaming."

"I totally agree, Billy. Totally agree."

"Dane, last month, Pat came over to Bangkok and
we met up for a few drinks."

"A bit more than a few drinks is what Pat said,"
Dane laughed. "He told me he couldn't remember the
last few hours of that night! Said it was all a bit hazy—
and he' had a real sore head the next morning!"

"Yep, it was a big night. All harmless—just two old
mates catching up again after twelve months or so. That
night, Pat told me my biggest weakness is that I trust
people too much. I always believe what they tell me is
the truth. I never imagine anyone would lie to me."

I leaned back in my chair as I spoke.

"I look back at Future Wealth and reflect on Tom
Carroll and Steve Roberts. I should have acted earlier
and got rid of those two corporate cowboys. I should
have acted on my gut instincts. It would have saved a
lot of stress and worry. Spinkle has many of the same
traits as Roberts. He's a control freak who doesn't trust
anyone. He's got it in for both Mandy Jones and
Johnny Kean. Why? Because they are both very close to
me—perhaps the closest two."

I paused, my brow wrinkling.

"So, why is he concerned by that? Maybe because it
doesn't give him the complete power he craves. He
knows I have the ultimate power to hire and fire as the
sole shareholder."

"I do sense that, Billy. I really do."

"There's more, Dane. Whilst Spinkle may be the
CEO, I've allowed both Mandy and Johnny Kean to

wield equal power to him in their respective departments. It's how I allowed both to run their business units before I appointed Spinkle as CEO. Johnny and Mandy are both creative, talented individuals who always put the company first. If you try and control them—always looking over their shoulder—you'll first lose that creative output from them, and eventually lose them as employees entirely. When I hired Spinkle, I told him both Johnny and Mandy had complete autonomy over their respective departments. He never indicated it was an issue before—but I've slowly watched him try and exert his influence over both departments. Mandy and Johnny have both been to see me individually, expressing their frustration with Spinkle's meddling. I'm now thinking he wanted both his wife and Gary Turpin working in the business so they could be his people on the ground and report back to him—his 'yes' people. He's now pissed off that I refused his request. I think Martin craves absolute power. It's like a drug to him."

"What should we do, Billy?"

"Let me think about it over the next few days whilst I'm here in Choeng Mon. I'll be back in the Bangkok office on Thursday morning. I'll call a meeting with Spinkle for Thursday afternoon, once I've had time to gather my thoughts. I don't want to make the same mistake I did with Roberts and Carroll at Future Wealth."

"What would you have done differently there?"

"I would have sacked them both *before* they'd had a chance to destroy our company culture."

IT WAS SATURDAY night, and I was walking along Choeng Mon beach to catch up with Lars, my Norwegian friend, who'd lived in Choeng Mon for the last few years. He and his Thai girlfriend, Dao, had asked me to join them for a few quiet drinks at the beach bar. I say 'quiet' with my tongue in cheek—because there's never a quiet drink with Lars. It normally turns into a *very* late night and a big sore head the next morning.

"Billy Houston! Great to see you!" Lars welcomed me in his best Australian accent—which sounded so un-Australian it always broke me up in laughter, much to Lars' dismay. I no longer bothered reminding Lars that I'd left Australia as a fourteen-year-old schoolboy and had lived in America for thirty-six years or so, before I finally moved to Choeng Mon. He just didn't seem to get it.

Dao excitedly told me she was using my yoga and fitness apps. She said she also knew at least thirty of her friends who were using the apps too—people who'd never taken fitness seriously before. Dao and her friends had set up a WhatsApp chat group to compare the benefits of the new dietary supplements, and they couldn't wait to see the new clothing range that we had planned for release in a few weeks' time.

Through previous discussions with Lars, I already knew Dao was an avid user of our fitness programs, so I surprised her with a special gift. As she unwrapped the present, the pretty Thai burst out into tears of excitement. She now had three complete 21st Century gym outfits—something she told me would make her friends *very* jealous.

"Billy," Lars interjected, "Dao and I have some very special news to share with you—and a special favor to ask." He paused, giving me the biggest smile I'd ever seen from him. "We're getting married!"

"Congratulations!" I raised my glass of beer. "Lars and Dao! Great news." I happily congratulated them both.

But Lars wasn't finished. "Billy, I would like you to be my best man."

"Of course! It would be my honor, Lars!" I turned to the bartender. "Sam, can we please have a bottle of your best champagne? To celebrate some special news with my good friends here!" Turning back, I asked: "Is this news public yet?"

"Not yet," Lars told me, "but it will be now." He pushed back his chair. "Everyone? I have some special news to share!" He shouted across the bar, where about forty or fifty fellow drinkers were assembled—some locals, some tourists. "I'm pleased to announce my engagement to my lovely wife-to-be, Dao."

The patrons at the bar all shouted as one: "Congratulations!"

"So," I asked. "What's the date for the special day?"

"Two years' time, Billy. Dao's divorce only recently came through. She wants to wait a while between the divorce and marriage. If it were up to me, we'd get married tomorrow." Lars smiled at Dao.

"Well, two years goes by very quickly," I shrugged.

"Billy, I hope this isn't a problem, but one of Dao's bridesmaids will be Chimlin. She's one of Dao's best friends, as you know."

It had been over two years since Chimlin and I had broken up. Ours had been a long-distance romance, with Chimlin running a successful retail clothing business in Bangkok and commuting most weekends to Koh Samui so we could spend time together. Her ability to travel to Koh Samui was dependent on her ex-husband being able to look after their young daughter. Chimlin wanted me to move permanently to Bangkok so we could be together—but I didn't want to live in Bangkok. Eventually, Chimlin gave me an ultimatum: Move to Bangkok, or our relationship would have to end. After six months together, our relationship ended.

I do believe she was in love with me—but she was eleven years younger than me and, deep down, I didn't want the responsibility of raising her young daughter with her at my age. Plus, I enjoyed living in Choeng Mon at the time, far away from the rat race, and I'd had no desire to live in Bangkok.

Chimlin eventually moved back in with her German husband—but Dao had recently told me she'd separated from him again and was now single. Lars had confided in me six months earlier—after a few too many drinks—that Dao always hoped Chimlin and I would get back together.

I hadn't seen or had any contact with Chimlin since the end of our relationship.

I shrugged: "That won't be a problem at all. It'll be great to see Chimlin again. We'll always remain friends." Then, to change the subject, I proposed another toast to the lovely couple.

CHAPTER 4

"MANDY?" I ASKED down the phone. "It's unexpected to hear from you this late on a Tuesday. You sound terrible. What's wrong?"

"I've been marched, Billy. I had my work phone and computer confiscated, and I've been told I'm on 'garden leave' until Martin's completed his investigation." Mandy was sobbing inconsolably.

It was Tuesday night at 6.30pm. I wasn't due to return to the Bangkok office until Thursday.

"Just hold on, Mandy. Calm down. Take a deep breath. What do you mean you've been marched? Marched from where?"

"Marched from 21st Century. Today, at 3pm. I was having my normal weekly meeting with my team—going through which fitness apps we needed to update, reviewing all the programs, and working out the deadlines for the month. As I always do, I'd left my private cell phone on my desk. While I was in that meeting, someone opened my private cell phone and looked at my personal messages."

"Hold it there, Mandy. I find this a bit incredulous. You mean someone in our office—one of your fellow workers—deliberately opened your private cell phone?"

"Yes." Mandy continued to sob.

"Calm down, Mandy. Tell me how you know this." I was thinking how I found all this all a bit hard to believe.

"While I was running my team meeting, Martin's PA knocked on the door and told me Martin wanted to see me immediately. I could sense by the look on her face it wasn't going to be a happy meeting—not with grumpy, old Martin. I hurried down the corridor to Martin's office. He was waiting at the door for me with a stern look on his face. He asked me to sit down, then shut the door behind me."

"Carry on, Mandy. Focus on what you're about to tell me." In my head, I pictured Spinkle waiting at his office door.

"Martin produced a screen shot of a message from my private cell phone. A message I'd sent to Cheyenne Holly earlier that day."

I could now sense where this conversation was going, but I didn't want to interrupt Mandy's train of thought.

"As you know, Billy, I talk to Cheyenne at least once a week. She was one of my best students at Sydney University and I'm forever grateful to her for getting me this job at your company. You know I love my job here. My family and I love living in Thailand—it's a dream come true for us, and I'm indebted to Cheyenne for allowing this to happen. Cheyenne and I often joked that we should have set up a business like yours five years ago in Sydney. It's a joke—nothing more, nothing less. You told me last week that you expected this company to list at around $500 million in three years' time. You laughed and said Cheyenne and I would have shares worth twenty-five million bucks each. I texted Cheyenne early this afternoon with a message Martin Spinkle has completely misinterpreted."

"What did your message say?"

"It simply sad: *Cheyenne - do you reckon we'll make fifty million if you and I set up in competition to 21st Century Fitness in Australia?* My message simply reiterated what you told me last week about the amount of money our shares would be worth."

I told her: "Spinkle wouldn't even know I've given five percent of the shares to Cheyenne. He assumes she has nothing, because she didn't stay for the full three years. I told you after your six-month review that you were each going to receive five percent of the shares when we list. Only Dane and I are privy to how much each key executive will receive."

Mandy continued: "So, Martin berated me, and told me he now had documented proof that I intended to set up business with Cheyenne in competition with 21st Century Fitness. I tried to tell him that he had it all wrong—but he wouldn't listen. He wouldn't let me talk. He told me I was on indefinite leave until he'd completed an investigation. I wasn't allowed back in my office and I was escorted out of the building by him and his PA, Sue."

She exhaled loudly.

"I asked him *who* had looked at my cell—as it's a blatant breach of privacy—and he refused to answer. He just said that he now had irrefutable proof I'd been conspiring to open a new business in Australia with an ex-employee, in direct competition to 21st Century Fitness."

"This is quite unbelievable, Mandy—quite unbelievable. It's a blatant abuse of privacy."

"Billy, I had to phone my husband, Sean, to rush to the office to pick me up. I couldn't even catch public transport home—I was an emotional wreck."

Her voice trembled with emotion as she continued:

"On the drive home, I told Sean about what had happened. He was flabbergasted. As you know, Sean was a law lecturer at Sydney University before we had kids—it's where we met. Sean used to lecture third year law students, and one of the topics he covered was Privacy Law. Sean says I could sue 21st Century Fitness—your company—and Martin Spinkle for a blatant breach of privacy. Someone in the office touched my private cell phone, opened my most recent messages, and took a picture with their phone and forwarded it to Martin."

Mandy sighed.

"Billy, I don't want to sue the company. Hell, if we list in three years' time, I may well make $25 million. I *love* working for this company, and I love being part of your team."

"I'll sort this out, Mandy," I promised her. "I can't get a flight tonight from Koh Samui to Bangkok, but I'll catch the first available flight tomorrow morning and I'll be in the Bangkok office by mid-morning. You don't have to worry about Spinkle, believe me. Please don't consult lawyers yet. Let me speak to Dane and I'll sort Spinkle out."

Bloody Spinkle, I thought to myself. He wouldn't accept my decision not to hire his mate, Gary Turpin, so he went spying in Mandy's private cell phone trying to dig up dirt on her so he could get rid of her the old-fashioned way. The man was a complete fool—a psychopath! How he ever got so far in the fitness industry, I had no idea.

For the next hour, I was on the phone to Dane—who happened to be in Hong Kong on other business—working out our strategy to deal with Martin Spinkle.

"HELLO, MARTIN," I said, entering unannounced into the CEO's office at our Bangkok headquarters. I instantly noticed the look of surprise on Martin Spinkle's face. He hadn't been expecting me back into the office until tomorrow. The CEO quickly adjusted the collar on his shirt, then fidgeted with his watch. I could sense he was nervous.

"Billy! I wasn't expecting you here until tomorrow,' there was a croak in Martin's voice, revealing how he'd been surprised by my sudden appearance.

Dane Turnbull walked in thirty seconds behind me. It had been fortunate that Dane happened to be in Hong Kong on business—so he could quickly hop on a plane and be present for this very important meeting with our soon-to-be-ousted CEO.

"Martin, I've heard first-hand from Mandy about someone looking at her private cell phone yesterday, without her consent or knowledge. That same unknown person took a picture of a message on Mandy's phone and forwarded it to you. You immediately reacted to that message—*incorrectly* reacted, might I add—and jumped to completely the wrong conclusion."

Martin said nothing—looking up, wide-eyed.

"Little did you know, Martin," I warned him, "that both Mandy and Cheyenne have been individually allocated five percent of the shares of 21st Century— which Dane and I are aiming to be worth a combined fifty million when we list the company. *That* was what the message was referring to, you fucking twit." I never once raised my voice as I explained this to him.

Dane and I had agreed I'd do all the talking, while he'd be the bystander, carefully noting everything I said and any reply Spinkle gave—just in case he'd intend to legally fight what was about to be his instant dismissal.

"Martin," I demanded. "Who was your cohort in this blatant breach of Mandy's privacy? Who looked at her cell phone?" I reached forward and snatched his company cell phone from his desk.

Martin didn't answer. His face flushed red—no doubt with embarrassment at the huge mistake he was realizing he'd made.

"I've been informed by the IT team that once they examine your work cell phone—which we have a legal right to look at, unlike Mandy's *personal* phone—they can tell me who forwarded you the picture of Mandy's private message." I narrowed my eyes. "Martin, you are *not* a fit and proper person to run this company.

You're destroying the culture of this business right before my eyes. You're *immediately* dismissed."

Martin recoiled in his seat.

I continued: "If Mandy decides to take legal action against our company for this blatant breach of her privacy—which, by the way, she has every right to do—the company will sue *you* personally for damages. The person who opened Mandy's private cell phone and took the picture will also be immediately terminated, once we discover who that person is. Either you tell us now—or we'll find out shortly from IT. Your call, Martin. It doesn't really worry me either way."

Martin stood up from behind his desk. He was a powerful man—six feet, four inches tall, and lean and fit. He looked as though he'd done some form of body-building in his youth, or perhaps just taken steroids. I'd learn the truth about that in the next eighteen months or so.

Martin was obviously not going to divulge who his partner in crime was. Instead, he picked up his car keys, grabbed his jacket, and walked toward his office door. There was stony silence, which seemed to last forever.

As he paused to open the door, Martin turned—and in a booming voice, said: "I'll *destroy* you and your business, Billy Houston. I'll destroy you." His mouth moved fast, and a bit of spittle and froth leaked from his bottom lip. He slammed the door as hard as he possibly could. It was amazing the glass didn't shatter.

Within an hour, Martin's PA, Sue, had also exited the business for the last time. She took her work cell phone with her. We could only assume Martin had phoned her after his less-than-graceful exit from the office, informing her that by the close of business, Dane and I would be aware she'd been the one who'd illegally accessed Mandy's private cell phone.

All Sue had left on her desk was a large, handwritten note, all in capital letters. It read: *I QUIT THIS FUCKED-UP COMPANY. YOU CAN ALL ROT IN HELL.*

Thereafter, Dane and I met with Mandy. We were obviously very concerned, since she had every right under Employment and Privacy Laws to take legal action against 21st Century Fitness. Fortunately for us, Mandy agreed she wouldn't take the matter any further—and she was happy both Spinkle and his PA had been terminated.

It had been an eventful day—but finally, it came time for Dane and I to share a drink and recap the events of the day.

"SO, *THIS* IS the bar you and Pat started that big drinking session at last month," Dane joked.

A sense of déjà vu flooded me. Dane was right. This was exactly how last month's bender had started for me and Pat.

It was going to be a fun night, I thought to myself.

CHAPTER 5

I WAS SITTING at the bar, overlooking the ocean at Pantai Cenang. I was on the island of Langkawi, Malaysia, with the key executives of 21st Century Fitness. We'd just completed a six-hour session reviewing what we'd achieved with the business over the last couple of years, and setting our goals for the next two and half. The end goal would be listing the 21st Century Group on the Hong Kong Stock Exchange.

After much research, Dane had decided the Hong Kong Stock Exchange was the perfect exchange for us to list our company. It's the third largest stock exchange in Asia, in terms of market capitalization, behind only the Tokyo and Shanghai Stock Exchanges. Dane also had lots of contacts in Hong Kong from his years of working in the banking and investment world there—contacts who'd assist us with our listing.

That evening, we were watching the sun set over the ocean in Langkawi. It was a beautiful, red sky.

"Red at night is a shepherd's delight. Red in the morning is a shepherd's warning." I was repeating a saying I remembered from holidays with my mum and dad, back in South West Rocks, Australia. I'd been a young boy—40+ years ago.

"We're in for a beautiful day tomorrow," I smiled.

EARLIER THAT DAY, I'd opened our strategy meeting. Sitting at the table with me was Dane, the chairman of the Board, Benz Watakeekul, my Thai lawyer, and my executive team consisting of Johnny Kean, Peggy Lane, Mandy Jones and Tommy Srisuk, along with my special guest, Sammy J.

"Guys and gals, it's been a tremendous six months for 21st Century," I announced. "We've successfully launched our fitness, yoga and dietary apps in the Philippines, Vietnam, and Singapore. We'll launch in Indonesia in three months. The final piece of the jigsaw will be China. That's the icing on the cake. We'll start entering the Chinese market—first in Hong Kong in six months, then mainland China in twelve months. We'll get twelve months of operations under our belt, then we'll be ready to list."

I could see the glowing smiles on all the faces around me. *If only Pat Gabriel was in this room with me right now,* I thought to myself. He'd loved it when I'd done these little speeches for the team at Future Wealth. He'd always say: *"Billy, it's as though you have the audience in the palm of your hand—ready to charge through burning doors to follow you on the journey."*

Not a week went by during which I didn't wish Pat was involved in this business with me. We were like brothers and had known each other since we were fourteen—when we'd attended Santa Monica High School in California together.

Pat and I had taught each other a lot. For example, I'd learned to always be fully transparent with my staff across all my businesses, sharing with them the key metrics of the company. It was now time to do that once again, with the team from 21st Century.

"We've cracked a very special milestone," I announced. "Last week, we hit 2.5 million weekly users across our fitness and yoga apps. At twenty cents a pop, we now have an annual revenue of $26 million from those two segments. We're expecting to pick up another million users over the next twelve months in Indonesia. After twelve months in China, we should have added a further five million users. That will give us an annual revenue of roughly $88 million. Once we add the license fees from the gymnasiums, plus the dietary food and supplement range, we'll be nudging a $120 million in annual revenue. After expenses and company tax, our NPAT—net profit—will be $50 million."

I paused for a drink of water, before continuing:

"Ladies and gentlemen, with an NPAT of $50 million, multiplied by ten, this company should list on the Hong Kong Stock Exchange at $500 million." I wrote the figure in large, bold writing on the whiteboard behind me.

"Forty percent of this figure is shared with the executives in this room, along with a couple of other key staff in the Bangkok office. $200 million—that's the amount your shares should collectively be worth in two years' time."

"Wow," Johnny Kean shouted. "Fucking unbelievable! Fucking *unbelievable.*"

Johnny was one of those guys who included the word 'fuck' in just about every sentence. I'd repeatedly tried to let him know it might offend people. While I didn't mind him saying it in front of me, I'd told him he should perhaps tone it down when speaking to others—particularly people he'd just met for the first time, who hadn't yet had a chance to become accustomed to his robust manner.

But I wasn't about to criticize him now. Instead, I turned to him and said: "I must add, Johnny, that you and your IT social media wizards are crucial to enabling us to list. We need to get those five million Chinese people signed up."

"Not a fucking problem, Billy." Johnny grinned. "We're fucking on to it already—already fucking working on stuff twelve months out, using some of China's most popular fucking social media platforms like WeChat, Sina Weibo, Tencent QQ, along with Toudou Youku: Which is the YouTube of China. We're working on the fucking translation and graphics. It's going to be pretty fucking powerful and eye catching."

"What about Chinese influencers? Have we got them sorted?"

"We have, Billy. We're in discussions with five influencers—one of them has thirty-five million followers. Can you fucking believe that? Fucking thirty-five million followers? Unbelievable!"

"Thanks, Johnny," I grinned at his enthusiasm. "The team and I have complete faith in your artistic talents. By the way, Johnny—I counted eight 'fucks' in those seventy-five words." My team burst out in laughter. We all loved Johnny's passion—and his incredible work.

"Mandy," I started, before she interrupted me.

"Everything under control, Billy," she held up her hand to silence me. "We've already started to recruit the Chinese instructors for the fitness and yoga apps. We've changed the programs slightly, considering the Chinese cultural differences. That's something we've always done for each country we design programs for. Just a slight tweaking for each market—nothing major—but it just makes it easier to get market penetration. The programs for Indonesia are all finished, and Johnny and his team are just building the final draft of the apps. The dietary and food supplements are all finished and performing well in retail sales across all markets. We have a panel of twelve leading dieticians who've all certified the health benefits of our food, drink, and supplements. We'll have the dietary and food supplements for China finished six months before we launch in that market."

I knew both Johnny and Mandy would have already thought of everything well in advance of my questioning. That was why they were such a joy to work with—and crucial to our success. I once again thought to myself what a complete fool Martin Spinkle had been, trying to control them and look over everything they did.

Peggy gave an update on the sales of the 21st Century Fitness license to gyms in our new markets, along with a detailed overview of the research her team had already completed on the Chinese gym and fitness instructor markets.

After hearing the updates from Johnny, Mandy and Peggy, I was already thinking I'd perhaps been a bit too conservative in my estimates. Maybe this business could list closer to *$600* million.

"I'd now like to formally introduce Sammy J. to you all," I announced next, gesturing towards my special guest. "Sammy J. and I go back many, many years."

I briefly shared the story of my foray into the surf clothing game in the American, European, Canadian, Australian and New Zealand markets, some fifteen years earlier.

"I'll be fucked," Johnny leaned back in his seat. "I used to wear Shortfuse clothing all the time! Never knew you were the man behind the label."

"It's a long story, Johnny. It cost me over four million bucks in the end, and my best mate, Pat Gabriel, just over two. Ever hear about the 'tipping point' marketing concept?" With a smile on my face, I looked across to Sammy J.

"Over a few drinks tonight, Sammy J. and I will share the 'tipping point' concept—and why it cost me so much money. However, our clothing label here at

21st Century will go much, *much* better than the results I got with Shortfuse."

Sammy J. stood, and I gestured to him and Tommy, the new General Manager of our clothing label.

"Over to you, Sammy J. and Tommy—to unveil the new '21st Century Fitness Clothing' range."

Tommy was a local Thai who'd been involved in fashion in Southeast Asia for the last twenty years. Once again, I'd enlisted the services of my old mate from California, Sammy J., to sort the production side of things. Sammy had 25+ years of producing clothing in China.

The team saw samples and images of the clothing line we were producing.

"Fantastic clothes, Tommy and Sammy," Mandy clapped her hands. "Love the active wear, tights, sports bras, shorts, and tops. I want some now!"

"Me too," Peggy added.

"I'll fucking have some, too," Johnny spoke in a high-pitched voice, and we all burst out laughing.

I shared the sales projections for our clothing range with the team. We'd decided to launch across all existing markets to coincide with the launch of the fitness and yoga apps in Indonesia. We planned to repeat this same strategy when we launched in China— a launch of all products, across the entire country, all at the same time.

After breaking for lunch, the last part of our Strategy Day was an overview of the stock exchange listing process, presented by Dane. He explained the lead up work required, along with the reasons for choosing the Hong Kong Stock Exchange rather than the mainland Chinese, Japanese, or Thailand exchanges.

It was a productive, if mentally draining, six hours of strategy. I hosted these days three times a year, roughly four months apart, with the key management team. We'd always go somewhere away from the office for two days. One day of meetings, and then one day of relaxation as a team. Tomorrow, we had jet skis booked for a four-hour tour around the islands of Langkawi with our personal guide. Each of the team would have their own jet ski. Tommy, Peggy, and Mandy were a bit apprehensive about hopping straight onto one—but I reassured them there was no training required. Jet skis were easy machines to manage.

LATER, WE GATHERED in the bar at the resort in Langkawi.

Johnny, after a good twelve scotches or so, embarked on a story which he assured us was true—about a friend of his English cousin whose father had passed away. The friend's family had got hit hard with death duties. I let Johnny tell the story on the condition he didn't use one 'f' word. The bar at the resort we were drinking at was quite crowded, and I didn't want the other guests—who weren't used to Johnny's colorful use of language—to get upset.

"One 'f' word, Johnny, and I'll close you down, mate. Okay?"

"Not a problem, Billy. Not a problem." He turned to address the team. "This is a true story. My cousin's best mate's father passed away twelve months ago.

He was a very wealthy man. A retired heart specialist—one of the best in London. He'd retired seven years earlier and moved to the Caribbean. Over the course of this life, this bloke had built a large fortune and was concerned about the impact of death taxes in the UK. He told his son there was no way he was going to drop dead in England and have those thieving bastards take away half his estate in death duties."

"He was single—his wife had died a few years earlier. So, he sold all his UK assets, all his properties and shares, and became a resident of the Caribbean—and lodged his tax return each year in the Caribbean. He'd visit the UK for four months a year to see his children and grandchildren, who were all still residents of the UK. Anyway, twelve months ago, this bloke passed away in the Caribbean. In his will, he stipulated his ashes were to be spread across the Thames River in Oxford, England. It's where he'd grown up, and where he'd met his late wife. Nine years earlier, he'd spread the ashes of his wife on the same river, at the very same location he wanted his own ashes spread."

"So, the good doctor passed away in the Caribbean. His eldest son flew to there to tidy up the estate, as per his will, and gather his dad's ashes in the urn to return to England so he could spread them on the Thames. The son walked through customs with the urn, and the customs official there stopped him and asked him what was in the urn. He replied: *My father's ashes. He was living in the Caribbean for the last seven years and passed away. In his will, he stipulated he wanted his ashes spread across the Thames, in Oxford, where he'd grown up.* With that, the English authorities assessed death duties on his estate. Can you fucking believe that? He went to all that trouble to avoid death duties—but because his ashes returned to England, they bloody hit his estate with death duties. It cost the estate millions of pounds. He'd been turning over in his grave if he knew those thieving bastards got hold of his assets in the end.' Johnny rolled his eyes. "True story. I'm not kidding."

"Do you have death duties in America, Billy?' Mandy asked.

I nodded—and thought I'd better check with my American lawyer if what Johnny said could equally apply to me. I doubted what Johnny was saying was true, as I thought it might be the twelve scotches setting in. At this stage in the game, anyway, I was enjoying living in Thailand—and had no plans to return permanently to America. I liked the Thai way of life. It was so different from my American lifestyle. Sometimes, I'd even considered that perhaps, in a previous life, I might have been Thai.

I'd left everything in my will for my three children, who were all living back in America. I'd also specified that my ashes be spread in the ocean at Malibu—where I'd surfed with my old mate from California, Chook Burns. I certainly didn't want my estate to be hit with death duties when my children returned my ashes to California. *Perhaps I should have my ashes spread at Choeng Mon beach*, I thought to myself, writing a note on my cell phone to speak to my American lawyer next week.

CHAPTER 6

JOHNNY KEAN AND I were sitting in the lounge bar, at the Intercontinental Hotel in Kowloon. From there, we could gaze across Victoria Harbour and admire the sights of the Hong Kong skyline at night. It was truly a magnificent city. The light shows every night were something incredible to behold.

Three months earlier, we'd undertaken the successful launch of our complete range of products in Hong Kong—our fitness and yoga apps, along with our dietary and clothing range. Johnny and I were here to oversee things with the team we'd recruited in Hong Kong. We were off to Beijing, China tomorrow to put the finishing touches to our mainland China launch, which was only three months ahead.

"You won't believe this, Billy," Johnny told me, "but I saw the infamous Martin Spinkle this afternoon. A black limousine pulled up outside the restaurant I was having lunch at with my Chinese social media gurus. Out hopped three smart-looking Asian guys, all dressed in black suits. Then the passenger door opened, and Spinkle appeared—wearing a dark suit, sunglasses and sporting a pony-tail. Can you believe that?"

"Interesting." I narrowed my eyes. "I wonder what he's doing in town? I haven't seen or heard from him since I sacked him as CEO. He left in rather abrupt circumstances—threatening me on his way out."

"Not a nice man, Billy," Johnny nodded. "A complete tosser, if you ask me. The guys he was with looked like gangsters, not businessman. I've always wondered if the guy was taking steroids. I heard a rumor he might have been selling steroids to some of his gym junkie mates. Only a rumor, mind you—from a friend of a friend, if you catch my drift."

"I'd often wondered if he used steroids, too," I admitted. "We checked his background fully before we hired him. He was clean—no criminal record. But I agree, Johnny, he's a complete wanker—excuse my French. I should never have hired him." I turned to Johnny. "Speaking of excusing my French—I must admit, I'm pretty impressed with the way you've managed to stop using the 'f' word since we've been in Hong Kong."

"Not a problem, Billy," Johnny nodded. "I told you I'd tone down my language. I realize how important both Hong Kong and China are to our goal of listing on the stock exchange. I don't want to upset any of our Chinese friends."

The waiter approached, and I held up two fingers: "Another two cold beers, please."

"You know, Billy," Johnny continued, "did I ever tell you who Spinkle reminds me of?"

He didn't give me a chance to reply.

"In New York, six years ago, I worked for an advertising agency. It was owned by a chap in his mid-fifties, Paul White. His son in law, Steve, also worked in the business. Talk about wankers! Those two were the ultimate wankers. My wife, Suzie, also worked in the business at the time. Paul was a complete control freak. He never trusted anyone. He had his own wife and son-in-law working in the business just so they could report back to him on everything and everyone working there. It was a soul-destroying place to work, believe me. I lasted two years, but in the end, I quit."

"What made you quit?"

"This isn't one of my tall tales, Billy. This actually happened." Johnny shot me a smirk of laughter. "I shouldn't laugh, though, because at the time, it wasn't funny."

He turned in his seat to face me.

"Suzie and I had broken up six months earlier, and we'd only just got back together. We were still working together whilst we were separated, and it was all quite amicable. After we got back together, she confided in me that that while we'd been separated, she'd had an affair with a married co-worker—a guy who reported to me." When he saw the look on my face, Johnny reassured me: "It was okay. We weren't together at the time, and I'd been seeing someone else too."

"Still tough, Johnny," I admitted. "But, as you say, you were both separated at the time."

"Exactly. But what made it difficult for me once we got back together was that she'd had it off with a guy I worked with—a guy who reported directly to *me*. Maybe it's a male ego trip. You know—I can fuck around, but you can't. It took me a while to get over it."

Our beers arrived, and Johnny took a long draught.

"We were on a road show in Chicago one night," he continued his tale, "doing a big pitch to win a large new advertising account. Suzie and I—along with Paul White, and three or four others. We'd all been out for dinner that night and had a few drinks, celebrating the work we'd done with the potential new account in Chicago. We were pretty confident we'd win the account."

Pain flickered across Johnny's face as he recounted old memories.

"Suzie and I got back to our hotel room later that evening, both having consumed *way* too much alcohol. We had a heated discussion about the affair she'd had with my co-worker. I told her how tough it was for me to go to work every day and see that grub—the married guy she'd been fucking."

He took another sip of beer, to steady himself as he continued:

"She pushed me, and I pushed her back. She told me to get over it, saying we weren't even together at the time. Then, she threw her hand across the back of my head, waving me away. Her bracelet cut the back of my head. It was an accident, Billy—but it drew some blood. I angrily told her I was going back to the bar.

I didn't want to sleep in the same bed as her, so I stormed off."

I listened intently as Johnny kept talking.

"So, I popped down to the bar—and Paul White was still there, drinking all by himself. White knew about the affair. He'd told me previously the guy Suzie had been fucking was a sleaze. He apparently had a history of fucking around behind his wife's back. I told Paul about the argument Suzie and I had just had, and that now I understood how some people cross the line with their temper."

He drifted into an aside:

"In fact, just twelve months earlier, there'd been a case in New York where a guy shot his next-door neighbor dead. The shooter had been sacked from his job that afternoon, after twenty-five years working there. He came home and found his wife in bed with the next-door neighbor. Apparently, the affair with the neighbor had been going on for years. The wife wasn't expecting him home so early."

Clearly not!

"So, the husband grabbed his gun from the bedside table," Johnny continued, "and shot the neighbor in cold blood—right while he was still in bed with the man's wife. The husband was about to turn the gun on himself but the wife—fearing for her own life—grabbed the gun off him. The cops came—he got life for murder. Never had a criminal record, and the guy was a leader in the community. His four kids all testified he was a gentle man, and had never displayed any violence towards anyone. They said theirs had always been always a loving, caring household—but the man had reached a breaking point and he just snapped."

Johnny breathed out contemplatively.

"Just think—if he hadn't been sacked from his job that afternoon, he'd never known about his wife's affair, and his next-door neighbor would still be alive. The neighbor was a single parent—his wife had died a few years beforehand, and he was supporting three kids, all under fifteen. Now they don't have a father. In a matter of seconds, the life of those two families changed forever. It was absolute disaster.

Johnny leaned closer to me, and confessed:

"I remember saying to Paul White when we heard about it: *At times, we're all capable of reaching that breaking point.*"

He reached over and placed a hand on my shoulder.

"Billy, you can understand that some people just loose it—completely out of character."

"I remember that case, Johnny," I nodded. "All such a tragic set of circumstances for everyone involved." I narrowed my eyes. "How does that relate to you and your wife, in Chicago?"

Johnny nodded, and continued: "The next morning, after Suzie and I had fought, we all hopped onto a plane and headed back to New York. Suzie and I were happy, actually. Everything from the night before had been resolved. We were holding hands, smiling—laughing with the team on the way home in the plane. For the next two weeks, we were all working together in the office and everything seemed fine."

I had a sense it hadn't been fine, and waited for Johnny to explain:

"A little while later, Suzie and I had a conference to attend in Florida, along with the rest of my team. The day before we were due to fly out, White comes to my office and says: *"Johnny—you and Suzie are to stay in different rooms at the conference. You're also not allowed to ever travel together on business again after this trip."* I asked him what he meant."

Johnny's face hardened.

"White told me: *"I have to look after the safety of my employees—and given the argument you both had in Chicago, I can't allow you to stay in the same hotel room when travelling on business together."* "I replied" "You're fucking kidding! We've lived together as husband and wife for fifteen years. We have three children together. Since we've both worked for you, over the last two years, there's never been one instance of any form of abuse. No fighting or harassment between either of us."

Johnny shook his head.

"I told White: "I'd told you about the argument we had two weeks ago. You saw us the next day, all happy, behaving like a normal couple. I only talked to you about that murder case in New York to illustrate how some people can reach their breaking point." I even said to White: "I'll go grab Suzie, and you can repeat everything you've just said to me straight to her face.""

"So?" I asked. "Did you get Suzie?"

"I did, Billy— and White repeated to her what he'd told me."

"What did Suzie say?"

"She was flabbergasted—dumbfounded. She basically repeated what I'd told White: That we've lived together for fifteen years and raised three children.

Neither of us came from backgrounds with any history of domestic violence or abuse. I told White that if he was so concerned, he should've spoken to our colleagues to corroborate his accusation—which they wouldn't do."

"What a complete wanker, Johnny." I shook my head. "So, what did you do then?"

"We both resigned on the spot. I told him to take his job and stick it up his arse. I'm a big believer in karma, Billy." The corner of his lips curled. "Once I told my team we'd quit, they all resigned within the space of six months—all twenty of them. They all started looking for jobs the moment I was gone."

He leaned back against the bar.

"Initially," Johnny admitted, "I had a bit of anger toward the guy. Now, I just feel sorry for him. He's obviously a tormented soul—some would call him a psychopath. Six years later, his business is insignificant. It's just him, his wife, his daughter and son in-law working there."

"I suppose no one else can put up with him."

"Pretty sad when the only people who'll work for you are your family," Johnny nodded. "His son-in-law, Paul, was a complete tosser as well. It was a running joke among the staff wondering how he'd ever managed to keep his job. He used to pay his private expenses on his business American Express card, and he never provided receipts to the accounting department. No one knew where he was during the day. It all but destroyed the culture in the business—not a happy place to work at."

Johnny sorted bitterly. "Paul White even confided in me one afternoon, over drinks, that he couldn't trust his son-in-law—that if he didn't start providing receipts for his business expenses, he was going to take his America Express card off him. White had already reduced his son-in-law's role from full-time to part-time, and removed him as a director of the company. White told me his son-in-law was on his last chance— he was sick of having to follow him up all the time to find out where he was." Johnny then raised his glass of beer to mine. "But the irony is that the son-in-law is still working there, because no one else will! That's karma for you, Billy. Bloody karma!"

"Yep, sounds like a horrible place to work," I nodded. "You get these people in charge who have no people skills—and they try to cover their own inadequacy by controlling everything. It makes for a very sad and sorry place to work." I shook my head. "Unfortunately, the world is full of people like that. They shouldn't be bosses."

"Suzie and I often joke that if you want to turn a big business into a small business, hire Paul White to run it," Johnny laughed.

I laughed with him—and then Johnny leaned closer: "Now, tell me this story you were going to tell me, Billy—about the couple you witnessed last week in Patong."

"Ah, yes. That's a funny story, Johnny." I sipped my beer. "I thought I'd pop down to Phuket to check the place out. It's been a few years since I've been there. I was staying at a nice little resort on the beach at Kata. I had an old mate with me, who'd never been to Patong before—so we popped down there for a few drinks. We walked into this bar just after ten. It was a small bar with a pool table, about ten to twelve people drinking, and a couple of bar girls working there. We met a couple in their late fifties from South Africa. They apparently came to Patong—this same bar, in fact—every year on holiday. We were having a few drinks with them when this *other* bloke suddenly appears from nowhere. He was in his fifties, missing teeth, covered in tattoos, with long, scruffy hair. He told us he'd just woken up from a big night the previous evening. The bloke muttered a few words to us with a deep, Irish accent—and then he's gone. He just vanished. Five minutes later, he reappears—but without long hair. He's bald now, and suddenly talking in a distinguished voice with a slight Irish accent. Turns out he's the owner of the bar and his initial appearance was one of the party tricks he liked to play on first time guests like me and my mate."

"Bloody funny, Billy."

"That's not the funny part, Johnny," I grinned. "So, we start drinking with the South African guy. Nice guy. His wife is sitting across the other side of the bar having a drink, chatting to a few different people. She was quite a large lady. Her husband asked us if we wanted to play a game of doubles pool. We agreed, assuming we'd be playing against him and his wife. Instead, he pointed to the young bar girl and said: "She'll be my pool partner.""

"We started playing and I noticed him and the young bar girl getting quite friendly, with their arms around each other and him giving her the occasional kiss on the cheek. I said to him: "*Mate, I don't want to interfere, but your wife is sitting right over there. Do you think it's wise to get so friendly with the bar girl while your wife is here?*" He replied: "*Not to worry. She fully approves.*""

Johnny stared at me as I continued with the story:

"I looked across to the wife, who gave me a big smile and a thumbs up. So, for the next thirty minutes or so, we played pool with the South African guy and the young bar girl—who, at this point, was now embracing him."

I shook my head, recollecting the experience.

"I'm somewhat perplexed by what's going on," I admitted to Johnny, "so I wander over to the guy's wife—the plump, middle-aged South African woman. I say: "*So, you're okay with your husband being with that young bar girl?*"" She replies: "*I certainly am. We share her. She comes home with us every night.*""

Johnny's eyes widened—just like mine had at the time.

"I must have had a look of bewilderment on my face," I admit, "because she then adds: "*Don't worry, it's always safe sex. I have more fun in the threesome than my husband!*" With that, the three of them disappear together on the back of a motor bike. I was left standing there absolutely gobsmacked."

Johnny was staring at me, his mouth wide open. He was speechless, waiting for me to continue.

"My mate and I got talking to the owner of the bar—the Irish guy who'd played the party trick earlier," I sipped my beer. "He tells us the South African couple have been coming to his bar every year for more than five years. Every holiday, they have a different girl for the week. My mate and I spent the rest of the evening trying to visualize what went on in the bedroom between the three of them." I elbowed my mate in the ribs. "Not a pleasant thought, Johnny!"

"Fucking unbelievable, Billy! Fucking unbelievable."

"Yep, but all true, Johnny—and still quite un-believable." I sighed, leaning back against the bar. "Anyway, that's enough storytelling from each of us. Let's call it quits for tonight. We've got a big day tomorrow with that early morning flight to Beijing."

CHAPTER 7

WHILE I WAS having a big day in Beijing, my best mate, Pat Gabriel, was having a similar day in Los Angeles. I wasn't here for the encounter he later related to me, but apparently it went like this:

"Hi, Fred! Good to see you. It's been a while."

Pat Gabriel shook hands with Fred, a senior investigator from the FBI's Los Angeles office—and a member of his own family through marriage.

"Yes, it's been over four years," Fred nodded as he was welcomed into Pat's office. "Four years since you and I—along with a couple of my contemporaries at the FBI—met with officers of the Securities and Exchange Commission for that two-day think-tank about cleaning up corporate America."

"Time flies, Fred. Four years. Hard to believe."

Fred nodded: "I was only saying to Jane this weekend: We must catch up with you and Sue, along with the kids."

Small talk out of the way, Fred gestured to the other man standing in Pat's office at Future Wealth.

"Pat, let me introduce Ivan Cameron to you. Ivan works for Interpol. He's based in their Bangkok office. I was telling Ivan on the way down here how your wife is my cousin—and while we all live in LA, we're still lucky to get together more than once a year."

Pat reached out to shake Ivan's hand. "Pleased to meet you, Ivan."

Ivan nodded—but it was clearly time to get down to business.

"Do you know this man?" Ivan showed Pat a photo of a large, well-muscled, middle-aged white male.

"I don't recall ever meeting him." Pat studied the picture. "Should I know him?"

"His name is Martin Spinkle," Fred explained, adding: "He worked for your good friend, Billy Houston. Spent twelve months in Bangkok running his fitness business."

"*Now* I know who you're talking about," Pat nodded. "The English guy. Billy had him running his company—but Billy ended up sacking him. A real crazy guy from what I understand."

Pat swiveled the paper around on the tabletop.

"But I'm somewhat confused, guys. How does Billy hiring this guy lead to both the FBI *and* Interpol coming to my office?"

"What I'm about to tell you, Pat, doesn't go beyond these four walls," Fred warned. "I shouldn't even be telling *you* what this investigation is about—but given you're family, and we've known each other for over twenty years, I know I can trust you. I just can't give you the details—only the bigger picture."

Ivan grabbed Fred's arm and warned: "I'd rather not share this confidential information with Pat. Not while the investigation is still ongoing."

"Okay," Fred nodded. "It's your call, Ivan."

Pat looked worried.

"I'm totally perplexed, guys. Fred, you phoned me out-of-the-blue, two days ago, to see if you could pop around with one of your colleagues for a brief chat. I remember starting to ask you for more details, and you said it was nothing. You told me you just wanted to run a few names past me—get some understanding of my encounters with those people, if any. You've now shown me *one* picture, of a guy I've never even met before, who *used* to work for my best mate, Billy. Why the fuck would you come to see me about a guy I don't even know?"

"We can't share that information with you, Pat," Ivan apologized. "But I would like to ask you a few questions about Billy Houston, though."

"Fire away." Pat shook his head with astonishment.

"How often do you see Billy Houston?"

"Billy and I have been best mates for over forty years. He left the States and moved to Thailand about five years ago. In the space of those five years, I think I've been to Thailand about three times to catch up with Billy. He's probably been back to California twice since he left. We speak on the phone every second month or so. I'm the chairman of Future Wealth—

a business Billy and I founded about twelve years ago. Billy is still a major shareholder, so he likes to keep in contact with me to ensure his investments are going okay."

"Have you noticed any change in Billy's behavior over the last few years?" Ivan asked. "Ever since he's been living in Thailand?"

Pat snorted.

"Billy is a unique character, Ivan. He loves the thrill of building businesses. He's got a goal of listing his current venture, 21st Century Fitness, on the Hong Kong stock exchange—and, knowing Billy, I'm pretty sure he'll achieve that goal in the next twelve months or so."

Pat leaned in closer, and admitted:

"When Billy left the States five years ago, he was utterly burnt out. Burnt out from all the hard work he'd put in travelling all across America, building Future Wealth." Pat gestured around him. "If it wasn't for him, all the people in this building wouldn't have a job." He shrugged. "If he's changed, it's only that Billy's a lot more relaxed and at ease with himself since he's being living in Thailand."

"To your knowledge, does Billy take any illegal drugs?" Ivan demanded.

"Never!" Pat responded instantly. "I mean, for sure—we used to smoke a bit of pot in our teens, like all the kids in California did in our era. Billy also likes a drink or two—but that would be the extent of his drug use." Pat chuckled at the memories. Ivan wasn't laughing, though.

"Has Billy mentioned any new sources of income he's recently acquired?" He asked. "Or spoken about any luxury boats or properties he's recently purchased?"

Pat raised his hands in frustration.

"Guys, Billy is an extremely wealthy man. We both made a truckload of money when we listed this business on Wall Street. Billy made roughly $150 million. He's not exactly short of a dollar—but he doesn't display his wealth. He's never mentioned to me any luxury boats, cars, or properties since we listed Future Wealth—though he could certainly afford those luxuries. He plans to list his latest business, 21st Century Fitness, on the Hong Kong Stock Exchange for about $500 million. His share will be about $300 million—and that's after giving away $200 million worth of shares to his team."

"So, you've seen no change in Billy's behavior since he left the States?" Ivan asked.

"The only change I've seen is that he has his old zip and passion for life back." Pat smiled. "The old Billy Houston is back."

"Is Billy a law abiding, honest person?" Ivan asked.

"I'm not sure where this line of questioning is going," Pat narrowed his eyes. "He's honest, he's law abiding—hell, he's somebody you'd trust with your last dollar."

"Is he easily led astray?" Ivan.

Pat paused.

"Billy's biggest weakness is that he always believes what someone tells him to be the truth. So, does that mean he gets led astray?" Pat pursed his lips. "Maybe—

but only because of the dishonesty of other people around him."

"Thanks for your time, Pat. I have no more questions." Ivan nodded to Fred, turning to leave.

"I'm not sure I understand what this is all about." Pat shook his head, shaking hands with both Ivan and Fred.

Fred, seeing the look of confusion on Pat's face, murmured: "Sorry, Pat. As per Ivan's instructions, I can't share with you the details of this investigation. It's an Interpol matter, not FBI."

"BILLY? IT'S PAT. Can you *please* call me as soon as you get this message? It's urgent."

I listened to the voicemail. Pat sounded anxious. I knew he wasn't sure where in Southeast Asia I was at that moment—but Pat probably remembered from our previous conversation, a couple of weeks earlier, that I'd be off to both Hong Kong and Beijing at some point.

Five minutes later, Pat's cell phone would be lighting up halfway across the world, with my name on the screen. Pat answered almost instantly.

"What's up, mate? What's so urgent?"

"Billy, I've just had my cousin-in-law, Fred, here."

"Who's Fred?" I asked.

"Fred—he's Sue's cousin. He works for the FBI in LA."

"Oh, yeah! I remember him. So, what's urgent about that, mate?"

"Fred was accompanied by an Interpol agent from Thailand—a guy called Ivan. They produced a picture of the guy you sacked from your business. The pommy guy, Spinkle."

"I'm confused, Pat. Why would the FBI and Interpol come to see you about Spinkle? You've never even met him—and you're not missing out on anything by *not* having met him, believe me. The guy's a complete wanker."

"Don't worry, Billy," Pat admitted. "I'm just as confused as you are. I told him that I'd never met the guy in the picture. Ivan then started asking me all these questions about you—like, if you took drugs, if you were honest. Weird stuff. In the end, I asked them what this was all about. Fred was about to tell me—but Ivan butted in. He said the investigation had to be kept confidential."

"The investigation? What the fuck? Have you got Ivan's number? I'll give him a call to find out what this is all about."

"He didn't leave me a card, but I'll phone Fred and get his number and text it to you. Once you've spoken to him, Billy, please call me and let me know what this is all about."

"I have no idea why Interpol or the FBI would come to see you about Spinkle, or me." I sighed. "I've got to go, mate. I'm in the back of a cab in Beijing with Johnny Kean, about to go to a 10am meeting with our Chinese lawyers. Talk soon, Pat."

After I hung up, I stared into space—sitting in the back of that taxi, pondering what Pat had just told me.

"Billy, you okay?" Sitting next to me in the taxi, Johnny demanded: "Has something happened? is someone in trouble?" He was shaking my arm.

"I'm good, mate," I promised—before adding: "When and where did you say you saw Martin Spinkle a couple of days ago?"

"Outside a restaurant in Hong Kong. He got out of a stretch limousine with three Asians guys who looked like heavies. Why do you ask?"

"Oh, it's nothing," I lied. "I was just wondering to myself what the guy was up to. What he was doing in Hong Kong."

"You sure you're okay, Billy?"

"I'm good, Johnny. I'm good."

Johnny was the sort of guy who never pried into people's personal affairs. He knew if I'd wanted him to know more about the conversation he'd just overheard in the taxi, I'd share the details in my own time.

I couldn't wait to call Ivan from Interpol, though. I was hoping Pat would have his number for me as soon as possible, so I could call the guy straight after our morning meeting. I was puzzled—or, perhaps, a better term would be anxious. Why were the FBI and Interpol talking about *me*? I'd never had a criminal record, never been in trouble with the police—other than caught peeing on a policeman's foot at Santa Monica beach when I was fifteen. But even then, no formal charges had been filed for that misdemeanor.

JOHNNY KEAN AND I were sitting in a Chinese restaurant having lunch. Our meeting with the Chinese lawyers had gone well, but there were still several regulatory issues we needed to overcome before we could launch our 21st Century Fitness products in the country.

I'd filled Johnny in about my earlier telephone conversation with Pat—and the meeting he'd had with the FBI and Interpol agents, asking questions about me and Spinkle.

"You know, Billy, to me, all Chinese look alike," Johnny admitted, "but I'm pretty sure those two Chinese blokes sitting at the table behind us—about thirty yards away—were in the hotel this morning having breakfast." He paused. "They were also in the downstairs lobby of the lawyer's building when we exited from the lift forty minutes ago."

I stared at my business partner and friend.

"Don't be silly, Johnny. There are over twenty-one million people in this city. The chances of seeing the same two people at three locations over a six-hour period are a billion-to-one." I snorted. "Probably even more than that!"

I laughed, staring down at my food.

"Plus, I'm like you, Johnny. All Chinese people look alike to me. I mean, I read we all look the same to them, so it's all fair."

"I'm serious, Billy," Johnny reached over and grabbed my arm. "I've seen them three times today, I'm sure of it. The scary thing is: Each time I've seen them, they've been wearing different clothes."

"Mate, this talk of Interpol and the FBI is making you think you're a super spy."

I glanced once again at my cell phone, to see if Pat had sent me the Interpol agent's number. I was keen to get to the bottom of this. It was chewing me up inside. I must admit, it had even taken away my focus during the two-hour meeting we'd just had with the Chinese lawyers.

"Let's finish our lunch, Johnny," I tried to sound determined. "We've got to be back at the lawyer's office in forty minutes. I'll go for a pee—and I'll have an inconspicuous look at those two on my way past. Where are they sitting?"

"Behind you," Johnny nodded with his head, like the spy I'd accused him of imagining himself to be. "Last table before the exit to the toilets. About thirty yards away."

"Okay, super sleuth, I'll be back in five." I rose from the table, trying not to look at the table Johnny had pointed out, thirty yards away. I headed toward the exit for the toilets as nonchalantly as I could.

It was a large restaurant, with Chinese people everywhere—most dressed in business suits. The chatter in Chinese was loud even to me, a man who was partially deaf in one ear. I assumed they were all conducting business over lunch, idly chatting away, all trying to put together business deals. I got to the back of the restaurant and the last table before the exit to the toilets was empty. I thought to myself: *I've fallen for another one of Johnny Kean's pranks. He's set me up again, the bastard.*

After a quick pee, I returned to our table and gave Johnny a high five. I admitted: "You got me, mate. I fell for your trick."

"What do you mean you fell for my trick? I was serious, Billy."

"There's no one sitting at the back table. Its empty."

Johnny stood up to peer over the top of the large crowd. He got a good view of the back table. It was empty—I wasn't lying.

"They were there, Billy! I'm serious. They must have left when they saw you coming toward them."

I shook my head, and sighed at him: "Come on, Johnny, let's go. I think all this talk about the FBI and Interpol has gone to your head." I chuckled. "Next thing, you'll be telling me when we walk out of the lift at the lawyer's office that you see the same two people again!"

CHAPTER 8

IT HAD BEEN two weeks since I'd returned to Bangkok. Our meetings with the Chinese lawyers had gone exceptionally well. Of all the countries we'd entered, China was by far the most difficult in terms of regularity requirements. Our businesses were big users of social media—but, unfortunately for us, there was no Facebook, Twitter or Instagram in China.

Nevertheless, Johnny and his 'social media gurus', as I called them, had successfully embraced all the leading Chinese social media networks. My team, including the Chinese lawyers, had several meetings with various Chinese government agencies and had managed to get approval for all our intended social media marketing. Johnny was still in China, overseeing the build of our Chinese social media platforms.

We never saw the two Chinese people Johnny was adamant had been following us. Two people he believed he'd seen three times in three different locations, each time wearing different clothes, all within the space of six hours. Thinking of Johnny made me chuckle to myself. He was our office prankster. He always had a story to tell—and always swore he was telling the truth when sharing one of his many tall tales.

To me, it had all sounded a bit farfetched. I'd thought it was just a common example how—to us Westerners—Asians all looked the same. Just like to Asians, all Westerners look the same—other than, of course, the obvious difference between males and females.

I would later discover, though, that Johnny *had* been correct—that there had been two people following us throughout our time together in China. If we'd been more observant, we'd have also noticed being followed in Hong Kong, Bangkok and Singapore.

So, how did I discover this? A couple of days after Pat's meeting with Ivan and Fred, Pat messaged me with Ivan's contact details. Fred apparently had to get permission from Ivan to provide his phone number.

After trying to contact Ivan for five days—leaving upwards of twelve messages for him to contact me—I'd finally got him to return my call.

It must have been because of the last message I left on his cell phone.

"Ivan? It's Billy Houston here, mate. You continually fail to return my phone calls, which I can only assume is on purpose. You have the audacity to travel from Bangkok to Los Angeles to pay a surprise visit to my best mate—asking all these weird questions about me. For some reason, you didn't have the common decency to contact me directly to

ask me those same questions, which would have saved Interpol a lot of money given that you're based in Bangkok and I spend most of my time there as well. Anyway, you're aware that I published a book a few years ago—which was a best-seller. I'm sure my publisher, who is very well connected with the American press, would love to run a story across the media in America about the mysterious way Interpol has been asking questions about me. You have twenty-four hours to contact me, otherwise I'll be calling Cynthia Fleming of World Focus Publishing. One last thing Ivan—I'm not bluffing."

It worked a treat, because less than twenty hours later, I received a phone call from Ivan. Now, I was on my way to his office in downtown central Bangkok for a face-to-face meeting.

I hadn't slept at all last night in anticipation. I arrived at the foyer of his building at 9:30am sharp, ready for our 10:00am meeting. That gave me just enough time to grab a coffee to give me some energy from the sleepless night. I was looking forward to this meeting.

"MR. HOUSTON! SO pleased to meet you. I'm Ivan Cameron. Please, take a seat." Ivan gestured to the couch by the coffee table in his large, expansive office.

As I glanced around the opulent office, I figured Interpol must be making some *serious* money catching crooks. This office looked more like the bureau of an interior designer rather than that of an employee of a government agency.

"You can call me Billy," I said coolly, before asking: "Tell me: Is it Ivan 'The Terrible'? Or Ivan 'The Great'?"

"Neither, Billy," he replied with a smile. "Just Ivan. Ivan Cameron."

"Well, Ivan," I smiled coolly back. "Let's get down to business. What's going on? Why does Interpol travel to Los Angeles and engage the FBI to ask my best mate, Pat Gabriel, questions about me?"

"Billy. Firstly, I apologize for not returning your calls over the last week. I just needed to tie up a few loose ends of our investigation before I could arrange to contact you for a meeting. I've now tied up all those loose ends, so I can share in *general* terms why I travelled to LA—and why I was asking questions about you in the first place."

"Investigation? You're kidding me, mate. Enlighten me, Ivan—I'm intrigued."

"Interpol has had Martin Spinkle under surveillance for the last couple of months. We now know that Spinkle was supplying steroids through many of the gyms your company was selling fitness programs to. We suspect he's now in cohorts with a local Thai bikie gang, who supply narcotics through some of the gyms—plus various street gangs in Bangkok."

"You're kidding me! Are we talking about the same Martin Spinkle? Who I sacked from my business because he was basically incompetent? The guy is a wanker!"

"This is the Martin Spinkle we have under investigation." Ivan produced a large headshot of Spinkle.

"Yep, that's him," I peered at the picture. "That's Spinkle."

"Because Spinkle worked for you, we needed to undertake an investigation to ensure you weren't also involved. We're aware of the massive distribution network you've built up with gyms in Thailand, Singapore, Malaysia, Indonesia, and now, Hong Kong. We understand you have plans to set up distribution of your fitness programs in China. We weren't sure if you were the mastermind behind the supply of steroids— and now narcotics—through all these gyms in Southeast Asia."

"Me? The mastermind?" I laughed bitterly. "You've got to be kidding. You should've just come to see me in the first place and saved yourself a lot of time and effort."

"We had to go through a process, Billy, before we could be satisfied that you weren't involved."

The memory of what Johnny Kean thought he'd seen in China two weeks ago came flooding back: The two people he'd seen three times in the space of six hours.

"Have you had people following me?" I asked.

"Yes, we have," Ivan admitted with a slight chuckle. "We've had people watching you in Bangkok, Hong Kong, Singapore and China. Different agents in each location."

He saw my expression harden, and continued:

"Unfortunately, our Chinese agents weren't as effective as those in Bangkok and Hong Kong. When you were heading to the toilet behind their table, they sensed their cover was blown and took off before you could get close to where they'd been sitting."

"Yep, the table was empty when I got there. I assumed Johnny was just playing a prank on me."

"Spinkle was in Hong Kong when you were there a few weeks ago. Up until that moment, we believed you were the Mr. Big and were there because you'd organized a rendezvous with Spinkle. We're still uncertain as to who or which group is behind selling the narcotics." Ivan stepped closer. "Billy—could you ever imagine Spinkle being a drug dealer?"

"Never ever in my wildest dreams," I admitted. "Sprinkle's a fool—a power-driven psychopath who I had to sack. I thought he might have been a steroid user, but I never thought he'd turn into a drug dealer."

"I'm very sorry, Billy, for any stress and worry we've caused you. We just needed to conclude some further investigations about you. We became aware of Pat Gabriel's connection to one of our FBI colleagues, and since I already had some other business to attend to in the States, I made the trip to Los Angeles to see him."

"So, what happens now?" I asked.

"You're free to leave this building, Billy. As far as we're concerned, you're clean—and not under any further form of investigation. Spinkle is under twenty-four-hour surveillance. He'd been in Hong Kong for the last two weeks—only yesterday, he flew to Phnom Penh, in Cambodia. He's been associating with some known criminals in Hong Kong and we believe his trip to Cambodia may be to meet the Mr. Big of the operations."

"Can't you tap his cell phone conversations? Or bug his hotel room? I see that happening all the time in the movies."

"Easier said than done, Billy. The people Spinkle is working with are very professional. They sweep his hotel room twice a day looking for bugs. Different drivers pick him up for his meetings—and even Spinkle is unaware where he's going for each meeting. We need to be *very* careful with any surveillance to ensure we're not discovered. If the people Spinkle is working with became aware he was under surveillance, they'd most likely kill him and dispose of his body where we'd never find it."

"This is pretty scary stuff, Ivan."

"These are dangerous, ruthless drug lords, Billy. Human life is irrelevant to them. That's why they have no hesitation in killing whoever they need to, in order to protect their business dealings."

"You know, Ivan, Spinkle threatened me after I sacked him. He told me he was going to destroy both me and my business."

"Spinkle is mixing with very dangerous people. I don't imagine there's any immediate danger to you, as the operations have now gone beyond supplying steroids through gyms. Just in case, here's my card with my direct number. If you sense any danger, don't hesitate to contact me—no matter where in the world you might be. I can dispatch an agent in just about any country in the world."

"Appreciate our chat, Ivan. Got to go." I stood up to shake his hand.

"One more thing, Billy," Ivan warned. "Please don't tell anyone about our conversation today. Not even your best mate, Pat Gabriel. We don't want our operation compromised in any way."

Two weeks later, Ivan and I would catch up for dinner.

"THANKS FOR THE dinner invite, Ivan. Any more news on Spinkle?"

"I can't say too much about our investigation, Billy. It's all highly confidential—plus, potentially very dangerous for you if you knew too much. These are very ruthless people Spinkle is mixed up with."

Ivan leaned toward me.

"I can share one update with you, though. Spinkle spent two days in Cambodia. We believe he was there to meet with the Mr. Big of the organization—who we now believe comes from Burma. Their headquarters are located there as well."

"So, you followed Spinkle in Cambodia and found Mr. Big?"

"Not exactly, Billy. We have no agents in Cambodia, so I had a couple of my men from here in Bangkok fly to Cambodia to follow Spinkle. Unfortunately, we lost Sprinkle's vehicle in heavy traffic in Phnom Penh. We only located him again at immigration, when he was leaving the country two days later. We're getting closer to Mr. Big—but our investigations require more work."

Ivan then turned and signaled a waiter.

"But enough about Spinkle, Billy. I thought to myself—given the stress and worry I caused you and your friend Mr. Gabriel, by appearing unannounced in Los Angeles a few weeks ago—the least I could do was to buy you dinner. Once again, I offer my sincere apologies for the unconventional way I tried to glean information about you."

"Apologies accepted, Ivan."

"Since I last met you, Billy, I've read your book. A truly fascinating story. Your book finishes with you living at Choeng Mon. No mention of your plans for the fitness world—though you must have had that business well underway whilst you were still writing the book. Or am I wrong in assuming that?"

"No, you're correct, Ivan. This business was well underway while I was writing the book. In fact, much to my publisher's dismay, I ceased working on the book for six months because my life got consumed by the money-making possibilities of my fitness ideas for Southeast Asia. My publishing agent nearly lost her job because of me. There were two weeks to go, and I'd only completed twenty-thousand words—less than one third of the book. Gloria, my publishing agent, told me if I didn't have the manuscript finalized within the next fourteen days, she'd be fired for backing me in the first place. Her managing director had it in for her. So, I dropped everything and feverishly typed away for the next fourteen days, to finish roughly sixty-thousand words. It ended up saving Gloria's career at World Wide Publishing."

"But why no mention of the fitness business? Or is that going to be in book two?"

"There's no book two, Ivan," I shook my head, chuckling softly. "I realized the enormous opportunity with my fitness idea in Southeast Asia. I didn't include that idea in the book because I didn't want anyone to steal it."

"I'm fascinated about 21st Century Fitness," Ivan admitted. "Mr Gabriel mentioned you had plans to list the business on the Hong Kong Stock Exchange for $500 million. That's a truly remarkable feat, Billy. Can you share the story of the business?"

I laughed. "It's really a pretty boring story, Ivan. Just a lot of hard work by me and some great people I have working with me."

"I'd love to hear the story, *and* the journey. In my life, Billy, I never get to meet entrepreneurs or business builders like you. I'm normally chasing crooks—most of whom are involved in drugs and money laundering. I don't get to meet successful businesspeople—who make a living an honest way, without lying and cheating and, at times, killing each other."

I leaned closer to the Interpol agent. "Well, I'm a big believer, Ivan, that to be successful in business, you need to focus on a few key things: Firstly, you need the right strategy. Secondly, you must be able to implement your strategy—there are plenty of people in the world who are smarter than me and who have great ideas. They'll just never become successful because they can't *implement* those ideas. They're what I call *dreamers*—and believe me, Ivan, there are plenty of dreamers in this world. I reckon it's five percent strategy and ninety-five percent implementation."

I started really getting into the subject.

"To have a truly great business, Ivan, it must have three, key pillars. Your business must have *systems*, it must have *processes*, and it must be able to be *easily leveraged*."

For the next ninety minutes, I took Ivan on the journey of 21st Century Fitness—all the way from its inception just over four years ago, to where we were today. He was feverishly writing down notes while I was talking.

"And so, Billy," Ivan eventually asked, "you plan to list the business on the Hong Kong Stock Exchange once you have your fitness and yoga apps—along with the dietary food, supplements, and clothing—all established in China. And, of course, the gyms..." He was pretty much repeating what I'd just told him.

"Correct, Ivan. $500 million will be the value of the company once we list."

"A truly remarkable achievement, Billy. I congratulate you on your vision and hard work." He paused. "And who are the shareholders, Billy? Who else gets to share in this wonderful achievement?"

"My private company is the sole shareholder. I plan to give away forty percent of the company to several of my key staff the day before we list. It's a way of motivating people who are crucial to the success of the business *and* the listing on the stock exchange. I'm a big believer that its best to have a small piece of a big pie, rather than a big piece of a small pie."

"Wow! That's a lot of money for those people, Billy. Money I, as a humble agent, could only dream of."

"Ivan, without their involvement, I couldn't have built this business—so, the shares the key staff will receive motivates them to work harder and smarter to fulfil our goal. When we list on the exchange, it'll be a win for me and a win for them."

"I'm not skilled in business matters, Billy, so, excuse my ignorance—but how do you give the shares to the staff?"

"It's a fairly simple and easy process, Ivan. My company is the sole shareholder of 21st Century Fitness. I'm the sole director of the company. It simply requires my signature on the share transfer document and the shares are transferred. I have ten key staff who'll be receiving shares, so I sign ten share transfer forms. A stroke of the pen by me and it's all completed."

"Wow, just like that?" Ivan leaned back in his seat. "A truly remarkable business you've built. Your life is so different to mine, Billy. I'm a humble agent. I started life as a Thai policeman before managing to fulfil my lifetime goal of working for Interpol. The money you talk about is mind-boggling to me. I only get paid enough to live week to week. My wage covers the bills and leaves only a little bit more to look after my elderly mother and support my sister and her three, young children."

This talk of money—or, rather, our very different relationship to it—started to make me uncomfortable.

"Gee, look at the time, Ivan," I glanced at my watch. "It's after eleven. I need to go—I've got an early morning flight to Koh Samui tomorrow. A friend of mine, Lars, is getting married on Saturday. Tomorrow night is his buck's party. A brave man having a buck's party on the Friday before his wedding, right?"

Ivan and I bid each other farewell. In the cab back to the hotel, I thought about what a nice guy Ivan was.

A man who fought crime throughout Southeast Asia—perhaps at times risking his own life as he tried to make the world a better place. He had a tough life—working hard for no great financial reward *and* having to support his elderly mother as well as his sister and her three, young children. Yep, I decided he was 'Ivan the Great', not 'Ivan the Terrible'. It's sometimes funny how first impressions can be so wrong.

CHAPTER 9

"NERVOUS?" I ASKED Lars as we stood waiting for the arrival of Dao, Lars' bride-to-be.

"No, not nervous at all, Billy. I'm the luckiest man in the world. I'm truly in love, Billy."

Lars and Dao were having a traditional Thai wedding. It was my first time attending a Thai wedding ceremony, and only the second time I'd been best man at someone's wedding. The first time was at Pat's wedding to Sue, back in Santa Monica, California—and that was nearly thirty years ago. It had been a traditional American-style, Catholic wedding ceremony.

"How's the head, Billy?" Lars asked.

"Not good, mate, not good," I grinned. "We didn't get home until after 3am. How are *you* feeling?"

"Ah, not good, Billy. My head is throbbing."

"I can't believe you decided on having the buck's party the night before the wedding. Whose stupid idea was that?"

"It was Dao's! She didn't want me to drink too much, and didn't want me to get into any trouble at my buck's party. She thought if I had my buck's party the night before the wedding, it would stop me drinking too much."

"Well, that didn't work out very well, did it?" I laughed. "You were blind drunk, Lars. Actually, the drunkest I've ever seen you!"

"Tell me, Billy, that I only dreamt it and it didn't really happen."

"What didn't happen, Lars? What are you talking about?" We were both whispering, so no one else could hear us talk while we waited for Dao and the bridal party to arrive.

"The girl, Billy! The girl."

"Oh, you mean the stripper?" I chuckled. "Lars, it *did* happen, mate. You wanted to bring her to the wedding with you!"

I shook my head.

"Believe me, Lars—if you bought her here today, Dao would *not* be marrying you. But in my country, there's an old saying: "W*hat happens on tour stays on tour.*" So, mate—nothing more will ever be said about what happened between you and the stripper."

"The last hour is such a blur, Billy. I didn't sleep with her, did I?" Lars had a worried look on his face.

"No, mate, you didn't sleep with her. Just a kiss and a cuddle," I grinned. Then I nudged him in the ribs with my elbow. "Quiet, Lars. Here comes Dao. Mate, she looks sensational."

I took a deep breath as Chimlin and I made eye contact for the first time in over four years.

Wow. I'd told myself four years ago I would never, *ever* see Chimlin again—and yet here we were, about to come face-to-face, standing within four feet of each other as Lars and Dao exchanged their marriage vows.

As she stepped up beside me, Chimlin smiled and whispered: "Hi, Billy. How are you?"

I smiled back. I was feeling dizzy. I think it was the effect of the alcohol from the night before, along with the feeling of unease at seeing Chimlin after all these years.

LARS AND DAO'S wedding went off without a hitch. It was a magical setting, with seventy guests mingling beneath the roof of the marquee set up specially for the wedding on Choeng Mon beach. The sun, setting gently across the ocean, generated a lovely pink sunset.

"A magical sunset for a magical couple." I muttered my first words to Chimlin since her initial whisper to me ninety minutes earlier.

"Hi Billy." She brushed a lock of hair from her face. "I've been so nervous seeing you. It's been such a long time."

"No need to be nervous, Chimlin. Well, to tell you the truth, I've actually been a bit nervous myself." Both of us burst out laughing.

The ice broken, I continued: "I never expected to see you again, Chimlin. I thought when you decided to finish our relationship, we were gone from each other's lives forever."

She looked sad for a moment.

"Billy, I couldn't carry on the way we were. It wasn't fair to me. I couldn't do this long-distance romance any longer. I wanted us to be together forever—but it was too difficult getting down to Koh Samui every week from Bangkok, especially while trying to run my business and look after my daughter. If my ex-husband couldn't look after my daughter, it sometimes meant I couldn't see you for two weeks. It was driving me crazy! So, I thought the simple solution was for you to come to Bangkok and live with me. There was nothing stopping you! You were writing your book, and you could have done that from anywhere in the world. When you said no, I realized that you didn't *really* love me. So, as much as it hurt me, I had to finish our relationship."

"Yes," I sighed bitterly. "Perhaps I *should* have come to Bangkok to live with you. Hindsight's a wonderful thing, Chimlin."

"I read your book, Billy—the story about your life. There were lots of things in the book I never knew about you. I didn't know anything about you being expelled from Santa Monica High. I didn't know about the car accident. I never asked where you got the scars on your face from—I just assumed it was a fight, or something. I never knew about the armed hold up, or the accounting franchise in America, or the clothing company. The only thing I knew was what you'd told me about Future Wealth. You're a man of many secrets, Billy Houston."

"Those things happened a long time ago," I told Chimlin. "I don't dwell on them. It was only because I had the book contract that I wrote my life story."

Chimlin told me a little of her life.

"I meet with Dao a lot—and sometimes, of course, with Lars. They shared with me what's been happening with your latest fitness business. I use your fitness apps at least twice a week, as well as the yoga app. I really enjoy them. Dao tells me you now spend most of your time living in Bangkok." She smiled. "Perhaps you should have moved with me to Bangkok four years ago, Billy?"

I looked at that smile—one I'd thought about many times over the last four years.

I sighed.

"We have an eleven-year age difference, Chimlin—plus, I'm too old to look after Kiah. She must be what, six-years-old now?"

"Yes," Chimlin nodded. "She turns seven in six months. I didn't expect you to become her father, Billy. She *has* a father. I also didn't expect you to look after her. That's my responsibility. I just thought she could live with us most of the time—and perhaps spend the weekends with her father."

I crossed my arms.

"I heard you got back with your husband shortly after our relationship finished." I said that knowing Chimlin had since separated from her husband once again.

"Yes," she nodded. "We got back together—but it didn't work out. Within two months, we were sleeping in different rooms. We agreed to share the same house for the benefit of our daughter. Eventually, we agreed he should move out—so now it's just me and Kiah again."

A new song came on, and I extended my hand.

"You want to dance, Chimlin?"

"Of course, Billy. Let's go." Chimlin grabbed my hand and led me to the dance floor.

As we started to move together, in time to the music, Chimlin murmured: "Remember, Billy, when we used to go to the nightclub in Chaweng? We used to dance like this most Saturday nights after going out for dinner."

"How could I forget, Chimlin?" The memories flooded back as we embraced, slowly dancing to the three-piece band. The smell of Chimlin's perfume was so familiar after all these years apart.

"It's been so long ago, Billy—but just holding each other again, it seems like yesterday. Isn't that weird?"

"Yes," I murmured in Chimlin's ear, thinking to myself that perhaps I should've moved to Bangkok to live with her—especially since I now spent most of my life there.

There was a loud clap, and the singing of a traditional Thai wedding song began. It now was the time for Lars and Dao to leave for their honeymoon.

After the bride and groom left the wedding, Chimlin whispered: "Billy let's go for a walk along Choeng Mon beach like we used to. It's a full moon. There's plenty of light."

"Okay, I'll just grab some drinks for us to take. Back in one minute."

Sixty seconds later, we started walking along the beach. Fifteen seconds after that, Chimlin grabbed my hand and said: "I want this walk to be like old times, Billy Houston."

I turned and looked into her eyes as she continued talking:

"Tell me about what you've been doing since we broke up, Billy. Tell me all about 21st Century Fitness and your plans for the future."

By that time, we'd reached the western end of Choeng Mon beach. We sat down on the dry, soft sand next to each other. I spent the next thirty minutes giving Chimlin a brief overview of the business. I left out the part about Martin Spinkle and Ivan Cameron.

It was then that Chimlin leaned over and started kissing me. I didn't know where this was going to lead—I wasn't sure if I wanted to rekindle our relationship. My heart told me to go for it, but my head told me: *"Billy, you have a bad track record with relationships. Three failed marriages and one failed relationship with Chimlin."*

That night, my heart won over my head. I wasn't sure if that was a good thing or a bad thing.

Afterward, as we walked back along the beach, Chimlin turned to me and asked: "Billy? Why don't we try getting back together? Not living together—but just seeing each other, like we used to. This time, it's easier—given how you now spend so much time in Bangkok."

I took a deep breath.

"Chimlin, I just have so much on my plate now. We're weeks away from entering the Chinese market, then in just over twelve months—fingers crossed—we should be able to list our company on the Hong Kong Stock Exchange. I've just got so much hard work ahead of me. If we get back together now, Chimlin, I won't be able to give you the attention you deserve—and I can't lose my business focus now. It wouldn't be fair to my key staff, who helped me get this business to the stage it's at right now."

I sighed.

"It's been like a marathon. Lots and lots of hard work, by lots of people. We're just on the last lap, with the finishing post in sight. I can't be distracted now. We're so close to achieving our goal."

Chimlin let go of my hand. She had tears streaming down her face. I didn't know whether to embrace her or give her space. I didn't know what to say.

I moved my hand to her waist, to hold her, but she quickly brushed my hand away.

"Billy, you have a problem," Chimlin hissed. "Whenever people try to get close to you, you push them away. You're fighting something," she stabbed her finger at my heart, "in *here*."

She wiped tears from her eyes.

"I love you, Billy. Every day for the last four years, I've thought about you. I cried myself to sleep every night for three months after we last broke up. I've been *so* looking forward to seeing you tonight—ever since Lars and Dao announced their wedding date. I've been hoping and hoping that tonight we could get back together."

She snorted bitterly.

"But I'm facing the same problem as four years ago: You don't love me, Billy. If you loved me like I love you, you'd say: "*Yes! Let's get back together!*""

She took a step away from me.

"I can't go on hurting inside, Billy. It's too painful." And, with that, Chimlin gave me a peck on the cheek. With tears running down her face, she murmured: "See you later, Billy Houston."

Chimlin walked away—but then stopped after five paces. Turning around, she said: "Billy, you only ever think about yourself."

"Farewell, Chimlin," I muttered. "I love you." But, by then, she was too far away to hear me.

I stood there, and wondered if perhaps Chimlin was right. Perhaps the problem was me. I remembered the words Pat had spoken to me, nearly two years ago when we'd met up at the Sky Bar in Bangkok: "*The happiest I ever saw you was when you'd retired to Koh Samui and started your relationship with Chimlin. She'd fly down each weekend to Koh Samui to be with you, and you finally seemed to have found inner peace with yourself. I felt happy for you, Billy—and I was hoping for your sake that the relationship would last.*"

I didn't know it at the time—but in ten months, my path would cross that of Chimlin once again, only under circumstances I'd never have imagined in my wildest dreams.

CHAPTER 10

THE CHAMPAGNE CORKS popped as the team from 21st Century Fitness celebrated our successful foray into mainland China.

It was just one month after our initial launch—and we already had over a million Chinese users of our fitness and yoga apps. Our target was five million users by the time we listed on the Hong Kong Stock Exchange, in eleven months.

I'd booked a private function room at the Bangkok Hilton for tonight's celebration. All the Bangkok staff were in attendance—and I'd also flown in another thirty-three members of staff from our offices in Malaysia, Vietnam, Singapore, Indonesia, Philippines, Hong Kong and, of course, China.

Along with our Thai bankers, lawyers, accountants, and some government dignitaries, there were over a hundred people in attendance at tonight's function.

Dane whispered in my ear: "Probably time for your speech, Billy, the way some of these people are drinking. If you leave it much longer, they may not be in a fit state to remember what you say!"

I shook my head, so Dane then added: "I'm joking, Billy, but it probably is time to share the good news with everyone."

"I'll go and get mic'd up Dane, then I'll start."

I looked up and saw Pat Gabriel enter the room, followed by Cynthia Fleming—the woman who'd published my first novel, my life story, some four years earlier. With a wave to both, I accepted that it was now time for me to say a few words and formally open tonight's proceedings.

"WELCOME TO TONIGHT'S celebrations," I announced to the assembled team, my voice amplified by the mic I was now wearing. "Just over four years ago, I saw an opportunity to take the world of fitness, diet, and gym apparel to Southeast Asia—a market of over six hundred million people, with one of the highest uptakes of new Internet connections on the planet. I sensed the digital revolution was about to hit the area, and I saw an opportunity to combine mobile apps with the fitness revolution I believed would soon sweep across Southeast Asia."

The entire room was watching and listening, so I continued:

"They say: In life, if you're in the right place at the right time, magical things can happen. Four years ago, I was in a bar in Choeng Mon talking to my Norwegian friend, Lars, about my business idea. Lars said I should talk to a young Australian girl who was working across the road—a woman with a master's degree in sports science. That young woman was Cheyenne Holly—and with Cheyenne's assistance, we created mobile fitness and yoga apps. Cheyenne was crucial to the launch of my business, because I wasn't sure, back then, that I could turn my dream into reality. So, a big thank you to Lars for introducing me to Cheyenne."

I waved to both Lars and his new wife, Dao. Then I turned to Cheyenne.

"And a big thank you to Cheyenne—because, without your assistance, I might have given up."

Pat Gabriel yelled from the back of the room: "You never give up, Billy! I'm sure you would've kept on going anyway." As people turned to him, he added: "I know you too well, Billy Houston".

Several people were laughing and nodding in agreement with Pat's comments.

"Yes. So true, Pat—I'd never have given up," I admitted. "But there are many people who've been part of this journey over the last two years... Three years... Four years..." I looked at the faces of those key people as I told them: "Your contribution to our success is incalculable. Your efforts, your knowledge, your work ethic, your skills... They've got us to where we are today. Without you, I wouldn't be standing here this evening."

I could see the look on Pat's face as he listened to me talk. I'd made speeches just like this one on numerous occasions for employees of our previous businesses: The Tax Refund Shop and Future Wealth. The look he was giving me now was the same look he'd given me back then; when he'd known I had the whole team hanging on my words, ready to run through burning doors.

"Yesterday," I continued, "we concluded our first month of operations in China—our final frontier. I'm pleased to say we hit one million Chinese users across our fitness and yoga apps—at 3:15pm, Chinese time, to be precise."

There was a resounding cheer across the crowd of eager faces. I heard an 'f' word uttered—and could only assume it had been spoken by Johnny Kean.

"We're now slightly ahead of our sales target in China," I grinned happily, "and we're tracking to budget in all our other Southeast Asian markets. In eleven months, we'll formally list the 21st Century Group on the Hong Kong Stock Exchange at a value of $500 million—give or take a few million."

At that news, there was a thunderous reception from all in attendance.

"Finally, there are two people I must single out and pay special thanks to," I gestured to two figures among the crowd. "Their expertise has been crucial to getting this far. Firstly, Mandy Jones—a woman who used to lecture Cheyenne Holly whilst she was completing her master's degree at Sydney University. Mandy moved her entire family from Sydney to Bangkok to take over from Cheyenne. She's the brains behind our fitness and yoga apps—continually developing and refining them for each of our markets."

Mandy received applause.

"The second person I must single out is Johnny Kean. We can have the greatest products on the market—but they're no good to our company unless someone buys them. Johnny and his team of fellow tech-heads have mastered social media, enabling us to sign new people up daily throughout Southeast Asia. The Chinese market was far more difficult for us to enter—as we had to use *their* social media platforms, which weren't familiar to us. Thank you, Johnny—and thanks to your team for a phenomenal effort."

There was further applause. I waited for it to die down before continuing.

"If I might just say some final words: Tonight's celebration is a way of me thanking everyone for their efforts so far—but we're not there yet. We still have eleven tough months ahead of us before reaching our goal and listing on the stock exchange. Let your hair down tonight, enjoy the festivities, and we'll be back at it tomorrow. Thank you."

"GOOD SPEECH, BILLY. It brought back so many memories." Pat cornered me as I removed my mic.

"How are you, mate?" I grinned at him. "I really appreciate you flying all the way from the States to celebrate this with me."

"I wouldn't miss it for anything. I owe you so much, Billy. If you hadn't asked me to join The Tax Refund Shop twenty-five years ago, I'm sure I'd still be slaving away as a lawyer." He laughed. "And probably *still* not being considered as partnership material."

Cynthia was standing beside him, so I gave her a peck on the cheek.

"Great to see you, too, Cynthia."

She grinned. "When I got your phone call last week, inviting me to come to Bangkok to celebrate with you, I knew I had to hop on a plane and get here. It's just about four years to the day since we last spoke, Billy."

I shook my head, amazed at how long it had been.

"I remember the last time I saw you, Cynthia. We had lunch at my favorite restaurant in Choeng Mon—celebrating the launch of my first ever novel."

"You nearly gave me a heart attack, Billy," she grinned. "We had less than fourteen days until the deadline and I hadn't even seen your manuscript—*and* you weren't returning my phone calls!"

"Your managing director was threatening to sack you!" I added.

Cynthia leaned forward. "You said to me over lunch in Choeng Mon, Billy, that this business was going to be bigger than Future Wealth—and you were right. It's bigger, listing at $500 million. I take my hat off to you, Billy. You just never stop building businesses. You're the textbook serial entrepreneur."

"It keeps me young, Cynthia." I smiled.

"You don't have another book you want to write, do you? The story of 21st Century Fitness?" Cynthia handed me her business card with a smirk.

I laughed. "No, Cynthia—my book writing days are over. That was a one-off." Nevertheless, I took a moment to examine her business card. "Managing Director of World Focus Publishing? Well done!"

"Yep," she grinned. "The previous managing director got the sack when your book was a success. Not sure if you remember, but he'd bad-mouthed me for months leading up to publication—telling everyone what a fool I was ever getting World Focus Publishing involved in a deal with you. Six months later, they appointed me managing director."

Pat interrupted us with a grin. "Chook Burns is on a flight over tonight. He'll be around for the weekend, so the three of us can catch up just like old times."

Pat Gabriel, Chook Burns, and I always caught up on the 21st of July—no matter where in the world we were. July 21st was the date, way back in 1988, when one of our best mates—Tommy Jones—had died in an ill-fated car accident in Los Angeles we'd all been involved in. Roger the Dodger had also been a passenger in the car that night, but unfortunately Roger had passed away a few years earlier, ravaged by cancer.

Yep, five boys who all went to Santa Monica High School together—all best mates. One dead at twenty-one in that car accident, another dead at fifty from cancer. Both far too soon. Only the three of us were left now.

"I'd better start to mingle," I told Pat and Cynthia. "There are a lot of people I need to personally thank. I'll catch up with you both later." I headed off to welcome the other guests.

That night, among my friends and colleagues, there'd been no way I could have known what lay ahead for me in the coming months. If you'd a crystal ball that had told me what was about to happen, I'd have looked at it and scoffed: "*You're dreaming man.*"

I wish it *was* all a dream—but unfortunately, it wasn't.

CHAPTER 11

Eighteen months earlier

ASIDE FROM WHAT Ivan and Johnny had told me, I'd had no idea what had happened to Martin Spinkle after I'd sacked him from 21st Century Fitness. Later, I'd learned about a meeting that had occurred eighteen months earlier; and I imagined him opening it like this:

"I was the CEO of Billy Houston's business for eighteen months," Spinkle angrily told a man he knew only as 'Larry.' "I despise the man *and* his two trusted lieutenants—Mandy Jones and Johnny Kean."

He was heated as he growled: "Billy sacked me and my PA right on the spot. I vowed that *one day* I'd get that bastard back for what he did to me. He had no right to sack me, and he ruined my career. He absolutely ruined my standing in the fitness and health industry in Southeast Asia. My name's mud. After any prospective employer checks my references, or speaks to anybody I used to work with, I'm screwed. No one will ever hire me again."

"So, why are you here talking to us, Spinkle?" Larry asked dryly.

"Because you guys have been supplying me with steroids for the last few years. I've always paid upfront—and it's been a nice little earner for you."

"I'm sure it's been a nice little earner for *you*, as well," Larry responded.

"Yes, it has," Martin admitted. "I need to make a living—and I'm unemployable in the only business I know—the fitness world—because of that arsehole Houston. For sure, I make a little money flogging steroids to the gym junkies, but hardly enough to be able to live an opulent lifestyle."

"So, let's get to the point, Spinkle—*why* are you talking to us?" Larry looked across to the other man in the room—his partner known as 'Tommy'.

"I have a plan that can make your organization a *lot* of money," Spinkle explained, "*and* will allow me to destroy Billy Houston and his two scrooges, Jones and Kean."

"Tell us your plan, then," challenged Larry.

For the next forty-five minutes, Martin Spinkle would outline his plan to destroy me, my business, and hurt my two trusted partners—and make a *serious* amount of money at the same time.

When he'd outlined his plan, Larry hadn't sound impressed.

"Spinkle, it's never a good idea to mix business with a personal vendetta. It tends to all go pear-shaped when that happens. I'll need time to think about this before I take it to Mr. X."

Mr. X was Larry's boss - the "Mr. Big" that Ivan had been after for years.

"Mr. X is always looking for ways to make money," Larry warned—but he doesn't take kindly to hairbrained schemes. Believe me, you *don't* want to get on the wrong side of Mr. X. People who get on the wrong side of Mr. X tend to disappear—never to be seen again."

Larry chuckled as he said that - and then looked across at Tommy, who also started chuckling.

Spinkle hadn't become a CEO for nothing. He read the mood of the room, and held up one hand.

"You know? Forget I even mentioned the personal vendetta against Houston. My plan still stacks up."

Larry pursed his lips. "This is a lot of money you're talking about, Martin. How much of it would you want?"

"Forty percent—of everything."

"Forty percent?" Tommy spoke for the first time—and he sounded incredulous. "For what? The idea? We do all the dirty work, you don't even get your hands dirty, and you still expect forty percent? That seems a bit rich."

"I'm the one with the idea," Spinkle shrugged. "Take it or leave it. I can always find someone else who'll want to take my idea and make it happen—and then *they'll* give me my forty percent."

The two men were silent for a spell.

"Okay," Larry eventually mused. "So, when do you suggest your plan is put in place?"

"In two-and-a-half years," Spinkle explained. "Just before Houston's business is due to list on the stock exchange. It'll list for $500 million, American."

Another pause.

"You know what concerns me, Martin?" Larry eventually asked.

"What?"

"It all sounds so fanciful. It's all too easy—it seems too good to be true," said Larry.

"It *is* easy," Martin responded. "It *is* simple. That's why I get forty percent, as the brains behind it."

"Two-and-a-half years is a long time to wait. Things can change, Martin." Larry leaned forward. "Things can go wrong in that space of time. What if Houston isn't successful in launching his products in all those countries? Then your plan means nothing."

"Gentleman, you don't know Billy Houston like I do," Martin snorted. "Billy Houston *will* be successful. He'll successfully launch his products over the next few years in *all* those countries." Martin leaned back in his seat. "As much as I hate the man, I have to take my hat off to him for his business acumen. Billy Houston is a successful entrepreneur—one of the best I've ever worked with. The guy never gives up. Since he's sacked me, he's now taken on my role as the CEO. He is the one driving the company. He has one of the best social media guys in the industry in Johnny Kean, enabling the business to sign up millions and millions of people across numerous countries."

Martin paused, and then held up one finger.

"Remember, I only take forty percent of the *upfront* amount. You guys get sixty percent of the upfront, *plus* all the ongoing money—and Houston's business is a license to *print* money, believe me. And you guys will get the license. All of it."

Larry and Tommy exchanged glances. Martin could tell they were hooked.

"So, why are you talking to us now?" Tommy demanded. "The first thing Mr. X will ask us is: "*Why is this guy talking to us now?*" Why wouldn't you wait until just before the stock exchange listing and talk to us then, if the execution of this plan is so easy?"

"Good question," Spinkle nodded. "But the answer is quite simple. I want you guys to continue to supply me with steroids for the next few years. The bikie gangs in Thailand are trying to muscle in on my territory, supplying steroids through the gyms the same way I do. It's only a matter of time before I cross paths with them. I only run a small team of distributors. For all intents and purposes—to the outside world, at least— I'm a respected retired businessman from the fitness industry. You guys have contacts with the bikies. As part of the deal, I need you to tell the bikies to leave me alone and keep away from my turf."

Another long pause.

"Why don't you tell them yourself?' asked Larry.

"Come on, guys," Martin scoffed. "Let's be serious. I'm no match for the bikies. If they wanted to take over my operations by force, they could do it—but they *won't* do it if your organization is backing me. They don't want a war with you guys. They're smart enough to know that no one will win."

Larry crossed his arms.

"Well, Spinkle—that would take a bit of negotiation. I'll tell you what we'll do—or, more precisely, I'll tell you the offer I'm prepared to take to Mr. X: You get *twenty* percent, not forty percent, of the upfront amount for being the mastermind of the plan. We'll organize for the bikies to back off. For that, we'll take eighty percent of the upfront *and* all the ongoing profits."

He paused.

"Your call. A deal or no deal, Spinkle. If you say no, we'll walk away now. If we walk away without a deal, the risk to you is that we execute your plan without you. If *that* happens, you'll get nothing—and we'll get it all."

"It's a deal, guys." With that, Martin Spinkle put out his hand and shook hands with both Larry and Tommy.

When I eventually learned about Spinkle's involvement, I often imagined how chuffed with himself he must have been. Twenty percent of the cut was all he'd ever been after. He must have thought to himself: *"I'm a far better negotiator than Billy Houston. I started the negotiation high, at forty percent, and made those guys think they'd walked out winners when I reduced my cut to twenty percent. It's so easy when you negotiate with thugs. They don't have the IQ to compete with me."*

Besides, the money hadn't been the entirety of the reward. I imagined Spinkle thinking: *"Billy Houston, your demise is not far away, you bastard. For that, I can wait another two-and-a-half years. Hell, what's a few years when I can walk away with $100 million?"*

Yep, I imagine Spinkle had been a happy man as he'd gleefully marched down the street away from that meeting, probably whistling to himself.

However, just like I'd had no idea of what lay ahead, little did Spinkle ever imagine what would happen to *him* in just over nineteen months' time.

Nineteen months later

"BILLY, I'VE GOT something I want to show you."

Ivan Cameron, the Bangkok head of Interpol, pulled a picture out of the top pocket of his blue suit.

One thing I'd noticed about Ivan is that each time we caught up for dinner, he was always impeccably dressed, and always wearing a blue suit. I assumed it was his favorite color.

"Do you know what this is?" Ivan showed me a picture of a forty-four-gallon drum, standing upright by the water. The picture appeared to show the Chao Phraya river, which flowed through Bangkok to the Gulf of Thailand.

"Is this a trick question, Ivan? It's a forty-four-gallon drum."

"Correct," replied Ivan.

"Let's not play the super sleuth with me, Ivan."

Over the last few months, Ivan and I had been catching up regularly for dinner in Bangkok. Ivan had taken a great interest in my business and wanted me to share the progress 21st Century Fitness was making toward our goal of listing on the stock exchange.

We'd actually become good friends—able to relax and enjoy each other's company.

"Billy, I know we agreed many months ago to not discuss my investigation into Martin Spinkle—or the 'Mr. Big' of the drug trade that Spinkle has got himself involved with." Ivan took a deep breath. "But, inside that forty-four-gallon drum, we found the decomposed body of Martin Spinkle."

"The *what*?" I spilled red wine on the table cloth in front of me.

Ivan studied my reaction, before continuing:

"We found the drum washed up on the edge of the water this morning, on the outskirts of Bangkok. I won't show you the pictures of what was inside it—it'll give you nightmares. But, someone—perhaps more than one person—had used a chainsaw to dismember Spinkle's body. The pictures are quite horrific, Billy."

"Fucking hell! Are you kidding me, Ivan?"

"I told you, Billy, that Spinkle was mixed up with a ruthless group of people—to whom human life is a simple commodity. We imagine Spinkle must have outlived his usefulness to this group. They had no further use for him—so they must have decided to just get rid of him." Ivan shook his head. "I'm sure they weren't expecting us to find the drum."

I gulped.

"How did you identify the body as Spinkle?"

"Quite simple, Billy—from dental records."

I shuddered.

"They'd failed to remove all his teeth," Ivan explained coolly. "A bit clumsy on their behalf. I'm sure Mr. Big won't be happy about that."

"Are you any closer to identifying who this 'Mr. Big' is?"

"Unfortunately, not—and with Spinkle now deceased, our job just got a lot harder."

"But—I thought you had Spinkle under twenty-four surveillance! How could you lose him?"

"We're dealing with professionals, Billy!" Ivan shook his head. "Ten days ago, one of our agents was uncovered following Spinkle. He had to abort his surveillance. Unfortunately, our other agents in the vicinity couldn't locate Spinkle before they got to him. It's as though he vanished out of thin air—there wasn't a single trace of him. We had his hotel room under surveillance, but no one entered his room since. His bank accounts haven't been touched."

"Perhaps he was murdered ten days ago," I wondered.

"Yes, that might well be the case," Ivan nodded. "Forensics are undertaking the required investigations now to determine *when* he was murdered." He paused, and his voice became more upbeat. "But let's discuss something far more palatable, Billy. Tell me—how is the Century 21st Group? I'm always fascinated to hear your journey—how you build these businesses. It's a very different world to the one I encounter in my role as Bangkok's head of Interpol."

It was difficult to switch subjects, but I tried.

"We're on track for our listing on the 14th of June, Ivan," I explained. "On the Hong Kong Stock Exchange."

"So, you've now set the date, Billy? Officially? How exciting! That's only ten months away."

"Yes. We've cleared all the Hong Kong regulatory hurdles. The prospectus will be out in six months—giving prospective investors an opportunity to purchase shares ahead of time. All my key executives have signed new contracts, to remain with the company for a further five years after we've listed."

"What's the importance of that, Billy?"

"I have a team of six key executives," I explained. "Mandy Jones, Johnny Kean, Peggy Lane, Tommy Srisuk, Dow Amudee and Stuart Taylor. They all have a wealth of knowledge about the business and are crucial to its continued growth. Them staying gives potential investors confidence that all key management are committed to the company for at least the next five years."

"What about *your* role, Billy?"

I snorted.

"As you know, Stuart Taylor assumed my role as CEO two months ago. He's been with the company ever since I sacked Spinkle. I recruited him with a clear goal of replacing me. I'd never planned on becoming CEO—but when I sacked Spinkle, I had no one else ready to step into the role, so I took it on. I told Dane, my chairman, that I'd only take the role until we launched in China—our final frontier. So, from here on, I'm only staying as a director; and Dane will remain as chairman."

"Won't the investor market be concerned with you stepping down as CEO?"

"Not at all, Ivan! My strength is building businesses, not running them. We've put the infrastructure in place in terms of people, systems and processes—so the business runs like clockwork even without my involvement. I learnt many years ago that all successful entrepreneurs share a common trait."

"What's that, Billy?"

"They know when it's time to move on—and hand the reins to others, who'll take the company to the next level. I'm a bit like the coach of the Dodgers."

"The what? Who are the Dodgers?"

"Sorry, I forgot you're Thai, not American," I chuckled to myself. "The Dodgers are a baseball team from Los Angeles. They compete in Major League Baseball. I'm like their coach. I can get the Dodgers to the playoffs, but I can't get then into the Championship series. They need a new coach to take them to that next level."

"I think I get what you're saying," Ivan nodded.

"Running a business is no different to coaching a sporting team," I reiterated. "You're a Premier League fan, right?" When Ivan nodded, I continued: "It's like me coaching Tottenham. I can get them into fourth place, but I can't get them to the top of the league. Business is no different. There are plenty of CEOs in the world who are fools—they don't know their own limitations. They don't know when it's time to move on and hand the baton to somebody else."

"So, whether you're still at 21st Century Group after the listing will have no impact on the value of the company?" Ivan nodded his head, indicating he'd finally got it.

"Exactly, Ivan, exactly," I grinned. "In fact, I'll let you in on a little secret." I moved closer to him and started to whisper: "As I've said to you before, great businesses are built on three key pillars; systems, processes and leverage. Our business is completely systemized and process-driven. That's why it's so simple to roll our business out into different countries."

Ivan listened intently. I continued:

"We've completed rollouts in eight countries: Thailand, Malaysia, Singapore, Vietnam, Philippines, Indonesia, Hong Kong, and now China. By having those systems and processes in place, it means we can leverage the business enormously. Our next market is India—one of the fastest-growing countries in the world, with a population of over 1.3 billion people. More importantly, India has an ever-growing middle class who can afford twenty cents each week for our fitness app."

Ivan listened, and I sensed how he was hanging on my every word.

"You know, this will all be outlined in the prospectus coming out later, Ivan," I murmured. "Here's a quick word of advice: I know how tough things have been for you financially, but you should still try and scrape together whatever spare cash you can and purchase shares in 21st Century Fitness."

I then reached into my jacket.

"And, to give your share portfolio a kick start, here's a check for $10,000."

Ivan's eyes widened. I held up my hand in warning:

"I give it to you on *one* condition—and that's you use the money to buy shares in 21st Century Fitness when the prospectus comes out."

"Billy, that is so generous of you! You don't have to do that!" Ivan shook his head. "I can't accept your generous gift. It probably breaches Interpol rules for a start, taking a gift from you."

"It's a personal gift, Ivan," I reassured him. "You've helped me out, we've become close friends over the last few months, and I know you've had people keeping an eye out for me in case Spinkle and his cohorts tried to endanger me."

Ivan looked impressed.

"How do you know that, Billy?'

I grinned: "I decided to hire my own private investigator—ever since our first meeting, when you gave me your card and told me to phone you any time if I sensed I was being followed. I contacted an old colleague of mine in California—he's a private investigator—and he put me in contact with an Italian guy in Bangkok. His name's Sergio Russo. He's got a team of investigators in Southeast Asia who have been watching me ever since. He confirmed I was being followed—so, I assumed it was one of your guys."

Ivan nodded quietly.

"Yes, we've had people following you intermittently," he admitted. "Just wanted to make certain that my good friend, Billy Houston, wasn't in any danger. We were aware you had your own people watching out for you."

"So, we've had spies following spies?" I chuckled.

"I didn't want you to end up like Spinkle, Billy."

CHAPTER 12

AGAIN, I WASN'T present for the aftermath of Martin Spinkle's untimely demise— but what he'd set in motion continued to progress unbeknownst to me.

I'd later learn of a meeting between Larry and Tommy, Spinkle's old criminal associates, and a third character with a sinister agenda. I imagined it went something like this:

"It's time to move, guys," Larry addressed the trio. "Billy Houston's business lists in three months. From all reports, the business is on track to list at $500 million, as expected." Larry smirked. "Spinkle was a genius, God rest his soul."

"He obviously wasn't too smart, Larry," Tommy scoffed. "Otherwise, he'd be alive today. Did he really think we'd let him live? Mr. X was always going to have him knocked off before the heist took place. The boss has saved himself a $100 million by getting rid of Spinkle."

"Yeah, I guess he was the dumbest genius I know," nodded Larry in agreement.

"Okay, guys," the third member of their group interrupted them. This was Brian—Mr. X's right-hand-man. "I want to run through the finer details of the plan before we pay a visit to Billy Houston next week."

Brian Goad—or Goady, as he was better known—was an accountant by trade. He'd racked up more than ten years' experience in corporate America before he'd been caught and charged with embezzlement. Goady had spent five years in jail in America for that.

Following his release six months earlier, Goady had been recruited by Mr. X. Brian had been starting a brand-new life in Pattaya, Thailand, when his path had crossed that of Mr. X. Through shared connections, Mr. X had quickly realized he needed an accountant or lawyer like Goady to help him with his business dealings—given the rapid growth in his drug trafficking and extortion revenue.

Mr. X needed someone who was smart, but bent—and therefore comfortable making large sums of money by undertaking less-than-legal activities. Specifically, Mr. X needed someone who could help him launder all his ill-gotten gains—a man with an understanding of accounting, law, and how those could be leveraged for his money laundering operations.

Mr. X's contact had shared the details of Spinkle's scheme with Goady—the one they'd been patiently waiting two-and-a-half years to execute. Spinkle's plan had been to force me into transferring all my shares in 21st Century Fitness to *their* company.

When he'd heard this plan, Goady probably couldn't believe how naive Mr. X and his team must have sounded. What? Take all of a man's shares in one hit—forcing him to sign them over through the threat of violence—and then expect no investigation by the Hong Kong Stock Exchange? Especially given that the listing was taking place in less than three months' time.

It was fully disclosed in the prospectus for the listing that I owned one hundred percent of the issued capital. Any substantial changes in shareholding—either prior or post listing—would have to be notified to the authorities. Goady must have thought to himself how dumb Spinkle was—and how dumb Larry, Tommy and Mr. X were to believe such a hairbrained scheme could ever have worked in the first place.

Unfortunately for me, Goady had a much simpler and cleaner plan to extort money from me. He wasn't aiming for the full five-hundred million that Mr. X had been hoping for—but twenty million was still a tidy sum by anyone's standards; especially for not too much work.

Goady explained to Larry and Tommy: "I've examined the prospectus for 21st Century Fitness in detail. This Billy Houston fellow is certainly one smart guy. It's a truly great business."

He shook his head.

"But Spinkle was a complete fool. If it was simply a matter of just taking someone's shares by making them sign a standard share transfer form, don't you think we'd be doing this every day of the week? To every business owner we come across?" He scoffed." Think about it, guys. It's the weirdest and stupidest scheme I've ever heard of."

For the next thirty minutes, Goady went through his plan—to 'steal' $20 million from me a much simpler way.

"So, next Monday morning," Goady explained, "Billy Houston will be walking along Choeng Mon beach at precisely 6:30am. He gets up at the same time every Monday morning when he's staying at Choeng Mon—the guy is a creature of habit. He'll do his normal walk for an hour, then he'll grab his paddle board and go out paddling for forty-five minutes. At 9:00am, he'll be sitting in his favorite café having his first cup of coffee of the day, reading his newspaper. The man operates like clockwork."

Goady grinned: "We'll pounce *then*. Larry and I will join him for 'coffee'." He laughed, illustrating that a hot cup of coffee was not what he had in mind for this rendezvous. "You, Tommy, will sit across the road in the car. We'll then escort Houston to the car and bring him back to our little bungalow here, at Maenem Beach. I'll run Houston through his options. We'll have him back at his café to finish his breakfast an hour later."

Options. Painful, humiliating or potentially deadly options.

"This is the easiest money Mr. X will ever make," Tommy laughed with excitement.

Larry and Tommy had been promised $500,000 each once the 'sting' had been completed—whilst Goady, as Mr. X's brains behind the scheme, would receive considerably more. They hoped this business with me would be completed within an hour...

...but, then again, they didn't know me, did they?

Billy Houston is *not* a man who caves in early.

I NEVER SAW them watching me.

"I can see him, Goady—just like you said, walking along the beach right at 6:30am," said Larry.

Goady nodded: "Let's sit here and watch him for the next couple of hours. We'll be ready to pounce once he's ordered his morning coffee in the café down the road."

For just over two hours, Larry and Goady would watch me undertake my normal, Monday morning exercise regime—and I'd have no idea.

"He's a pretty fit guy, Goady. How old did you say he was again?"

"Fifty-four—about to turn fifty-five." Goady admitted: "Yep, pretty fit guy."

Eventually, they'd watch me order my first coffee of the day in the café across the road from where Tommy was parked.

"Time for us to go and introduce ourselves to Mr Houston, Larry." Goady gave the thumbs up to Tommy, who was seated in the black Mercedes fifty yards away.

"BILLY HOUSTON, I assume?"

That was how I become acquainted with Brian Goad—when he stretched out his hand to introduce himself.

Engrossed in reading yesterday's Bangkok Times, I looked up somewhat startled. Locals rarely approached me while I was having my first coffee of the day—knowing how immersed I always was in my morning newspaper. It was yesterday's news, as that day's Bangkok Times didn't normally arrive in Koh Samui until sometime after lunch, but I was still riveted.

"Yes, I'm Billy Houston." I looked up at the stranger. "I don't think I know you."

"I'm Alan Jones and this is Steve Bird." Goady used aliases for both him and Larry, which was something I'd only learn later. "May we join you?"

At first, I assumed they were harmless— maybe keen entrepreneurs looking for advice.

"Listen, guys," I sighed, "I'm just relaxing—enjoying my first coffee of the day. I do like my own space first thing in the morning. I've just been out walking and paddling for the last couple of hours."

"Yes, we know," Larry replied coolly. "We've been watching you."

That's when I started to get uneasy.

"Watching me? Are you guy's Ivan's agents from Interpol?" I asked.

It had only been two weeks since I'd ended the contract with Sergio's bodyguards—who'd been following me to make sure I wasn't in danger or under surveillance. Ivan, too, had informed me only recently that he'd stopped having his Interpol agents follow me—arguing that I didn't appear to be in danger any longer.

Or, so we'd thought.

"No, we're not from Interpol," Goady, pretending to be 'Alan Jones', explained. "We're private citizens—businessman, just like you."

"So," I narrowed my eyes. "You've been watching me? Should I find that concerning?"

"Maybe," replied 'Alan' bluntly.

I stiffened, but tried to hide the anxiety I was suddenly feeling.

"Well, sit down then, guys," I gestured to the chairs across the table from where I was sitting. "Enlighten me as to what this is all about. Would you both like a coffee?"

"No, we don't have time for a coffee," the man calling himself 'Alan' purred. "See that black Mercedes parked down the road?" He pointed toward a parked car about fifty yards away, while he and his colleague took seats on either side of me.

"Yes, I see it," I tried to keep my voice even. "Nice car."

"Thanks," he grunted. "Well, we'd like you to quietly call the waiter over and pay for your coffee. Tell him you'll be back in an hour or so for breakfast. We'd then like you to join us—and hop into the back of that nice car."

I stared at him silently for a second, before murmuring: "And, if I don't?"

"Um," 'Alan' pursed his lips. "That's not our *preferred* option, Mr. Houston—or may I call you Billy?" He gestured towards his companion. "You see, my good friend Steve Bird, here, has a gun in his jacket. If necessary, he'll use the gun to *force* you to join us."

As those words were uttered, the man referred to as 'Steve' opened his jacket slightly to reveal the grip of a small pistol inside a holster under his armpit.

I was a man of anti-violence—having never touched, let alone *used* a gun before. I didn't know what sort of gun the man sitting next to me had in his jacket—but it certainly looked real.

Reading my expression, 'Alan' warned:

"Billy, we don't want any problems. We just want you to come with us for an hour. Just a quick business meeting. You'll be returned here within the hour, safe and sound, free to carry on with your normal life."

"Do you guys know the late Martin Spinkle?" I asked, looking for any flash of recognition on their faces when I mentioned his name.

"No," 'Alan' replied coldly. "We don't know anyone called Martin Spinkle." He added: "Come with us, Billy. It won't take long. You'll be back here in an hour."

One of my strengths is being able to act coolly and calmly in the most extreme of situations. When under pressure, I've always been able to think logically and clearly. I knew that if I didn't go with these two gentlemen, they'd be back at some point to reacquaint themselves with me; this time where there might not be witnesses.

Ivan Cameron had reassured me there was no evidence to suggest I was being followed by his fabled 'Mr. Big' or any of the crime boss's cohorts. For that reason, I was somewhat intrigued to know what these two gentlemen wanted. So, I nodded in agreement—ready to hop into the black Mercedes with them.

They're not going to kidnap me, I thought to myself. *We're on an island, for God's sake!*

It would turn out to be one of the worst decisions I ever made in my life.

Hindsight is, of course, a wonderful thing. As my best mate, Pat Gabriel, has always said: *"Your biggest flaw, Billy, is that you always trust whatever people tell you as the truth. In Southeast Asia, you're a million miles away from home. It's a different culture—a different way of life. I've always been concerned you'll end up trusting the wrong people and come a cropper. You're in a different jurisdiction here, Billy. Different laws, where it may be harder to right a wrong. In America, we were lucky that the authorities picked things up and penalized Carroll and his cohorts. But here, Billy, it's like a jungle—where you or I don't understand the lay of the land.'*

Pat Gabriel was one smart guy. He'd never spoken a truer word.

TO MY SURPRISE, 'Alan' and 'Steve' immediately blindfolded me as soon as I climbed into the back of the car. I initially refused—until, after flailing my arms, a gun was pointed at my stomach. The man who called himself 'Steve Bird' said words which I can still hear in my head today:

"I'll have no hesitation in shooting you, Houston—just like I shot Spinkle."

It was then that I realized I was in deep shit.

Who *were* these people? What did they want? It had been over twelve months since I'd first met Ivan—when he'd first informed me about Spinkle and the bad people he'd been mixed up with. But during the following twelve months, during which Ivan's agents had been looking out for me, no one had ever threatened me. No one had ever followed me, other than those Interpol agents and the private investigators I'd hired myself.

So, why now?

I had no idea what this was all about—but I didn't have many choices. I obeyed Steve Bird's instructions—although I didn't see the benefit of being blindfolded, since I'd have had no trouble identifying either 'Alan Jones' or 'Steve Bird' again. At this point, though, I'd obviously assumed those were not their *real* names.

I hadn't seen the face of the driver, yet. He was wearing a baseball cap and large, dark sunglasses.

After fifteen minutes or so of driving, the car came to a stop. My blindfold was removed. I looked out of the window and saw we were parking in a clearing surrounded by thick foliage. I assumed I was somewhere in the jungle behind Choeng Mon. Fifteen yards away stood an old, non-descript building—to which I was escorted from the car.

Inside the small building was a large table and three chairs. I was forced to sit at the head of the table, and on either side sat the men identifying themselves as 'Alan Jones' and 'Steve Bird'. The driver of the car remained somewhere outside.

"Billy," the man calling himself 'Alan' explained, "we work for a major criminal organization. Our web of influence reaches many, many countries. Our network of contacts also reaches the highest echelons of governments—police, security, armed forces, and even the judiciary. We have many people in high places on our payroll. You need to know that before you listen to what we want. This meeting today can be peaceful and short—providing you obey our demands."

"What *are* your demands?" I asked with a soft voice. I was now quite petrified—perhaps more so than I'd ever been before in my life.

"Our demands are quite simple, Billy. We're aware that you're the sole shareholder of the 21st Century Fitness Group, and that you plan to list that company for $500 million shortly. We're also aware that you're a man of considerable means from your previous business dealings in the United States."

Alan paused to let his words sink in, before explaining:

"We expect you to transfer $20 million from your private bank account to ours. Here are our account details."

'Alan Jones' flashed a cell phone in front of my face, with the screen showing a routing code and account number.

I blinked.

"I can't just transfer $20 million like that. You think I'm made of money?"

'Alan' snorted.

"Billy, we know you have more than $20 million sitting in bank accounts both in the United States *and* Thailand. I have your personal iPad here." He held up my iPad.

"How did you get my iPad?"

"Quite simple, Billy. While you were out paddling this morning, one of my men entered your house and opened your office to retrieve it."

"But I have the latest security system guarding my house! It's impossible to enter unless you know the code."

"Billy, as I mentioned, we're a *very* sophisticated organization—with contacts in places you wouldn't have imagined in your wildest dreams."

To demonstrate that, the man calling himself 'Alan' entered a pin-code into my iPad, and it instantly unlocked. My jaw dropped.

"How did you know my code? *Nobody* knows that. My IT team told me it was impossible to crack. How did you *do* that?"

'Alan' smirked.

"Don't underestimate who you're dealing with, Billy. We don't know the code to your bank accounts, but we *do* know that within twelve hours of notifying the relevant bank, you can transfer $20 million to whichever bank account your heart desires."

I gulped. "And, if I don't?"

"Then someone very dear to you—somebody *very* close to you—will be kidnapped and tortured until you *do* transfer the funds to us." Alan said the words almost robotically.

He continued: "Your old mate, Martin Spinkle, brought you to our attention. That man had an immense dislike for you, Billy. He had a hairbrained scheme that involved forcing you to transfer all your shares in the 21st Century Group to us. I soon put the codgers on that idea—but it *did* inspire me to undertake some further investigation into who you were, Bill Houston."

'Alan' leaned back in his seat.

"You're certainly a successful man, Billy. Well done on the businesses you've built. Let me recall: There was the Tax Refund Shop in the States that you started with your best mate, Pat Gabriel. I recollect you guys sold that for roughly $30 million. Then, of course, there was the big one—the big fish you landed, when you and your mate, Pat, successfully listed that business on the New York Stock Exchange for roughly $480 million."

Both 'Alan' and 'Steve' whistled through their teeth.

"A big pay day for you," 'Alan' nodded. "I admire your noble gestures of cashing in most of those shares and helping those less fortunate around the world. I believe you've given away most of your wealth. But there *is* a lazy $20 million sitting in your bank accounts, Billy. What's $20 million when, in a few months' time, you'll receive close to *$300* million? That's what your sixty percent share of 21st Century Fitness is worth, right? And that's *after* giving away forty percent to your key staff."

I narrowed my eyes. "Most of that money will be given away to the Future Wealth Foundation to help— as you so rightly said—those less fortunate."

'Alan' shrugged, as if he clearly didn't care about the 'less fortunate'.

I sat there, stock still— wondering how much of this was real, and how much of it was a bluff. I didn't wonder for very long.

"Oh, we *did* discover Code 8888, Billy—when I initially investigated Spinkle's hairbrained scheme."

'Alan Jones' chuckled menacingly.

I gulped dryly.

Code 8888.

How did they enter my house? How did they get the code to my iPad? And how on Earth did they know about Code 8888? No one other than Dane knew that code!

Four years ago, I'd organized some security experts to review our internal security in case of cyber-attack. It was, in effect, a full audit of our internal systems. Over dinner one night, with the director of the cyber security firm—a woman called Elisabeth —I'd shared with her my plans to list 21st Century Fitness and gift forty percent of the shares to members of my key executive team.

Elisabeth had immediately probed the security of this—asking questions about the process of transferring shares. I'd told her it just required a directors' meeting between Dane—the chairman of the board—and myself.

Furthermore, given that I was based in Thailand and Dane was in America, the shareholders' minutes could be signed by me, scanned to Dane, and simply signed by him off site. Once a transfer document was signed by both of us, it was legally binding—it was as simple as that.

In business, you can often overlook the simplest of things. Elisabeth ran through a possible scenario with me:

"What if, Billy, you were drugged—and yet still able to sign your signature? What if someone had you sign a share transfer form, and then a shareholder's minute, and both were scanned to Dane? Would that then be enough for the share transfer form to be legally enforceable?"

At the time, I'd replied: "I guess it would—although I could lay criminal charges against anybody who drugged me and forced me to sign the form. That would make it null and void."

Elisabeth responded: "I get that, Billy—but why don't you introduce a further process to stop a fraudulent transfer of shares? I assume you fully trust Dane?"

"Absolutely."

"Well, why don't you introduce a code—known only to you and Dane—which would be required to be sent before he or you sign any minutes or transfer forms? So, in the situation I just described, Dane wouldn't sign the form unless he'd received the code. No one will know the code other than the two of you—and the people who drugged you wouldn't know anything about the need for a code, so Dane would never sign the forms because no code was even offered."

Elisabeth had explained: "It's a simple but *very* effective safeguard, Billy."

So, that's how the code system had come into place. Every three months, Dane and I would change the code whenever we met face to face. Never by text, or email, and we never had the discussion in the office—in case it was bugged. This was all a process suggested by our security experts.

But how did *these* people know the code? Or even the *need* for a code, for that matter? Dane and I had only changed the code three weeks ago.

"I WON'T TRANSFER any money to you, thugs." I raised my voice—but it sounded nervous. "Not even if you threaten to shoot me."

I immediately thought about the armed hold up I'd experienced, some thirty years earlier, when a gunman wearing a balaclava had tied me up and threatened to kill me and my two co-workers. I was even more scared now.

"We're not going to shoot you, Billy," 'Alan' snorted. "If you're dead, you're no use to us. But we *will* torture—and eventually kill—people close to you until you *do* transfer the money." He paused. "Are you a selfish man, Billy?"

I opened my mouth to speak, but 'Alan' cut me off.

"Don't answer the question, Billy. I'll answer it for you: If you *don't* transfer the money, you're a selfish man—because we *will* kidnap, torture, and kill someone close to you if necessary."

The way he said it left no doubt about his sincerity.

"You'll be aware of it," 'Alan' continued, "because we'll send pictures to your phone of the person being tortured. If that's not enough, we'll phone you—and you'll *hear* your dear friend on the end of the line, crying out in pain."

I was trembling.

"I have contacts in high places," my voice cracked as I spoke. "In Interpol, the FBI, and the Thai police. You'll never get away with this!"

Alan snorted.

"Billy, you seem to have forgotten what I told you earlier. Our web of contacts reaches the *highest* echelons of governments, police, security forces, armed forces, and the judiciary. We have many people in high places on our payroll. If you speak to Interpol, the FBI, the police, or any other official, we'll know about it. We'll then kidnap and torture not one, but *two* of your closest and dearest friends."

He paused, before asking: "Are you a gambling man, Billy?"

I was silent.

And then, suddenly— just like that— 'Alan' stood up from his chair.

"Well, you're free to go, Billy."

I looked up at him incredulously.

"You'll have seven days to transfer the money to our account—which, by the way, is untraceable." 'Alan' smiled wickedly. "I'm a qualified accountant, just like you, Billy. I'm highly skilled in fraud and embezzlement. In fact, it's how I've made a living for the last fifteen years." He warned: "If you don't transfer the money within seven days, we'll kidnap and torture someone very close to you. If you go to the authorities, we'll kidnap not one, but *two* people you're very close to."

I was visibly shaking. I'd never experienced anything like this before in my life—nothing remotely like this situation.

Oh, I've endured many business entanglements in which you bluff, you don't show all your moves at once, and you try and gain a competitive advantage. But were these guys bluffing? How could they *possibly* have people on their payroll in the highest echelons of the government, and police? Surely it was impossible!

But, if what they were saying was true, then this was a life or death dilemma. At least, in business, it's never *really* life or death.

There was silence for a few moments. Finally, 'Alan' spoke:

"We know everything about you and your business, Billy Houston. We know all about your old businesses, your mates—Pat Gabriel and Chook Burns. We know about your three-ex-wives, your three children living happily in California, and your mum and dad in Melbourne."

How the *hell* did these people know all this? How could they *possibly* know?

The man calling himself 'Alan' produced a folder and pulled out some color photos.

"To show we're serious people, Billy, I suggest you look at these pictures for a moment."

I immediately started gasping for air.

'Alan' was showing me what had been inside the forty-gallon drum that Ivan Cameron and his Interpol agents had fished out of the Bangkok river system. I nearly threw up.

"That is the late Martin Spinkle—the man who once worked for you," 'Alan' explained. "It's amazing what some of my team can do with a chainsaw, Billy."

He paused menacingly.

"It's your call, Billy. You have seven days. And remember—if you tell *anyone* about our meeting today, we'll know about it. We have eyes and ears in places you'd never imagine."

'Alan' turned to 'Steve.'

"Let's take Mr. Houston back to his café now, so he can have his breakfast and contemplate things over the next seven days."

I was led back out to the Mercedes, and in silence we drove back to Choeng Mon village. Once again, I was blindfolded for the journey. When the blindfold was eventually removed, the man named 'Alan' gave me a piece of paper and warned: "This is the bank account number, Billy. You have seven days. The bank account is untraceable. Don't talk to anyone about our meeting today."

He locked his gaze with mine.

"We're not kidding, Billy. We *will* find out if you tell anybody, and the repercussions will be the start of your worst nightmares *ever*."

CHAPTER 13

WE ARRIVED BACK in Choeng Mon village. I exited the car. As the three of them drove away, I knew I was in no mood for breakfast. I needed time to process what had just happened. I glanced at my watch, and realized I'd been gone with these thugs for just sixty-five minutes. It had seemed like an eternity at the time.

I headed solemnly to the beach, which was empty. That's where I always did my best thinking—walking alone on the beach. The sound of the waves, the smell of the ocean, and the feeling of the soft sand under my feet—it was when all my weird and wonderful business ideas came to me. This was no time to be thinking of business ideas, though. I was entering a zone I'd never entered before.

After walking for twenty minutes, it was apparent what my next steps *had* to be. Irrespective of what the kidnappers had warned me, I *had* to speak to the two people I trusted most with my life.

Actually, there were *three* people I had to speak to immediately—and in this order:

The first person I needed to call was my best mate, Pat Gabriel. I looked at my watch to work out the current time in Los Angeles. It would be late Sunday night in LA, so Pat would still be up and about.

The second person I needed to speak to was my good friend, Ivan Cameron—Head of Interpol in Bangkok. I'd phone him after I'd spoken to Pat, and let him know what had just transpired. He probably knew of 'Alan' and 'Steve' from his investigation into Martin Spinkle. Hell, I'd probably help him solve his whole investigation *and* find his Mr. Big!

Mr. Big, I thought. Those two guys referred to their boss as 'Mr. X'. I'd let Ivan know he was looking for the wrong guy.

I'd then catch a plane to Bangkok, later today, to meet up with Ivan in person. I was sure Ivan could have his forces mobilized to protect all those people who the thugs might try to kidnap.

I thought to myself who the people closet to me were. My three children in California, obviously. They needed protection. That's why my third phone call today was going to be to Pat's relation, Fred—a senior officer with the FBI in Los Angeles.

I needed to race back to my beach house and open my iPad, which I was still carrying, and make a list of the people closest to me. They were all potential targets for these criminals to kidnap and torture. I shook my head as I walked, still wondering how those thugs had accessed my data. I'd need to get my iPad to my IT guys in Bangkok this afternoon to check it wasn't bugged. Then I thought: "Stuff it, I won't turn on my iPad. I'll write on a notepad in case my iPad *is* somehow bugged."

I PHONED PAT first, and his cell phone went to voicemail.

"Pat, it's Billy, mate. This is the most important phone call you've ever received from me. *Please* call me back immediately—no matter what time it is."

I then phoned Ivan. However, his cell phone also went to voicemail.

"Ivan, it's Billy. Please call me immediately. It's urgent. Thanks."

I opened my cell phone to check flights from Koh Samui to Bangkok. There was a 1pm flight. Perfect. Just enough time to pack a few clothes, gather some possessions, and get to the airport.

As I sat in a taxi on the way to Koh Samui airport, my phone rang. It was Ivan. I felt my mood immediately lift.

"What's up, Billy? What's so urgent?"

"Mate, you're not going to believe what's happened to me this morning. I got kidnapped!"

"What did you say? Kidnapped?"

"Yep! Kidnapped and threatened by some thugs. The same thugs who killed Spinkle. By the way, Ivan, it's not a 'Mr. Big' you should be trying to find: It's 'Mr. X'. He's the leader."

Ivan said nothing.

"Mate, I'm in the back of a taxi—and while my Thai taxi driver assured me he doesn't speak much English, given what's happened this morning, for all I know, he could be one of the bad guys posing as a taxi driver. I'll be at the airport in ten minutes. I'll call you then so we can speak in private".

We arrived soon after. I paid the taxi driver and then looked for a nice, secluded part of the airport, so no one could overhear me when I phoned Ivan again.

He answered immediately. "Ah! Billy! Kidnapped and threatened? Are you okay?"

"No, I'm not, Ivan. I'm shit-scared. I'm also scared for some of my closest friends."

For the next five minutes or so, I shared with Ivan everything that had transpired—including the threats the thugs had made if I didn't transfer the $20 million.

"Ivan, I've made a list of all the people closest to me. You need to organize around-the-clock protection for them. I also need to contact Pat's relation at the FBI, Fred, and get protection for my kids and my three-ex-wives—plus Pat, and Chook Burns."

"Billy, leave the FBI to me," Ivan suggested. "I'll contact them directly and give them a briefing. Text me the full names and addresses of the people in the States I need to organize protection for. Don't open your iPad—it's probably been bugged, and they can probably see every message you send, and every piece of information on your PC. When we meet in Bangkok later today, bring your iPad and I'll get my security guys at Interpol to clean and de-bug it. You may well have a mole inside your own IT team at 21st Century Fitness. That might be how they got the code for your iPad, the security codes for your house, and the special code you and Dane share." Ivan paused. "We can't trust anybody now, Billy. Who needs protection here in Asia?"

"Dane, my chairman," I told him, "plus my executive team—Mandy Jones, Johnny Kean, Peggy Lane, and Paul White." I paused. "Wait, that probably includes my bankers and lawyers as well."

"Who else, Billy?"

"Well, *you*, of course, Ivan—you've become one of my closest friends. There's Cheyenne Holly, who used to work for me. Lars and Dao, in Choeng Mon. There's also a woman called Chimlin. I never told you about her. She was very close to me. She lives in Bangkok."

"Okay, Billy. Text me their details. I'll have surveillance organized on all these people within seventy-two hours—both here in Asia, and in the States."

"Fuck, why seventy-two hours, Ivan? Can't it be done within the hour?"

"Billy, it's a big task! We have to search databases and find these people. We'll then have to communicate with them and explain what's happening. We can't tell them the true story—otherwise, they'll be petrified. I'll have to get my experts on the case to make something up that sounds plausible, without making people scared."

"I think we need to move within the hour, Ivan. We *need* those people protected as soon as possible."

"Billy, those thugs gave you seven days to transfer the money. That means we've got seven days of breathing space."

"Okay," I reluctantly nodded. "I trust you. My plane is about to board. I'll be in Bangkok in an hour or so."

"Billy, I don't want to alarm you, but you're most likely being followed right now. We need to make certain that these people don't see you meeting with me, or any of my agents. Remember that little bar we met at last month? On Sukhumvit Road, near Soi 14?"

"Yes."

"Meet me there at 4pm. Check into the Sofitel, then exit via the service exit. Walk around the block and double back to the little bar. I'll be sitting at a table in the back, watching for any unwanted intruders."

WHILE IN THE air, flying from Koh Samui to Bangkok, I had two missed calls from Pat. As soon as I landed, I grabbed my luggage and then hailed a taxi to take me to downtown Bangkok. I quizzed the taxi driver as to whether he spoke English. He shook his head 'no', so once in the back of the taxi, I immediately phoned Pat—comfortable that the guy driving wouldn't understand a word I was saying.

After he'd heard my story, Pat exclaimed: "Fucking hell, Billy! This is big shit, man! What are you going to do?"

"I need time to think."

"Luckily, you've become friends with Ivan—and if anyone can protect you, it's him. Hopefully, they'll catch these thugs quickly."

"That's the scary thing, Pat. I don't think they *will* catch these thugs in a hurry. It must be the same group that Spinkle was involved with—and look what happened to him! He's dead." I sighed. "Ivan's been chasing these guys for over two years and hasn't got any closer to catching this 'Mr. X'."

"Why don't you come back to California, Billy? We can get the FBI to protect you here—plus hire some private security for you and the kids."

"No, I need to remain here. I've got the listing in three months. My involvement is needed here. We're *so* close to the finishing line, Pat. I have two choices: One, I can transfer the money over to these thugs. Or, two, I can carry on as normal—in the hope that the authorities track down these thugs and put them in jail where they belong. I think it has to be option two, Pat."

"I agree, Billy. We can't let these thugs intimidate and threaten people. They do it to you now, and next week, it'll be somebody else. They *need* to be caught and thrown in jail to rot. Plus, if you give in to their demands and transfer that twenty million, they'll probably just come back looking for more once you list your business. They're vultures, Billy. Animals. Despicable human trash."

"I'm heading to Bangkok Central now to meet up with Ivan, and hopefully identify the two thugs who kidnapped me. I'll assist Interpol in catching these no-hopers."

"Do you want me and Chook Burns to fly over to Bangkok?"

"No, you're better off staying in LA. Make certain both you and Chook have the FBI surveillance until we grab these guys. Ivan is going to phone Fred, your relative at the FBI, to organize surveillance."

"Will do, Billy. I feel for you, mate. A worrying time."

"We've been through plenty of shit together, Pat. As I always say: Life's two steps forward and one step back. If you're always going forward, no matter how slow, then that's good."

I chuckled humorlessly.

Pat finished: "Take care, Billy. I'll call you tomorrow for an update."

"Cheers, mate."

CHAPTER 14

I STOPPED WALKING to read the text message I'd just received from Ivan.

"*Change of plans, Billy. To ensure you're not followed: When you get to the bar we were going to meet at, cross the road at the lights and you'll see a Thai guy wearing a straw hat, brown pants and carrying a large, white plastic bag. He'll be watching out for you. When he sees you cross the road, he'll start walking down the street and will turn left into a building numbered 190. Follow him to that building and you'll be greeted by two men entering the lifts going to floor 14. Follow them to the lift and get off at floor 12. They'll make certain no one follows you. Walk down the corridor and press the button at Suite 15. I'll be inside with some of my team. Sorry for the cloak and dagger approach, but we need to take certain precautions to ensure these people don't know you're speaking to the authorities. Regards, Ivan.*"

I followed Ivan's instructions, and eventually hopped out of the lift at floor twelve of this mysterious building.

It was a busy building, with each of the four lifts full. Fortunately, no one hopped out at the twelfth floor with me. I walked down the corridor as instructed and pressed the buzzer on the plaque outside Suite 15. The door was immediately opened by a young, attractive Thai woman who introduced herself as Ivan's private secretary.

"Mr. Cameron is waiting to see you," she said, and gestured for me to follow her down the long, dimly lit corridor.

I assumed this must have been some form of Interpol office. There were no windows, no pictures—only large, security-type doors in the hallway. I assumed some form of interview or work rooms were located behind each of those doors.

Ivan's secretary punched some numbers into a keyboard located on the door at the far end of the corridor. The door sprang open—and there was Ivan, plus two other men seated at a large, oval-shaped glass table with large computer screens on all four walls.

"Welcome, Billy," Ivan stood. "Sorry for the 'James Bond' approach. We just needed to ensure nobody knew you were here. This is an Interpol building only used in extreme emergencies. It's completely off the grid. No one at Interpol—or any other government agency, for that matter—will know we've been here today. The staff here have the highest security classification. There are no cameras. Nothing whatsoever is recorded here."

In the space of twelve hours, I'd gone from being a mild-mannered, successful business entrepreneur to a man kidnapped, threatened, and facing the loss of my life *and* the potential torture of those dearest to me. It all felt a bit surreal—a bit like a nightmare.

"Billy, this is Ted Anuwat." Ivan gestured to his left. "This is Bing Botwong." He gestured to the man at his right. "They're two highly-skilled agents who've been working with me for over two years, trying to find the 'Mr. Big' of the drug world that the late Martin Spinkle was involved with. We need to know everything that happened today. We're also going to try and identify the two people who kidnapped you."

For the next three hours, I endured an intense grilling from Ivan, Ted, and Bing about everything that had transpired that morning—along with the story of how I'd originally met Martin Spinkle, and numerous other matters; about both my personal and business life.

Ivan, Ted, and Bing were concerned that my business might have been infiltrated by Mr. Big and his cohorts. They were as confused as I was as to how somebody had known about the code used between Dane and I before any share transfer could be approved—let alone knowing the *actual* code, Code 8888, which had only been changed a few weeks earlier.

They were also confused as to how someone had learned the security code needed to enter my house at Choeng Mon, or the code to access my iPad.

I was required to give a run down on every person I'd ever had dealings with since I'd started 21st Century Fitness nearly five years earlier—along with any old enemies I might have made during my previous business dealings in America. There were a few old enemies from the previous business Pat and I had formed in the States, Future Wealth. Tom Carroll and his cohorts—guys who were now banned by the US Securities Commission from ever acting as directors of companies in America.

Carroll was a nasty piece of work—a liar, and completely corrupt. Yet, I couldn't imagine even *him* running a drug empire and being part of a group that would torture and kill people. I shared this thought with Ivan, Ted and Bing.

"I don't believe Tom Carroll or any of his cohorts could be involved in a crime like this. Corrupt, yes. But killing and torturing people? No, I can't ever imagine even Tom doing that."

"But Billy," Bing demanded, "you said this is the guy who tried to fraudulently take Future Wealth from you and Pat. He's got a track record of doing this kind of stuff."

Ivan nodded. "As a precaution, Billy, I'll contact my counterparts in America and put a trace on Carroll. We might as well call him in and check what he's been up to. As Bing says: Carroll has prior history with this type of crime."

There was a knock on the door. Ivan's PA entered, holding my iPad. She whispered something to Ivan.

"Okay, good work." Ivan nodded as his PA exited the room. He turned to me:

"Your iPad has been compromised. It's been hacked. Files have been downloaded and they've been tracking you emails for the last month. Do you keep passwords or codes on your iPad, Billy?"

"None of my personal information is saved on the iPad," I breathed a sigh of relief. "The cyber security experts we engaged were very particular about how staff, including me, stored classified and personal information. My passwords are stored on a separate, private phone."

More importantly, I clarified: "Dane and I never store or write down our code. That's why we use something easy to remember. That's why we used Code 8888. The code before was 3333".

Ted Anuwat turned his computer screen to face me.

"While we've been talking, I punched 'Tom Stuart Carroll' into the Interpol database. Is this the man, Billy?"

He showed me a headshot of the one and only Tom Carroll.

"That's him, all right," I nodded.

"An interesting character, this Mr. Carroll," Ted mused. "Banned by the US Securities Commission from being a director in the United States of America. Banned from ever acting as an investment advisor in any jurisdiction in the United States. It further describes him as: *"A person of dubious character known to engage in fraudulent corporate activities. Last known fraud was attempting to bribe government authorities in Laos to organize a casino license. Previously part of a consortium which failed to obtain a casino license in the Congo, due to confirmed criminal background checks. Possible links to major crime gangs. Last whereabouts UNKNOWN'."*

"He could be our man," said Ted.

"Certainly," added Bing.

"Okay, I'll alert our counterparts in the States," Ivan nodded. "It's interesting that his last whereabouts are unknown. What's the date of the last sighting of him?"

"Two years ago," replied Ted.

"About the time we became aware of the Mr. Big syndicate," Ivan pursed his lips. "Interesting."

CHAPTER 15

I WAS DEEPLY engrossed reading my newspaper, sipping on my first coffee of the morning, when I heard hurried footsteps heading towards me. I'd only arrived back in Choeng Mon late the previous night, after spending the best part of the last two days with Ivan Cameron's right-hand men at Interpol—Ted Anuwat and Bing Botwong.

With one of their trusted lieutenants, we'd managed to draw an accurate picture of the two goons who'd kidnapped me—the ones who'd called themselves 'Alan Jones' and 'Steve Bird'. Apparently, their identities didn't appear on any Interpol databases.

The footsteps grew louder—and before I had a chance to look up, a white envelope dropped into my lap. I raised my eyes and saw a young, dark boy hurriedly exiting the café. I only ever saw the back of him—and he appeared, judging by his size, to be no more than 13-years-old.

I glanced around the cafe and noticed nothing untoward. There were a dozen or so other people in the café with me, having breakfast. No one glanced at me—and nobody had apparently noticed the young boy enter and abruptly leave the café.

I stood and walked to the front of the café, holding the envelope as I scanned the street outside, looking for any signs of those goons who'd kidnapped me a few days earlier.

The street was empty, aside from a handful of local shopkeepers setting up for the day's trade.

I glanced back, looking at the people in the café. No one was watching me. No one was taking the slightest interest in me. I returned to my seat and nervously opened the envelope. Inside was a typed letter:

> "Billy. We told you we had contacts in places you'd never imagine. We told you we would know if you spoke to the authorities. We're aware of your movements over the last three days, and the people you've met with. You now have four days remaining to transfer the money before we kidnap and torture not one, but two of your closest friends. Your every move is being watched. A word of advice, Billy: Don't talk to the authorities again. If you do, we'll not only kidnap and torture your friends, but we'll also kill one or both of them. Ask yourself, Billy, are you a selfish man?"

My head was spinning. How could these people have possibly known I'd met with Ivan Cameron and his officers? Was there a leak in Ivan's office? Could it have been the Thai guy with the straw hat, carrying the large plastic bag? The one who'd been waiting for me to cross the road and take me to the Interpol office? Or was it one of the two guys waiting for me in the foyer? The ones who'd escorted me to the lift. Perhaps it was Ivan's PA—or any of the other people in that office who'd seen me enter.

Heaven forbid, could it have been one of Ivan's trusted lieutenants, Ted Anuwat or Bing Botwong? That all sounded a bit too incredulous.

I reread the typed note, and focused on the last paragraph:

> "*Your every move will be watched. A word of advice, Billy: Don't talk to the authorities again. If you do, we'll not only kidnap and torture your friends, but we'll also kill one or both of them. Ask yourself, Billy, are you a selfish man?*"

HINDSIGHT IS A wonderful thing. I often wonder: If we had our time all over again, would we do things differently in the same situation? I was in the same situation as I had been two days earlier—threatened, and warned not to go to the authorities. But what was I supposed to do this time around?

Many people might think I should've got straight on the phone to Ivan Cameron and told him what had just happened. Looking back, that *is* what I should have done...

…but it's not what I did.

Five years earlier, I'd had a bit of a breakdown. It had come on because of a combination of many things: Working too hard, too much travelling away from home, having a business that was being railroaded by a couple of corporate cowboys, and lots of additional things all building up at once. I even saw a shrink for a few months in LA. He was a guy who'd helped my ex-wife deal with the breakdown of our marriage.

He'd told me my problems were quite common among successful business people, because successful business people were always looking for the next opportunity. They were never satisfied with what they'd already achieved. That has been the story of my whole life—from my three failed marriages to the building of two very successful businesses, along with the failure of my clothing company. While my shrink, Dr. Draper, hadn't put a label on my condition, deep down, I'd realized I was experiencing some form of a breakdown. It was as though my brain was fried.

It had helped talking to Dr. Draper, and it had reinforced that I needed to escape my home in Malibu, escape from America, and relieve myself of all business-related stress. I'd realized I'd needed to pause and enjoy life. At the time, I'd told Dr. Draper about my car accident and the armed robbery I'd experienced some thirty years earlier—and how, back then, I'd felt the need to get away for a few weeks. I'd mentioned my trip to Choeng Mon in Thailand. Dr Draper had suggested I leave America and return to Thailand—or, more specifically, Choeng Mon. In fact, that's how I'd eventually come to live here.

The only part of Dr Draper's advice I hadn't followed was relieving myself of all business stress. Heck, once again I'd built a massive business from scratch—and I was about to list it in three months, for some serious money.

The way I was feeling now, given recent events, was very similar to how I'd been feeling five years earlier. I was stressed out, and when people are stressed out, their decision making is often less-than-good.

Yep, I realize now that what I was about to do was unbelievably stupid—but it's what I did anyway. I'll regret it for the rest of my life.

"IVAN, I'M GOING to head off to Singapore for a few weeks. I'm not taking my phone, I'm not taking my laptop. I just need to get away until all this crap blows over and you catch those thugs. I'll be uncontactable for the next few weeks—and I'll leave it in your capable hands to continue surveillance on all my closest friends and family. By the way, I haven't heard from the thugs. Probably all talk and no action. Cheers, mate. Talk soon."

That was the message I left on Ivan Cameron's cell phone.

The truth be told, I wasn't going to Singapore. Instead, I was going to head up to Chiang Mai for a few weeks—maybe wander across to Laos and basically become invisible while all this commotion was going on.

Ivan and his cohorts at Interpol had suggested I didn't succumb to these thugs. They believed if I gave them the twenty million now, they'd probably only come back after the stock exchange listing and try and extort more money. Their advice was to let Interpol catch these people in the course of their investigation. Nothing untoward should happen to my close friends or family, as they were all under constant surveillance by Interpol or the FBI.

I could have ignored Ivan's advice and simply transferred the money—but then I'd always be living with the risk that these thugs would come back to extort more money from me at a later point.

Until this morning, I'd been seriously considering that second option. Not now, though. Now, I planned to get way and leave Ivan and his trusted lieutenants to capture the people threatening me, and my friends and family.

I sent Pat Gabriel, Chook Burns, Ivan Cameron, and all three of my kids a text messages advising them that I was heading off to Singapore for a few weeks. I'd only have my private cell phone with me. Only Pat, Chook, my mother, and my children had that number…

…or so I'd thought.

CHAPTER 16

I HADN'T SLEPT a wink for the last three nights.

I'd flown directly from Koh Samui to Chiang Mai. I was sure I hadn't been followed. I'd kept a low profile in Chiang Mai, only coming out at night time to have a few too many beers. The more I drank, the better I felt while I was drinking—or so I thought.

But it actually worked in the opposite way. Too much alcohol meant I couldn't sleep—and I only ever woke up feeling groggy, tired, and stressed the following morning.

It was mid-afternoon of day eight of my self-imposed exile. I was tempted to call Ivan to see if he had any news, but I decided against that. *No news is good news*, I thought. I was running away from my problems. I was a classic case of someone suffering the first symptoms of acute depression. I was in self-denial of everything around me—hoping others, in this case

Ivan and his fellow Interpol officers, would solve my problems.

But that morning, a new thought entered my mind: *Should I call Ivan just in case something has happened? Maybe they've caught these thugs.*

No, I reasoned. If Ivan had any news, he'd have at least called Pat and organized for him to call me.

As if on cue, my private cell phone lit up. It was a photo with an accompanying message.

"Billy, you failed to follow our orders. We have Mandy Jones with us. As you can see from this picture, her torture has commenced. The next picture we send may be that of her corpse. We know you flew to Chiang Mai. You're very smart, Billy. You checked into two different hotels and managed to fool our men by exiting out of the back door of the first hotel, never to return. We will find you before too long, though. Send the money now—or Mandy Jones will be killed. The kidnap of the second person will start very shortly. Are you a selfish man, Billy?'

How the hell did they get my private cell phone number?

What have I gotten myself into? Poor Mandy! With three beautiful children!

I was distraught. I broke out in a deep sweat and my heart began to race. I'd give into their demands—instantly, and with no question. They could have the money, and who cared if they came back asking for more later? Nothing was more important than the safety of those close to me.

I was nauseous, and suddenly felt dizzy. I collapsed to the ground, knocking my temple on the side of the fridge in my hotel room.

I was woken later by the sound of my phone ringing. The right side of my face was covered in blood. I glanced at my watch and realized I'd been unconscious for at least sixty minutes. The force of my temple hitting the fridge must have knocked me out cold.

It was an unknown number, and I quickly answered the phone: "Hello?"

"Billy, you're a selfish bastard. Mandy Jones has now been killed. We've kidnapped and are about to torture a second person. I'll just put them on the phone, so you can hear their lovely voice. If the money isn't transferred today, this person will be killed by midnight."

Then I heard the voice of their next victim:

"Billy? What's going on? I'm scared! These men say they're going to kill me! Please, Billy! Help me!"

It was Chimlin, crying uncontrollably. "Please! Help me!"

Then the kidnapper returned to the line: "What's it to be, Billy Houston? Her dead? Or the money transferred?"

"I'll transfer the money now. Let her go now."

"If you carry out your part of the deal, Billy, then your lady friend won't be harmed."

"Why did you murder Mandy Jones, you bastards?"

"You failed to respond to our request. We wanted to make you aware we were fair dinkum."

I gulped.

"I didn't respond to your request immediately because I bloody fainted, after I saw the pictures of Mandy. I knocked my head against the fridge and knocked myself out. I've got blood pouring from my face."

They didn't seem to care.

"This is the plan, Billy: You transfer the money to our account *now*. It will take twenty-four hours to appear in our account. Once received, we'll release your lady friend—unharmed. You are then to catch a plane tomorrow morning, at 10:45am, from Chiang Mai to Bangkok. Check into the Hilton hotel there, where a room will be reserved under your name. You are to depart your hotel at 5:00pm and walk to the train station. Catch a train to Queen Sirikit National Convention Centre. Opposite the station is Benjakitti Park. Walk toward the lake and you'll see a row of seats. Sit on the seat to the far right as you approach the lake. Then wait."

My head was trembling as I held the phone. The voice continued:

"You will then receive a text message from us, while you're seated in the park. The text message will advise you as to where your friend will be. Note: You'll be under surveillance from the moment you arrive at Chiang Mai airport right up until you're seated in Benjakitti Park. Our surveillance of you in the park could be from a position *in* the park—or it could be from a highrise building a kilometer away. You'll never know."

Bastards.

"We will know, though," the voice warned, "if you've contacted the authorities again. If so, your lady friend will be killed. We'll then come and kill you, Billy Houston. You should now realize that we *don't* make idle threats."

"Okay! Okay!" I screamed into the phone.

I never heard that man's voice again.

A DAY LATER, I was sitting on the furthest-right seat at Benjakitti Park. It was approaching sunset, and there were many people in the park—some walking, some running, and others idly chatting. Young couples were embracing, others were holding hands. All were walking with what appeared to be no worries in the world.

Fortunately, the seat I'd been directed to sit in was vacant. Each row of seats was about eight feet long. The four adjacent seats were fully occupied. I wondered if the seat I'd been told to sit in had been left vacant on purpose. Had people tried to sit there and been told to move on? I'd never know.

I glanced at the people on the adjacent seats. A mixture of Thai and expat office workers, who'd finished working in one of the surrounding office buildings. Sitting on the grass in front of me was what appeared to be a multi-generational Thai family. The bespectacled grandfather had a cigarette in his mouth, and he was gazing at what I assumed were his three grand-kids; all running around and chasing each other while Mom, Dad and Grandma also looked on.

Thirty yards away, at the edge of the lake, stood a man with a cane feeding the ducks. Another couple, who appeared to be in their thirties, stopped on their bicycles to watch the congregation of ducks battling for the man's bread as he aimlessly tore the loaf apart and threw it into the shallow water a few feet from where he was standing.

Were any of these people part of the kidnappers' gang?

There was suddenly a loud ruckus from behind me, and the people in the adjacent seats stood up and started to point. I rose from my seat, somewhat reluctant to turn around and see what all the noise might be about—terrified it might be the tortured, bruised body of Chimlin they were peering at.

Thank God, it was a false alarm. The ruckus had been caused by a group of office workers playing soccer with each other; which had erupted into an argument. Two men stood chest-to-chest, pointing at each other. One was bare-chested, while the other wore a torn t-shirt. Tempers soon calmed down, though, and the game recommenced.

There were literally hundreds of people in my immediate area—including the masses of office workers getting some fresh air in the park after being cooped up in one of the dozens of office buildings surrounding the park.

I snorted bitterly. One thing I normally enjoyed about Bangkok were the beautiful parks dotted throughout the sprawling, urban landscape. They offered a sense of serenity amidst chaos, I guess.

It was now approaching 6:00pm and the lights of the park had been turned on. It would be dark in twenty minutes, and the park closed at eight. I was starting to feel impatient, and I was trembling nervously. I couldn't keep my right leg still—it was as though it had developed a mind of its own. I clasped both hands on my knee to keep my leg from jittering up and down, then started to massage my calf muscle to ease the tension. The day was still warm, and while I was dressed in a singlet with running shorts and shoes,

I was still sweating profusely. I hadn't slept at all the night before.

My cell phone suddenly buzzed. It was a text message from one of the unknown thugs.

> *"Your money has been received. Your lady friend is in Room 214 at the Grand Fortune Plaza in Soi Six. There is a key waiting for you in the foyer in the downstairs locker. The code to the locker is 8888. Your friend is tied up and unharmed. I see you are in your running gear, so if you leave now and jog, you should be there in fifteen minutes. Remember: One word about any of this to anyone, then we kill you. Understand?"*

I ROSE FROM my seat, looking across at the people I'd been observing for the last sixty minutes. Everyone was still carrying on as they had been previously. Nobody showed the slightest interest in me. I had no idea how these kidnappers could possibly have been observing me. Maybe, as they'd suggest, they were in one of the dozens of tall buildings that surrounded the park.

I looked around the skyline. Trying to find the person or people observing me was like trying to find a needle in a haystack. The only location I did have was where they'd claimed to have left Chimlin.

I'd never heard of a building called the Grand Fortune Plaza before. I quickly Googled it to find the exact address. Yep, one glance at the map and I knew where it was.

I ran as though my life depended on it. I quickly reached the building, which was a rather run-down, nondescript three-story building with a faded, broken sign outside flashing: 'Fortune'.

The word Plaza was hard to make out, as the lights meant to illuminate that part of the sign weren't working. I turned to enter, and was greeted on the front steps of the building by a slim lady wearing a miniskirt and a lot of makeup—obviously to make her look younger than she was.

She asked me: "I want lady?"

I ignored her and pushed open the door to the foyer. It had obviously seen better days, with the paint on all four walls peeling off. There was a damp-smelling stench as I entered the foyer. The Grand Fortune Plaza was certainly no longer Grand. I wondered if it had ever been Grand, even in its prime—which must have been decades ago.

Across, on the furthest-right wall, were a row of lockers. Some were dented, some were covered in rust. I found the locker for Room 214 and punched in code 8888.

Nothing happened.

I searched my phone for the message to confirm I had the right code: 8888. How could I forget that number? I punched it in again—and again, nothing happened. In frustration, I pulled the handle—and the door to the locker opened by itself.

Smartasses, I thought. The lockers were all so old the codes hadn't worked in years. The lockers no longer had *any* working locks.

I grabbed the key that was inside and looked around the foyer for the elevator, or stairs to the second floor. There was only one elevator, with a sign painted on it which read: "Lift isn't working."

I wondered if the lift had ever worked. To my left was a sign marked: "Exit". I wrenched open the door and the damp, musty smell was even worse in the stairwell. I climbed the stairs and quickly reached the first floor. There, I was greeted by another prostitute. She smiled at me, and asked: "You want boom boom?"

I rushed past her and opened the exit door to the second floor. The hallway floor was carpeted with pink, worn carpet. The walls were badly in need of paint. *What sort of hovel was this place?*

I finally found room 214.

I took a big breath as I slowly pushed the key in the door lock. I heard the click of the lock and turned the door handle gently. Slowly, I pushed open the door. Inside was the same, pink carpet, and the same walls, covered with peeling paint. Who lived in such conditions?

I screamed: "Chimlin! Chimlin?"

I was met with silence.

I was standing in a lounge room, with a television still turned on. The kitchen showed no signs of habitation. I assumed the television had been left on to ensure no passersby in the hallway would hear any muffled sounds from Chimlin.

There were three doors in the room, all shut. They lead off from the lounge and kitchen area.

I tried the door closest to me.

Empty. A bathroom and laundry.

The next door I pushed open was also empty: A bedroom with a double bed.

There was one more room to try. I hurriedly rushed to the door and shoved it open, screaming: "Chimlin?"

It was empty—a bedroom with a double bed. Other than the television being turned on, there was no sign of anyone having been in this hotel room.

I fell to the ground, gripped my hair, and started shaking. Tears welled in my eyes.

What the hell had I done? Mandy Jones was dead, and now it appeared Chimlin had also been murdered by these thugs.

Perhaps I should have got back with Chimlin after Lars and Dao had got married. I thought about the words she'd said to me that night, before she'd run off: "Billy, you only ever think about yourself."

My phone buzzed. I was scared to look at it—since surely it would only confirm my worst fears; that Chimlin had been killed.

After about fifteen seconds, kneeling there, feeling sorry for myself—regretting everything I'd done—my phone lit up again with the same message.

I peered at the message, having trouble reading it at first from the tears in my eyes.

Did it say what I thought it said?

I frantically rubbed my eyes, so I could see properly:

"She's in the room next door: Room 215. The door's unlocked. See ya, buddy."

I rushed to my feet and ran out of the door. I quickly turned back, realizing I was running the wrong way, and barged through the door of Room 215.

THE ROOM WAS dark as I entered. I could make out a body lying on the bed in front of me. I madly searched for a light switch. Chimlin was lying there, limp on the bed. Her feet and hands were bound, and tape covered her mouth.

"Chimlin? Wake up! Wake up!"

Her eyes slowly opened, then focused with a look of astonishment, bewilderment, and confusion. Her eyes opened and closed several times—no doubt adjusting to the sudden light in the room. A nervous smile appeared on her face once she finally recognized that I was in the room with her.

"I'll find a knife to cut these bandages!"

Chimlin shrieked in pain as I tore the tape from the bare delicate skin around her lips and cheeks. As she lay there, I rushed into the kitchen, searching the drawers madly—looking for anything sharp enough to cut the bandages. I finally found a knife and, while old and blunt, it did the job in removing the bandages from Chimlin's ankles and wrists.

"Billy! Billy, what's this all about?" Chimlin sobbed while hugging me.

"I'll tell you soon. Let's get you back to your house, so you can have a shower, changes clothes, and we can then sit down and I'll tell you everything. Let's get out of this horrible building."

CHAPTER 17

"YOU NEED TO tell the police everything you've told me, Billy. You need to get your $20 million, and we need to find Mandy."

I had tears in my eyes.

"Mandy's dead, Chimlin."

I buried my head in my hands for a moment, and only looked up at the sudden, unexpected touch of Chimlin's hands on my neck. Her touch brought me back to reality.

"I killed her, Chimlin," I sobbed. "I let those thugs take her life. I would've paid the $20 million straight away when they'd followed through with their threats and kidnapped Mandy. If only I hadn't collapsed and hit my head. If only I hadn't been knocked unconscious."

Tears rolled down my cheeks.

"It's my fault, Chimlin! It's all my fault that Mandy's dead!"

"Maybe she's alive, Billy. Maybe she'll be found!"
I sobbed.

"I doubt it. These guys are absolute monsters. I saw
what they did to Spinkle. The pictures I saw still make
me want to vomit." I wiped the wetness from my
cheeks. "But I'll go and see Ivan Cameron, my Interpol
contact, later tonight. I'll let him know what's
happened over the last couple of days."

I looked up at Chimlin.

"Do you want to come with me?"

"Of course, Billy." Her fingers tightened on my
shoulder. "I want to be by your side during this horrible
ordeal."

I wiped more tears from my cheeks.

"How did they kidnap you, Chimlin? You were
meant to be under 24-hour surveillance by Ivan and his
team. Didn't Ivan contact you? Didn't he tell you he
was placing you under surveillance?

"No. No one contacted me from Interpol."

"That's strange," I blinked. "We'll ask Ivan why
nothing happened..." I took a shuddering breath. "But
how did they kidnap you? What happened?"

"I was shopping at the local grocery store, pushing
the trolley toward the car. A Thai woman approached
me with a clipboard. She asked if I'd answer a few
questions for a survey she was undertaking. She
introduced herself as a market research person. I
obliged, and for the next few minutes, she asked me
several questions about my shopping habits. She then
thanked me—and that's when a car suddenly appeared.
It had dark, tinted windows—and she told me to get in
the car. She then produced a gun from her purse."

I gulped.

"Were there people around you? I mean, it's hard to kidnap someone in the middle of the day, in the middle of a busy shopping centre."

"Yes, there were people around," Chimlin nodded, "but it all happened so quickly. One minute, I'm talking to this professional-looking woman holding a clipboard. The next, I'm being pushed into the back of a car by force. I remember thinking I couldn't just leave my shopping trolley in the middle of the pathway. I looked out the window, and saw another woman appeared pushing the trolley away.

"Was your daughter with you?"

"She's away with my ex-husband."

"Thank God she wasn't with you."

"Yes, who knows how it all would have ended if Kiah was with me."

Chimlin shuddered.

"I was given an injection of some kind, and the next thing I knew, I was tied up and gagged in the hotel room where you found me. I have barely any memory of what happened to me from when I was forced into the car. I barely remember speaking to you on the phone. I remember they told me if you paid them the money, then nothing would happen to me. They didn't mention what the money was for, or how much it was. After I spoke to you, they allowed me to use the bathroom and gave me some food. Shortly after that, I was given another injection and I fell asleep. I'd wake up, but each time I did I felt so drowsy I'd soon fall asleep again. It's weird. It felt like a dream—one in which I was the star character. It was as though I was watching my own movie." She shook her head. "I still feel drowsy now." Then her eyes focused on me. "You look horrible, Billy—as though you haven't slept in days. That's how I feel."

"Let's go and see Ivan Cameron. I texted him earlier to let him know I was in Bangkok and I had some further updates for him."

"BILLY, WE DIDN'T have an address for Chimlin," Ivan explained when we finally met to speak with him. "I tried to call you numerous times, but you weren't returning calls. You'd left a message earlier that you were going to Singapore and wouldn't have your mobile phone with you. We had no way of contacting you, Billy! We had no phone number for Chimlin—only an old address. I suggest you check your messages on your phone, Billy."

Chimlin hugged her arms around herself, and admitted: "That's right, Billy. I did move three weeks ago."

I was reeling as I learned all this.

"Okay, I accept that." I turned to my friend from Interpol. "But, Ivan—what a fuck up! What do we do now?"

In all the excitement of locating Chimlin, I hadn't returned to my Bangkok apartment. where I'd left my business phone. I hadn't checked my messages since I'd left.

"We need to put out a missing person report on Mandy Jones," Ivan said gravely. "Until we find a body, there's a faint chance she's still alive. It's only a slight chance—but while there's any glimmer of hope, we must never give up looking for her."

Ivan sighed.

"Mandy was under 24-hour surveillance by my team, so I need to find out how the fuck she got kidnapped." He looked up at me. "I'll personally go and see her husband and tell him that his wife is missing. I must be careful how much I tell him—but, nevertheless, I need to tell him that you were the victim of an extortion attempt, and that these people might have kidnapped his wife. Mr. Jones is probably worried sick already as to what's happened to her for the last 36-hours. I wouldn't be surprised if he's already filed a missing person report with the local police."

"I'll come with you, Ivan. Should we show him the pictures of Mandy's tortured body?"

"No, Billy—there is no reason for him to see the pictures of his wife. If she's been murdered, I don't want the last image he has of her to be that of a tortured body. Plus, there *is* a chance—however slim—that Mandy is still alive. There's also a chance these people will come back and try to extort more money from you, Billy."

"That's not a problem, Ivan. All my wealth—every cent—is going to be given to charity. I don't want the money. It's only brought me trouble. It will all go to charity, aside from a few million left in trust for my children. If Mandy has been murdered, I'll be leaving money for her family as well—and I'll make that public, so these thugs can read it first-hand wherever they may be." I gulped dryly. "So they'll realize there's no money left to extort me for, or hurt my friends and family."

"Billy, it's a bit too early to be thinking about things like that..." said Ivan.

"No," I shook my head. "I thought about it all last week—ever since those guys kidnapped me in the café at Choeng Mon. Money just seems to get me in trouble, Ivan. I had those corporate cowboys try and take Future Wealth illegally from Pat and me—and now I build another successful business, I have more thugs using extortion to threaten me." I sighed bitterly. "I've had enough. Money is the root of all evil."

I took a deep breath and added: "Let's go and see Mandy's husband. I'll let you do the talking, Ivan. I don't think I'm capable of talking to Sean about Mandy, anyway. But I got her into this mess, so I've got to be there to share the bad news."

MANDY'S HUSBAND, SEAN, clearly didn't know how to take the news when we met with him. He focused on me, as Ivan and I stood there.

"This is unbelievable!" Sean growled, glaring at me. "You've had criminals threatening to extort money from you, Billy—and they've now kidnapped my wife! And you can't even locate her?"

Next, he turned his anger to Ivan.

"You're telling me there's a chance she's been *murdered?*" Sean was practically trembling. "Mandy hasn't been in touch for the last 36-hours. The last time I saw her was 8:30am on Tuesday, when I dropped her off at Bangkok airport to catch a plane to Beijing for work."

He turned back to me: "*Your* work, Billy."

Sean slumped into his chair.

"I was surprised I hadn't heard from her for the last day and a half. Not *concerned*, because I'd just assumed she was hard at it, finalizing things in China before the listing of Billy's business."

"We'll find her in the next 48-hours," said Ivan.

"So, you don't even know where she is, then?" Sean turned to me. "Billy—you said a moment ago that the kidnappers said they were going to torture Mandy if you didn't hand over $20 million. Just… Just confirm to me, Billy. You immediately transferred the $20 million, right?"

There was a moment of silence as I pondered what to say next.

I've never been a liar and didn't want to turn into one now. I glanced over at Ivan, who was staring at me anxiously, waiting for my answer.

I took a deep breath.

"Sean, mate… They told me they'd started to torture Mandy—and that if I didn't immediately transfer the money, they'd kill her."

"So, you *did* immediately transfer the money— right, Billy?" Sean stared intently at me.

I gulped.

"I fainted Sean."

His expression was like a mask.

"I fainted looking at the pictures of Mandy's tortured body," I stammered, "and I knocked my head on the fridge on the way down. I was unconscious!"

Sean just stared at me as I tried to explain:

"I... I awoke an hour later, Sean—with blood down the side of my face and the phone ringing. It was them calling me back."

"What did they say, Billy?"

"They said..."

I stopped, choking on my words—tears now swelling in my eyes.

"They said *what*, Billy?"

"They... They said they'd murdered Mandy, Sean—because I hadn't transferred the twenty million to them quickly enough."

There was silence. Sean buried his head in his hands and started sobbing uncontrollably. After a moment or two, he stood up, shaking—his fists now clenched together, tears running down both sides of his face. He lumbered over toward the window of the apartment and stood there, staring out into space.

Finally, Sean Jones turned around, shaking his fist at me.

"Houston," Sean spat, "you fucking *killed my wife*—the mother of my three children! Why the *fuck* didn't you just transfer the money when they wanted it in the first place? Why put all these people in danger? Because of your own greed? You are a fucking *murderer*, Billy Houston!"

The words of those thugs came back to haunt me: *"Billy, are you a selfish man?"*

Sean then demanded: "Show me the pictures of Mandy's tortured body."

"You don't want to see them, Sean," I stammered. "It's not good for you to see them."

Ivan interrupted: "Sean, there's no need for you to see the pictures of Mandy. There's still a chance Mandy is alive. Until we find a body, we'll continue searching for her. I'm confident we'll find her alive—I really am."

I knew Ivan didn't believe this. He knew better than me how ruthless these thugs were.

"Show me the fucking pictures!" Sean began to scream, walking toward me and reaching to wrap his hands around my neck.

I hesitated once again, and Sean screamed again: "Show me the fucking pictures of my wife, you murderer!"

I grabbed my private cell phone from my pocket and opened my messages to the pictures of Mandy. Reluctantly, I handed the cell phone to Sean.

Sean immediately started to dry heave. Ivan moved over to the couch as Sean collapsed onto it, trying to comfort Mandy's distraught husband.

I knew it was time for me to leave when Sean screamed once again: "Houston, you're a fucking *murderer*! You'll pay for this, you bastard!"

And that I would.

I'd certainly pay for it—for the rest of my life. I'd pay for not transferring that money when I was first threatened. I'd pay for the rest of my life for fainting and hitting my head against the fridge—delaying the transfer of the money for the crucial period that cost Mandy her life.

Every night since then, I've woken up covered in sweat, shaking—at times uncontrollably. The nightmare of what happened to Mandy Jones remains vivid in my mind. Every night, I replay the events of those few days—cursing myself for not acting sooner. I still cry myself back to sleep, huddled in the fetal position like a baby. There are times—many times—when I've wished it was me they'd taken, instead of Mandy Jones. Wishing it was me they'd murdered, and not Mandy.

How many times do we all wish we could go back in time and change things?

Hindsight is a wonderful thing.

CHAPTER 18

Five months later

WHILE THE LISTING of 21st Century Fitness Group on the Hong Kong Stock Exchange was a resounding success, the staff were in deep mourning for months following the kidnapping and assumed murder of Mandy Jones.

Mandy's disappearance became a Thai police matter—and, to this day, Mandy's body has never been found. After a couple of months, the authorities ceased their search for her—announcing that she was, unfortunately, most likely dead.

A week or two after that announcement, Mandy's husband was found dead himself—in his car, in their garage. Sean's body was found by their cleaning lady. He'd apparently gassed himself. The loss of his wife in such tragic circumstances had been too much for him to bear.

Mandy and Sean left behind three young children, all under the age of fourteen. He also left behind a suicide note, sharing his thoughts during his last few hours—the hours before he decided to take his own life.

There were more than a few scathing paragraphs about me in Sean's suicide note. Unfortunately, though perhaps not unfairly, he blamed me for Mandy's tragic disappearance.

Whether he was right or wrong didn't really matter—it was never going to bring Mandy back either way. Venting his anger toward me, however, only added to how wretched I was feeling about this whole, horrible, tragic mess.

I'd engaged one of the leading public relation companies in Bangkok to ensure widespread coverage, across all the Southeast Asian media, that I'd given away the entire fortune I'd made listing 21st Century Fitness to charity. I did so because of what had happened to me, what had happened to Mandy, and because of the threats that gang of thugs had made towards my loved ones. I never wanted those people to have a reason to come back, trying to extort more money from me—and threatening those closest to me if they did so.

I had established a special Trust Fund to ensure there would be $5 million set aside for each of my three children in the States—along with the same for Mandy's three children. I made sure I was in no way connected with the Trust Fund. I had no access to the funds and no role with how those funds were invested.

As for me—I had an ongoing annuity of $100,000 per year for the rest of my life, all from money I gave to Pat Gabriel—invested in his name, with no recourse back to me.

With the income from listing 21st Century Fitness, plus all my existing investments, my total fortune totaled close to $320 million—all of which was left in a charitable foundation to help the underprivileged in all the Southeast Asian countries that the 21st Century Group operated in. Other than the annuity income, that meant I had no other income or assets.

After Sean's suicide, I also resigned from all involvement with the 21st Century Group. I now had no board position, no shares, and no involvement in both Future Wealth or the 21st Century Fitness Group—the two companies I'd started from scratch, that combined were now worth more than a billion dollars.

I informed all the staff at 21st Century Fitness that I was taking a long vacation—uncertain myself where I'd be going, or what I'd be doing. Johnny Kean suggested a farewell dinner for me to celebrate what we had achieved in building 21st Century Fitness—which had become the region's leading fitness, yoga, and dietary company.

This was the conversation we had, one night in Bangkok, over a couple of drinks:

"YOU LOOK FUCKING horrible, Billy. Absolutely horrible."

We'd met in a nondescript bar in Bangkok, and I'd forgotten that Johnny hadn't seen me since I'd announced my departure via email to all the staff a few weeks earlier.

I could tell he'd been quite taken back by my appearance when I'd arrived at the bar he'd suggested. It wasn't one of our usual haunts. In fact, I believe he'd chosen it knowing full well that nobody here would recognize me.

Johnny whistled through his teeth: "You don't look anything like the proud businessmen I came to know so well over the last few years."

I snorted bitterly in agreement.

The extortion—along with the murder of Mandy, the unexpected death of her husband, and the kidnapping of Chimlin—had meant that the whole, horrible chain of events remained featured in the press for many months after it had happened.

When I met with Johnny, I hadn't shaved for several weeks, my hair had grown long, and I'd lost a lot of weight. I wasn't eating properly, and I wasn't sleeping at all—but I'd refused to seek professional help, since I'd thought I could tackle and overcome my demons myself.

Johnny placed a hand on my shoulder.

"I know you've been through a lot of shit, Billy. I know you blame yourself for Mandy's death and Sean's suicide but none of it is your fault, Billy."

"It *is* my fault, Johnny. If I'd transferred the twenty million the first time I was kidnapped in Choeng Mon, it would have been the end of the story. Mandy wouldn't have been kidnapped, or murdered—and Chimlin wouldn't have been kidnapped either."

"Billy, you did what *any* sane, normal person would have done. You immediately informed the authorities, and it was *their* professional judgement that you didn't cave into the demands of those criminals. You did what you were told to do, Billy."

"But I shouldn't have gone away for those few days!"

"I would've done the same, Billy," Johnny reassured me. "Given the pressure that extortion attempt put you under, it's a normal reaction for a person to want to get away and leave the authorities to deal with everything. Whether you went away, or stayed in Bangkok, it wouldn't have made any difference. When you found out Mandy had been kidnapped, you immediately transferred the money."

I felt tears well in my eyes.

"But I didn't, Johnny, that's the problem. I *didn't* transfer the money straight away."

"You didn't transfer the money straight away because you knocked yourself unconscious—and that was because you fell after seeing the pictures *they'd* sent you of Mandy. Fuck, you've still got the scar on your head to prove it." Johnny pointed to my head, where I had the scars of the seven stiches I'd had to get after hitting my head on the side of the fridge.

Johnny sighed.

"Billy, you need professional help to deal with what you've been through. If anyone is to blame, it's the authorities. How did Mandy manage to get kidnapped, if she was meant to be under surveillance by the authorities? You gave the authorities the names and addresses of all the people that required round-the-clock protection. The authorities fucked up! Not you!"

"Yes," I sighed. "Ivan and his team, while not admitting it, did stuff up Mandy's surveillance. She was kidnapped at the airport while waiting for her flight to Beijing. All Ivan said was that there would be an internal investigation. It's taking place right now, and he promised heads would roll once it was concluded."

I looked up at my friend and former colleague.

"I get what you're saying, Johnny—but ultimately, I was the boss. I was the guy being extorted. I had the money and I should've just given it to those thugs when they first demanded it."

"What? Given it to them on day one?" Johnny shook his head. "I bet they'd have just come back and asked for more. It would've kept on going, Billy. Only two things have stopped them coming back again and trying to extort more money from you as it is. Firstly, your very public announcement in the press that you've given away your entire fortune because of what happened. There *is* no money for them to come back and take. Secondly, once they tortured and murdered Mandy—and Sean committing suicide as a result— these criminals are now Public Enemy Number One. The whole of Southeast Asia now knows what they did—and that they're utter scumbags."

He leaned closer.

"Billy, it's not just me who sees things this way— it's everyone at 21st Century Fitness. No one blames you—not at all. Sean only blamed you because he had no one else to blame. He was inconsolable, looking for a scapegoat—and you, in his eyes, were the obvious choice."

He lowered his voice.

"You didn't hear this from me, Billy, but Sean suffered from severe depression. He'd been professionally diagnosed with depression—it was part of the reason he stopped working and became a stay-at-home dad. It was also why he and Mandy left Sydney. They'd thought a change might help him, and save their relationship. I don't know the full details, but he came from an abusive family—his father was an alcoholic who beat him up. He had a lot of emotional shit to get over. Mandy was his pillar. She provided him with his safety net. Once she was gone, Sean lost that safety net. In his warped eyes, he had nothing to live for—not even the kids."

Johnny's eyes were filled with empathy—for both me, and Sean.

"He couldn't function without Mandy," Johnny admitted, "but you weren't to blame for that, Billy. Those criminals are to blame—and the rest of the company agrees with me."

I was silent for a second, before murmuring:

"I wasn't aware of the personal issues Sean was dealing with."

"Mandy and I were close, Billy. She'd shared with me all the troubles she and Sean had in Sydney—and whilst things were still tough for Sean, he was finally getting on top of his demons here in Thailand." Johnny sighed. "Mandy shared this in confidence with me, so I'd please ask you to keep this to yourself."

I nodded, but said: "I understand what you're saying about blame. Pat Gabriel and Chook Burns had the same conversation with me a few months earlier—but it still doesn't take away the pain, Johnny."

"Nothing takes away the pain," he nodded. "Not when you're mourning. Nothing does, other than time. We all feel pain for what's happened—to Mandy, and Sean, and their lovely children. The only thing that will heal your pain—my pain, and everyone's pain—is time. Time eventually heals all wounds, Billy."

I smiled weakly.

"Thanks for your words of wisdom, Johnny. I think I only counted two 'f' words in that whole conversation." It had been a long time since I'd work a smile on my face.

"Correct, Billy," Johnny grinned himself. "I've cured my problem with the 'f' word, thanks to you. It was hard work, Billy, but I seldom use the 'f' word now—and that, Billy, is the first smile I've seen on your face the whole time you've been sitting here."

He squeezed my shoulder.

"Billy, you're a lovely man. You're caring, honest, fun, smart, and the best bloody businessman I've ever met. You've not once, but *twice* built companies from start-up to over four-hundred—*five-hundred*—million dollars each. Not many people in the world could have done that."

Johnny then added: "But you've got to get off the grog. You look horrible—nothing like the Billy I knew before this horrible ordeal. What about a farewell dinner with the team, Billy?"

"Nah, I'm not up to it at this stage. Maybe later."

I lied to Johnny. I knew there would never be a later.

Get off the grog, I thought. Easier said than done when you're dealing with internal demons like I was.

CHIMLIN WAS IN a bad way from her kidnapping ordeal. I was paying for her to have counselling. Initially, she appeared to be okay—but a few weeks after what had happened, she had an emotional meltdown. She'd been in the middle of a busy Bangkok shopping centre when she'd started screaming, collapsing in the middle of the shopping mall.

Ambulances had to be called, and Chimlin had been admitted to the hospital—which she'd then been in and out of for the previous few months. Apparently, she'd thought she saw one of her kidnappers walking towards her at the mall—and it bought back all the details of her horrible ordeal all over again.

I was in a dark place, too. Mandy had been murdered. Sean had committed suicide—and now Chimlin had suffered a breakdown. As much as Johnny Kean, Pat Gabriel, and Chook Burns had said it wasn't my fault—deep down, I still blamed myself.

I'd been through one nightmare, and I was about to go through another one. At the time, if you'd told me things could only get worse, I'd have laughed at you.

It would have been the last laugh I'd have for a while.

Chapter 19

I AWOKE FROM a coma-like sleep, still intoxicated from the night before. My head was throbbing. I searched blindly for my watch, dragging my right hand across the bedside table, expecting to find it there.

It wasn't there.

I sat up and swiveled to drop my legs over the edge of the bed. The room was still in semi-darkness, with the curtains closed. I waited for the throbbing in my head to settle down before I attempted to stand upright. Still sitting there, I leaned over and turned the bedside table light on. Then, slowly, I stood up—the blood vessels in my head beating in rhythm with my heart.

Wow, this was going to be a long day of recovery.

I found my cell phone and checked the time. It was 11:30am already. What had happened to me last night?

Water. I needed water—and a shower. I padded into the kitchen and opened the fridge, grabbing a fresh bottle of water. I gulped it all down. Man, that felt good.

I walked over to the curtains and pulled them back to reveal the skyline of Bangkok. The light was blinding. Why was I still in my clothes?

Then it came back to me with a shuddering jolt.

"MAN, I'LL PAY the bill! I just want one more drink."

"It's 3:30am in the morning. You're drunk. We can't let you buy any more drinks. You need to *go*, sir."

"Just one more drink—then I'II go."

"No. You've upset too many people here. No more drink for you. Come over to the counter and pay your tab now, or I'II call the police."

I'd attempted to get up from my bar stool and fallen to the ground. The manager had rushed over and helped me up, bringing my bar tab with him.

"Fourteen thousand, five hundred baht. You pay now. You pay *now*."

I looked around for the young bar girl who'd been sitting with me a few moments ago. She was nowhere to be seen.

"You pay now, sir—or I call the police. Pay now. Pay now."

"Okay, okay," I muttered, "I'II pay now." I searched my pockets for my Thai money and pulled out some loose coins. I searched my back pocket—nothing there. Then I searched both my front pockets again. There was nothing there other than a twenty baht note.

I've never carried a wallet. I've always carried cash in my pocket with an ATM card and a credit card as back up. I used to go out with my cell phone, but I'd stopped that practice a few years ago, after I'd left my cell behind in a bar when I was out on the town for an innocent night with Pat Gabriel. That had been the third time I'd lost a cell phone, so I decided my cell phone should stay home when I went out on the town. I'd never lost a cell phone since.

"You have no money? I call police," said the Thai barman—who I assumed was also the owner.

I'd never been in this bar before. Bangkok was a big city, and I'd been staying in a part of the sprawling city that I'd never stayed in before—purely because I didn't want to stay in a part of town where anyone would know me.

"I have money. That girl must have taken it from me. Where has she gone?"

"No girl! You drink, you get drunk, you not pay! You bad man! I call my friends over." The owner of the bar looked across to the far side of the room, where some locals were drinking. A couple of burly, western men, covered in tattoos and wearing singlets, stood up and approached us.

"What's the problem, Tan? This guy causing trouble?" They spoke in thick accents. I assumed they were Russian.

"He gets drunk. He drinks with lady. He owes fourteen thousand, five hundred baht. No money. Not pay." The man identified as Tan showed them my tab on the piece of paper.

"You pay Tan now, man—or we'll take care of you." The smaller of the three guys pushed my shoulder back firmly. "Pay *now*, man."

"I came here with a lot of money in my pocket," I blustered. "My money's gone! Either lost, or someone has taken it. I'll go to the ATM right now and get money out. I'll come straight back and pay."

"No! You not go. Not pay. You bad man," said Tan.

"I have a credit card. I'll pay now with that."

"No, I not take credit card, only cash."

"Okay, what I'll do is this: I'll give you my credit card to hold while I go to the ATM down the street and get money out."

"No! You give me *that* as well," said Tan, pointing to my gold Rolex watch. It was a present from the board of Future Wealth for my fiftieth birthday.

"Okay," I nodded. "You hold my watch—which is worth a lot of money—and my credit card. I'll walk down the road to the ATM, get the money, and come straight back. Done deal." I was slurring my words as I put my hand out to the man called Tan.

He shook my hand, and the Russians—who were there to threaten and possibly beat me up—walked away, muttering words in Russian as they no doubt laughed at my drunken state and my naivety at being fleeced by the bar girl.

I walked out to the street, the fresh air finally making me realize how drunk I was. I had no idea where I was. I looked down the street both ways. It was full of bars with people milling about on the pavement outside.

I thought I may as well go left. I was sure to find an ATM somewhere along the journey, right?

I'd walked at least two hundred yards down the street and must have passed at least thirty similar bars to the one I'd been drinking at. Both sides of the street were lined with bars—some large, some small, but all with lots of people in them; mainly males drinking and partying into the wee hours.

I was stumbling as I walked along, searching for an ATM. I'd walked into a few people on the pavement, simply a sign of how drunk I was. I apologized profusely and was gently pushed away, most times at least—with the occasional outburst from a couple of people telling me to "fuck off" in no uncertain terms.

Across the road, I finally saw a local convenience store. *It was sure to have an ATM*, I thought.

I crossed the road, thinking at the time I'd better make sure I wasn't hit by a passing car as I weaved in and out of traffic. A few drivers hooted their horn at me. This was a busy street, even at this hour.

I withdrew thirty thousand baht from the ATM—more than enough to settle my tab and pay for a taxi home. *I might even have a few more beers,* I thought. It might help me get to sleep. I looked across the road from where I came from. The street was lined with bars as far as the eye could see, all full of people, all with brazen lights flashing.

There was the 'Goodtime Bar', 'The Happy Bar', The Sexpot Bar', 'The Lonesome Bar', 'The Stay Home Bar', 'The Dickey Bar'—they all looked the same.

How was I ever going to find the bar I'd come from? Particularly in the drunken state I was currently in? *It can't be that hard,* I thought. I'm sure to recognize the bar when I walk past it.

I crossed the road. I was confused. Which end of the street was the bar on?

I don't know about you, but when I'm this drunk, I tend to lose all sense of direction. It must be *this* way, I thought—no more than two hundred yards down the road. I walked and walked. I wasn't sure for how long, as I no longer had a watch to tell me the time.

Where the fuck was the bar I came from? Surely it wasn't *this* far down the street.

Fuck it, I needed a beer. Time to gather my thoughts. I walked into the bar I was standing in front of. A few hours later, I remember being asked to leave the bar as it was closing. I'd forgotten all about my watch *and* my credit card. I'd just wanted to get back to my hotel room. I was exhausted.

One thing I'd learned over the last few months—as I continued to drown my sorrows every day, thinking about Mandy, Sean, and Chimlin—was I needed to always carry the card of the hotel I was staying at. I'd had a couple of experiences in which I hadn't got home until daylight, as I'd had no idea where my hotel was.

Having some brain cells still left—even after months and months of consuming far too much alcohol—I soon realized the solution was simply to always carry the business card of the hotel I was staying at. In my drunken state, I simply passed the hotel business card to the bar manager of whatever bar I was intoxicated at, and then asked him to hail me a taxi to take me to that address.

The previous night, twenty minutes after leaving that final bar, I'd stumbled out of the taxi outside my hotel. I remember seeing the first glimpses of sunrise as I somehow made my way to the lift.

I'd made some house rules while I was drinking to excess. I hated getting home from a bar in daylight the next morning, so I always ensured I got home before sunrise. I remember thinking to myself that morning: "*I only just made it.*" The first glimpses of the morning sun had been visible, but I'd still give myself a passing mark. It hadn't been *totally* daylight.

I'd hit the button for the sixth floor, exited the lift, walked down the corridor and fumbled for my keys. As I pushed open the door, I'd fallen straight onto my bed. I was too exhausted to even take off my clothes. This might have been one of the few nights—or, more correctly, mornings—in which I went straight to sleep.

"YES, I NEED to cancel my credit card. I lost it last night while I was out."

I was talking to a lady on the other end of the phone, located in a call center who-knows-where. Maybe the Philippines. Maybe India. Who knew—maybe even America.

After spending a few minutes on the phone, my credit card was finally cancelled and a new one was issued to my mailing address at home in Choeng Mon—though I wasn't sure when I'd be going to Choeng Mon next. Too many people there would want to know how I was feeling, how was I coping, or if I was suffering from stress. No doubt, as soon as they saw me, they'd would say I looked bloody horrible and needed to see a doctor.

I could survive for the next few months of my travels paying cash. It would make things a bit more difficult when booking flights and travel, but not impossible.

I sat at on the couch, looking across the skyline of Bangkok, and thought what a fuck up last night had been. I'd lost my gold Rolex watch, which was worth a considerable sum of money—probably fifty times the value of my unpaid bar bill. The owner of the bar had made a nice little return from me last night.

It wasn't the cost of the lost watch that upset me, though—it was the sentimental value attached to it. It had been my fiftieth birthday present from my colleagues at Future Wealth. Many good people had contributed to buy me that watch—people who were instrumental in helping me and Pat build the company.

Yep, I'd fucked up again. I thought of my kids in the States—and of Mandy Jones, Sean, and their own three children, who now had no parents. Then, of course, I thought of Chimlin.

Tears started to well in my eyes, and I muttered to myself: "Billy Houston, you've had a fall from grace here, mate."

I looked at the clock on the wall. It was only 12:30pm—too early to go to a bar for a drink.

Then, I thought: *"Stuff it."* Alcohol was the only thing that made me feel better—plus, as strange as it seems, perhaps a cold beer would be the only thing that could sober me up. I grabbed my ATM card, along with my remaining cash, and thought to myself as I closed the front door: *"Perhaps I'll buy myself a cheap watch on my way to the bar. Perhaps I need to go and try and find the bar I left my watch at."*

Then I realized I didn't even have an idea what street that bar was on. It would be like searching for a needle in a haystack.

CHAPTER 20

I WOKE UP startled.

A near-naked body was touching my naked body beneath the sheets of the bed.

I looked up to see a dark-skinned Thai woman with long, black hair lying sound asleep in my hotel bed. She was wearing only a G-string and a bra.

My movements woke her from her slumber. Yawning, she stood up and headed toward the bathroom door.

What happened to me last night? I remembered buying drinks for a few people in a bar—and then being asked to leave in the wee hours. The rest of the night was a complete blank, though. I couldn't remember a thing. How did I meet this woman? How did she end up in my bed?

The woman reappeared from the bathroom. I gathered she was no older than her early thirties. I hoped I hadn't had sex with her. When I was hitting the grog hard, I made it a rule not to sleep around. The thought of catching some sort of sexual disease scared me off the temptation of casual sexual encounters. I'd met plenty of guys in the various bars I'd been frequenting during the last few months who'd take home a different bar girl every night for casual sex. They all told me they used condoms—and none had come forward yet to tell me they'd ever caught some form of sexual disease—but I knew from my college days, some thirty years ago, that condoms sometimes break, sometimes they come off, and that they're far from fool-proof.

While they reduced the odds of contracting a sexual disease, they certainly didn't eliminate the risk.

This mysterious Thai woman walked across to the bed, then hopped on top of the sheets, giving me a big smile. "How are you feeling, Mr. Billy?"

She knew my name—but I had no recollection of hers. She was gorgeous, though. Stunning.

I sat up, with my private parts still beneath the sheets, somewhat embarrassed that I had a beautiful Thai woman in my bed—a woman whose name I didn't even know. Hell, a woman I had no recollection of even meeting—and she was wearing only her underwear!

"I'm sorry, I've forgotten your name."

"My name is Boonsri."

"Boonsri! Yes! How could I forget?" I lied. "That's a nice name."

"It's my nickname. It means beautiful."

"You speak very good English."

"Yes. I went to English classes for three years to improve my English. I can speak a little bit of German and a little bit of Russian as well."

My head was throbbing. It seemed I woke up with a sore head every morning lately—all of them self-inflicted as a result of consuming too much alcohol. I'd normally start off with a few beers and good intentions, but end up in the early wee hours drinking whiskey. The whiskey seemed to make it easier for me to fall asleep—and got rid of the flashbacks about what had happened to Mandy, Sean, and Chimlin.

"I don't want to be rude," I told the beautiful young woman, "but I have no recollection of meeting you last night. Did we... ahem... have sex?" I prayed the answer was no.

"We didn't have sex," Boonsri laughed. "You told me you wanted someone to hold you and cuddle you for the night, until you fell asleep. You tossed and turned for a long time in bed. You were talking in your sleep—and at one point, you woke up screaming words I couldn't understand."

"I'm sorry. I'm very sorry."

"You told me that some bad things had happened to the people you loved, because of something you did. You started crying in the bar I was working at. I comforted you, and you asked me if I'd come home with you and hold you. You seemed like a nice man—and you told me you were the man who started 21st Century Fitness. I use the 21st Century Fitness app, and I wear the gym clothes."

She laughed: "At first, I thought you were lying about who you were—but I googled your name and your picture came up: The man who started 21st Century! So, I trusted you—and I agreed to come to your hotel room with you. You seem very sad and lonely, Mr. Billy."

"Thank God we didn't have sex. I thought you must have been a bar girl."

"No! I'm not a bar girl. I manage the bar on behalf of the owner. I'm not a sex worker, Mr. Billy—and normally I wouldn't *ever* go home with a man. But there was something about you, Mr. Billy. Something I trusted. I can see something in your eyes. It's only a glimmer—but there's something there. You were asked to leave the bar across the road and came to my bar. You were very drunk, Mr. Billy."

I was silent for a moment, before saying: "Thank you for holding me—for giving me a cuddle. At times, we all need a cuddle, I guess. I do drink too much, and I'll stop soon. Just not yet."

Boonsri got up from the bed. She was wearing the smallest G-string I'd ever seen. Her body was sculptured. Obviously, she was someone who took care of her fitness and diet. I assumed someone had once paid for the boob job she'd clearly had.

Boonsri saw me glancing at her body and asked: "You like my body, Mr. Billy? I use your fitness and yoga apps at least three times a week. I also use your dietary supplements. I can't believe I met the big boss of 21st Century Fitness!"

I laughed bitterly. "I'm not the big boss of 21st Century Fitness any longer. I don't work anymore, Boonsri. I just drink and try and forget what happened in the past."

Boonsri put on a tight pair of black shorts, matched with an expensive, white tailored shirt. She put on her silver earrings—and I thought she'd make a nice girlfriend for some lucky man.

"You have a boyfriend, Boonsri?"

She giggled. "Mr. Billy, do you really think I would've come back with you if I had a boyfriend? There's no boyfriend, Mr. Billy. Oh, there was a few months ago—a German man who was twenty years older than me. We spent three years together, but I found out he was going to bars when I was working and playing up with other women. As much as it hurt me, I decided to break up with him."

I pondered that, before asking: "Without sounding rude, how old are you?"

"What age do you think I am, Mr. Billy?"

"Please, just call me Billy. Thirty-two?"

"Older."

"Thirty-five?"

Boonsri laughed: "I'm forty-one, Billy."

"Wow! You're looking good."

"And you, Billy. How old are *you*?"

"Fifty-five—but the way I've been living the last few months, I feel seventy-five."

"Who is Chimlin, Billy?"

I froze.

"What did I say about Chimlin?"

"Not much," Boonsri said coolly. "You said she was suffering because of you. You kept on saying it was all your fault she was suffering—and then you started to cry. That was at the bar when I first met you."

"Chimlin was someone who was very special to me. It was a long time ago, but yes—because of me, she has suffered."

"Are you a bad man, Billy? Who hurts people?"

"No, Boonsri, I'm not a bad man who hurts people. I got caught by some people who tried to kill me and demanded a lot of money from me. Other people—people close to me—got hurt by those animals. Google my name, Billy Houston, and you can read all about it. It was big news in the press."

Boonsri would later Google my name and read all about my ordeal. Our paths would cross again, very shortly.

I HAD A shower, which got my body back into equilibrium. In fact, I was left feeling good as I reflected on my encounter with Boonsri. She was a stunning woman. She reminded me a lot of Chimlin. It's probably why, subconsciously, I'd confided in her during my drunken stupor.

I searched into the pockets of my pants to see how much money I had left from last night. I'd gone out with 20,000 Thai baht—or about $700. I still always converted Thai baht back to dollars. Some habits never die—even though I'd been living in Thailand for over five years.

I only had one-thousand Thai baht left. Yep, an expensive night. I still had my ATM card. I felt something else in my pocket. It was a card—a business card. I read the name on the business card, wondering how I'd got it. Then, I read the name again to make sure I wasn't dreaming.

There it was, in bold print: *Griffith Peters, National Manager of Westport Shopping Centres, Los Angeles, California.*

How the hell did I get this business card? I hadn't seen or heard from Griffith Peters for over fifteen years!

I'd first met Griff twenty-five years earlier, when I'd started the Tax Refund Shop. He was the leasing manager of the Westport Group, one of the largest owners of shopping malls on the West Coast of America.

He'd backed me to set up my Tax Refund Shop-fronts in his shopping malls—about eighty or so of them all across the States. Having my Tax Refund Shops in his shopping malls was good for his business, but it was also good for the business I'd started with Pat Gabriel. After meeting with Griff, Pat and I suddenly had over eighty of the Tax Refund Shop franchises to sell—which gave us our big start. If Griff hadn't backed me all those years ago, I'm not sure whether the Tax Refund Shops would have ever taken off.

But how on earth did I get Griff's business card last night? Then—like a blinding flash—it all came back to me.

The night before

I WAS SITTING by myself in the corner of the bar, watching the football game on the big screen. It was only 10:00pm and the bar was yet to fill with late-night revelers. I'd been drinking beers since lunchtime and had only wandered into the bar about an hour earlier. The beers weren't numbing the pain in my brain, so I'd decided to start drinking straight whiskey.

A man approached me, speaking with an American accent.

"Billy? Is that really you? I'll be damned—it must be at least fifteen years since I last saw you!" The man reached out his hand to shake mine.

I looked up from my half-full whiskey glass. I was unshaven—not having shaved for the last five days. My hair was straggly and long, and I searched for recognition as I looked at the middle-aged guy shaking my hand.

"Sorry, mate. I can't place you. You sure you've got the right person?"

"You *are* Billy Houston, aren't you? The founder of the Tax Refund Shops? It's Griff Peters! National manager of Westport Group. The shopping mall owners?"

My eyes widened.

"You're fucking kidding me, mate! Griff Peters! Bloody hell! Long time since we last saw each other!" I stood up to give Griff a big, warm, intoxicated embrace.

"It must be at least fifteen years since we last saw each other, Billy. Since you and Pat sold the business, I guess."

"Yep, that'd be at least fifteen years." I was slightly slurring my words, the effect of consuming too much alcohol over the last ten hours. "What are you doing here in Bangkok, Griff?"

"I'm looking for sites to build our first shopping mall in Southeast Asia. Well, more specifically, Bangkok. There's a large, vacant industrial site I'm looking at a few miles down the road. I always like to spend a few weeks getting out and about in the local neighborhood to get a feel for the area before we decide to spend the money and undertake a full-blown feasibility study."

"I'll buy you a drink, mate." I waved to the barman. "What will it be? A whiskey?"

"Yes, whiskey will be fine, Billy. I'll just have a couple with you. I've got to be in bed nice and early First meeting is at 10:00am tomorrow."

Griff had heard about what had happened to me in the American press. For two hours, I shared with Griff my remorse about the events of the extortion—and, for two hours, he sat on the edge of his seat, glued to every word. I told him in minute detail all about my encounter with the thugs, and the damage they'd caused to those I cared about and loved.

I remember toward the end of my story, tears had welled in my eyes—specifically as I described the torture and death of Mandy, and Sean's subsequent suicide. Griff suddenly embraced me. I think he was about to cry himself, feeling sorry for me and everything I'd been through.

"Billy, you look shit, man," Griff admitted, as he released me from his hug. "I'll be honest, Billy—I hardly recognized you. I sat in this bar for a good twenty minutes, looking across at you—thinking that it *can't* be Billy Houston."

Griff looked me up and down.

"Christ, you've aged so much. But, when I heard you speak to the barman with that accent—that slight Australian twang—I realized it must be you. That's when I came over."

Griff grinned wryly.

"You're a smart man, Billy—but you need to clean yourself up. Have a shave, cut your hair—but most importantly, give *this* up." He picked up my glass of whiskey.

I snorted bitterly.

"I can't, Griff. It's the only thing that keeps me sane. It's only by drinking copious amounts of alcohol that I can even get to sleep."

"Billy, it's going to kill you, man. You're too young to die. You still have too much to offer the world."

"I have nothing to live for, Griff."

"You've got your kids, Billy! Your mates. Your friends. You've got everything to live for! What about Pat? Do you and him still keep in contact?"

"No one knows where I am, Griff. I got rid of my phone and picked up a new one. I've deliberately gone off the grid. I speak to no one from the past—not even my kids. I got sick of people asking me how I was doing, and telling me none of this was my fault." I snorted. "Look at this."

I produced a copy of Sean's suicide note.

"He blamed me for everything, Griff. I destroyed his life—and the lives of his kids."

Griff stared at me incredulously.

"Billy—why the fuck would you be carrying this guy's suicide note around?" He shook his head. "Stupid stuff, man. You told me the man had suffered from depression for years. He was delusional—not in a fit state of mind to deal with anything. He blamed you because it was *easy* to blame you for his own shortcomings. He wasn't strong enough to see the truth—to see reality."

Griff squeezed my shoulder.

"Billy, come with me tonight. Stay in my hotel room and I'll get you cleaned up. I'm here for another three days. Hang with me. We'll have breakfast and dinner together tomorrow. You can spend the day lazing around the hotel pool, soaking up some sun— getting some color back into you…" He paused. "And staying off the grog. I'll help you, Billy."

"I can't tonight, Griff. I've got to meet someone later tonight," I lied. "Give me your card, though, and I'll call you tomorrow."

Griff knew that would never happen. He replied: "I don't have a card on me, Billy. What's your cell number? I'll call it now, so you have my number." He grabbed my cell phone.

He knew I was never going to call him—and he knew no one had my phone number. Griff knew the only way he'd ever be able to contact me again was to get my cell phone number at that moment.

It's funny how sometimes we do things against our better judgment—but, me reluctantly giving Griff my cell phone that night is probably the only reason I'm still alive today.

Thirty-six hours later, Griff finally managed to contact my best mate, Pat Gabriel, to let him know he'd met me in a bar—and that I wasn't doing too well. In fact, Griff doubted I'd last another six months if I continued to live my current lifestyle.

CHAPTER 21

The next day

I THOUGHT LONG and hard about what Griff had said to me.

I knew I had to give up the alcohol, or it was going to kill me. I decided that I'd wean myself off the grog. I wouldn't have my first drink until 7:00pm. I'd do that for a few weeks, and then attempt to go cold turkey.

But I'd start in a weeks' time, I said to myself.

I also had a bit of a spring in my step that morning. I was quite taken with Boonsri. I'd always refused to be with a bar girl, so she ticked that box. She was glamourous—although *stunning* was probably a more apt description. Boonsri seemed to have a caring nature, too. I mean, she took care of me in my time of need— apparently offering to take up my suggestion of holding me through the night.

But I had no recollection of our encounter, and I'd had to rely on what she'd told me as being the truth.

But Boonsri was also single, or so she'd told me—so, yep, she ticked a lot of boxes when it came to being a potential companion for me. But I had to clean up my act first. I wasn't a good catch for anyone in my present state.

Next week, I'd cut my hair, have a shave, and check into a far better hotel—a five-star hotel, with a beautiful pool. After a couple of days lying around the pool, I'd start to look nice and tanned.

I'd also decided that next week, I'd set a curfew on my drinking. I'd have to be home by 12:00am, far better than the previous curfew I'd set of being home before sunrise. I'd then start to use the hotel gym and get myself back in shape. Yep, it all sounded good.

Sometimes, the best laid plans just don't work out.

I'D MET SOME new-found friends around the pool at the three-star hotel I was staying at. Three English couples, about my age, who were holidaying in Bangkok before heading down to Phuket.

Low and behold, one of the English couples had been living in Noosa, Australia—where my cousin owned an accounting firm. I'd visited him several years earlier.

"One of the nicest places in the world to live," I told the couple. "I loved the north-facing main beach, and the street called Hastings Street—with all the restaurants and cafes. A couple of great point breaks for surfing."

"I know your cousin, Billy," said the husband, Clive. "He's actually our accountant." This English couple had settled in Noosa, but not lost the accent.

"What a small world," I considered.

Well, that one beer with my new English friends turned into about twenty beers. At 10:00pm, I bid farewell to my new English friends and headed to my hotel room to get changed. I'd decided to head out on the town.

Alcohol tends to give you a distorted view of the world. At times, everything just seems so logical that you feel almost invincible. I'd said to myself that tonight would be my last big night on the town before I cleaned up my act.

Unfortunately, I wouldn't clean up my act. Someone else would do that for me.

I'D STUMBLED ACROSS a bar with loud music blaring from the open windows. It was jam-packed with people—people of all ages, some dressed in suits, no doubt having left work for a few drinks and continuing to party on late into the night.

There were attractive women as far as the eye could see. I've always been a personable person—never had problems making friends when I went out on the town by myself. There'd always be someone who wanted to talk to me—always someone else out on the town like me, who I'd bump into when we both needed a drinking pal.

Tonight, I was certainly intoxicated—by then drinking straight whiskey. There was a table at which two ladies stood sipping champagne, so I saddled up to the table and introduced myself—asking their permission to join them for a drink. I finished my whiskey and asked them if they'd like me to buy a bottle of champagne for all of us to share.

It turned out these two women were sisters, who were in Bangkok for the long weekend. They lived in Chaweng, Koh Samui. That meant we had something in common straight away, as I lived twenty minutes down the road from them in Choeng Mon.

The older of the two girls was called Kamon, and her younger sister was called Malee. One thing I'd learned from Chimlin was that all Thai girl names had a further meaning. When I asked the two girls the meanings of their names, Kamon—who was thirty-nine—told me her name meant: *"From the heart."* Malee told me her name meant: *"Flower."*

We were on our second bottle of champagne very soon. The bar was choc-a-block with party revelers. It was now standing room only, with all vacant chairs and tables already occupied.

The girls were starting to show the effects of the champagne, so I suggested they ease up the drinking and switch to water. I was drunk, but no one could tell *me* when to stop drinking. I'd promised myself tonight would be my last all-night bender—so I was going to make the most of it.

I suddenly felt an elbow in my back. It appeared to be more than an accidental blow. I turned around and, standing no more than two feet away from me, were two young guys. I guessed they were both maybe in their late thirties, with big smiles on their faces, laughing at me. One raised his glass to me and smiled—saying something in a foreign language, which I assumed was Russian.

I turned around to continue my conversation with Kamon and Malee, who both raised their eyebrows indicating what 'dicks' those two guys were.

Straight away, I received another elbow to my back—this one harder than the last. I ignored it and continued to talk to my two new friends from Koh Samui.

I assume that because I didn't react to the second elbow, I received the third and final blow. This time, I turned around and both guys were laughing at me—the smaller one, about my size, raising his glass to me and once again muttering words I could only assume were Russian.

"Guys," I held up my hand, "I don't understand what you're saying—but please stop elbowing me in the back, or I'll call security."

They then muttered something between themselves and raised their glasses toward me again. I thought: These two guys are out looking for trouble.

I've always been a lover, not a fighter. I've never once hit a person—and, at the age of fifty-five, I had no intentions of starting now.

Malee said: "Billy, let's move away from these guys. They're trouble. We saw them here last night. The smaller, blonde guy attacked and beat up another guy outside on the steps after the club had closed. Let's move away from them before they cause trouble with you."

We shifted to the other side of the club and continued talking and drinking for the next two hours, right up until the club closed at 3:00am. I had no romantic inclinations towards either Malee or Kamon, but we exchanged phone numbers. They were two nice, attractive Thai ladies—and I promised to catch up with them both when I was back in Choeng Mon.

I couldn't give them a timeline of when that might be, because in my present state, I didn't even know where I was going to be tomorrow—let alone in three months' time.

Unknown to me, those two young Russian guys had followed the three of us across to the other side of the club—and they'd spent the last couple of hours observing me from a distance. They were looking for trouble—and, for some reason, had taken a dislike to me in particular.

I WALKED OUT of the door of the club and down the stairs. I started to make my way down the laneway toward the road. I wasn't sure if I'd hail a cab and head home, or if I'd have a 'roadie' on the side of the road— which was an expression I'd used for the last thirty years to refer to the one, or sometimes two, last drinks you'd have before you finally headed home.

Suddenly, I heard someone yell in my direction: "Old man! What the fuck are you doing?"

While the words were spoken in English, they had a thick accent to them. I heard the same words again. This time, they were louder. I instantly knew they were directed towards me.

I looked up to see the two Russian guys approaching me, with big smiles on their faces.

I kept on walking, not wanting to get into an altercation with them. I felt relatively safe as there were hundreds of other night club patrons walking down the laneway towards the main road.

I kept my head down and walked past the two guys, who were now standing ten feet away, against the wall.

Then, I felt a hand on my shoulder.

It was the smaller of the two guys. "How old are you, fuckwit? Seventy?"

"Leave me alone, mate. I don't want any trouble."

His mate pushed me from behind, closer to the wall they were standing by.

The younger guy, who I now *knew* to be Russian, said: "You must have a lot of fucking money man—hanging around with those two young girls. How old are they both? Twenty?"

"Leave me alone, mate—and they're not twenty. They're both in their late thirties."

I pushed the guys hand off my shoulder and tried to walk away.

The bigger guy, also Russian, spoke for the first time: "You're fucking *old*, man." He spat at the ground in front of me.

I warned: "Get your hand *off* me and leave me alone."

I walked no more than five paces before a massive blow struck the back of my head from behind.

I instantly fell to the pavement. I couldn't believe what had just happened to me. I was in a state of shock—

but I was still conscious. The first thought that came to my mind was: *"My teeth! Are my teeth still intact?"*

Thirty-four years ago, at the age of twenty-one, I'd been a passenger in a car that hit a telegraph pole. A mate from Santa Monica High School had died in that accident. I'd broken every bone in my face—and nearly lost my left eye. I'd required bone grafts from my right hip to rebuild part of my face and replace the shattered bones. The most painful part of my injuries were my teeth, though. They were damaged extensively in that accident, and for eighteen months I'd required a massive amount of dental work, which had cost my mum a small fortune.

My teeth! My teeth! I grabbed my teeth to make sure they were all intact. Yep, they appeared to all still be there.

Then I felt blood running down my face. I looked down at my shirt. It was no longer white—it was covered in blood. There were people milling around me now, all talking in different accents. I heard several people yell: *"Get an ambulance! Call an ambulance!"*

I heard a familiar voice scream: "Billy? Are you okay, Billy?"

I tried to place the voice, as I put my hand on the ground and tried to lift myself off from the pavement.

Somebody grabbed my arm and comforted me, murmuring in a hysterical voice: "Billy? What's happened, Billy? Are you okay? Oh, Billy... Billy..."

I looked up and recognized the face and voice. It was Boonsri.

"Boonsri? What's happened to me?"

"I saw you leave the bar, Billy. I was there too. I tried to follow you down the steps to say hello, but I lost you in the crowd. I searched for you among all the faces and saw you over there against the wall, talking to those two guys. I yelled out to you, but you couldn't hear me with all the noise. Then I saw one of them grab your shoulder. He looked angry. When you walked away, he followed you—and threw a *big* punch at your head. You fell straight to the ground."

"I'll be all right. Can you help me up and get a cab for me? I want to go home and have a shower."

"You can't go home, Billy. The back of your head is covered in blood. You face, your nose, your mouth—they're all bloodied. There's an ambulance coming."

"No ambulance. I'll get up now. I'll be all right." I put my right hand on the pavement and tried to force myself up—but it was hopeless. I had no strength, no energy. I heard the sirens of the ambulance approaching, and then heard muffled voices as two men in blue uniforms started lifting me onto a stretcher.

I screamed as loud as I could: "Boonsri!"

"I'm here, Billy." She held my hand tightly, tears streaming down her face.

"Can you come with me? In the ambulance? Please?"

"Of course, Billy—of course I'll come with you."

At that moment, I had the weirdest thought enter my mind. I suddenly wished Chimlin was there. I wished she was here to hold my hand and look after me. Twice now, I'd ended our relationship and broken her heart. What a fool I'd been.

I looked up at the faces in the back of the ambulance as I was being whisked away through the streets of Bangkok. I had no idea which hospital I was being taken to. I had a male paramedic tending my wounds, and a drip had been attached to my arm. Boonsri sat on the other side of me, tightly holding my hand and whispering: "You'll be okay, Billy. You'll be okay."

I WAS RUSHED through the emergency entrance, with people in nurses' uniforms darting all around. A man dressed in a white gown, holding a clipboard, approached me as I lay on the stretcher in the entrance foyer. Boonsri was by my side, still holding my hand.

"We need your credit card, sir, before we can admit you to our hospital."

My credit card? I thought. *I don't have a credit card!* I'd lost my last one—and the replacement was posted to my Choeng Mon address. I hadn't returned to my Choeng Mon house for months.

"I don't have a credit card," I mumbled from my swollen mouth, touching my lips after I uttered those words, my fingers now covered in blood.

There was an exchange of words in Thai between Boonsri and the man in the white gown.

"Billy, unless you have a credit card, they won't admit you. They want to make certain you'll pay the bill. I've told them who you are—but they're adamant that without a credit card, they won't operate."

"I've lost my credit card. How much cash do they want?"

A quick exchange in Thai between Boonsri and the man with the clipboard occurred. Boonsri said: "One-hundred-thousand baht, cash."

"My ATM card is in my left pocket. Take it and go to the ATM and withdraw the money. My code is 8888."

After no more than five minutes, Boonsri returned, paid the cash, and I was wheeled into a room with a large x-ray machine. I'd later learn that I'd needed an MRI to determine whether I had any brain injuries or not.

Then, I was whisked away on the stretcher to the operating theatre—with Boonsri in the room with me, still holding my hand. My head and face were painfully stitched back together. They gave me a local anesthetic to numb the discomfort as they stitched merrily away.

Here we go again, I thought. *More stiches to my face.* I'd had over two-hundred-and-fifty stiches on my face after my car accident—so I was certainly *not* going to end up an oil painting with my scarred face.

I ended up having thirty-five stiches in the back of my head. The guy who'd hit me must have been wearing a ring, as it had torn the skin right off my skull. I'd fractured my nose when I'd fallen to the ground and my teeth had exited through my bottom lip with the impact of my fall. I had to have stitches on both the inside and outside of my bottom lip.

Fortunately, there were no signs of brain damage. My clothes were wrecked, though, and had to be discarded due to the massive amount of blood all over them.

At 6:00am, I was finally wheeled to a ward. Boonsri told me they wanted to keep me there for a few days to observe my head and ensure I didn't have a concussion, or any other delayed symptoms of brain injury. She said the police would be there later to take a statement from me. I gave her the key to my hotel room and asked her to bring a change of clothes and my cell phone back, later in the day.

Boonsri squeezed my hand and said goodbye. As she left, I whispered: "Thank you, Boonsri. Thank you for looking after me."

As I finally drifted off to sleep, I reflected on my life over the last few months. It had been a downward spiral, which was now running out of control. At 55 years of age, I'd been beaten up by some thugs in a bar at 3.00am. How much worse could my life get?

CHAPTER 22

BOONSRI WOULD LATER tell me about what had happened when she'd gone to my hotel room to collect my spare clothes and cell phone.

She'd unlocked the door to my hotel room—and, as she'd entered the room to gather my clothes and cell phone, she'd heard the ringing of my phone.

Boonsri told me she'd walked over to the desk by the window and picked up the phone. It was still ringing—and the name Pat Gabriel was displayed on the screen. She'd thought she'd better not answer my private cell phone.

From our time together, Boonsri knew that Pat was my best friend from America—but she didn't know much else about him. As she'd picked up my phone, Boonsri had noticed there were thirteen missed calls from Pat in the last hour, along with three messages.

Boonsri had scrolled through the missed calls to see if this woman known as 'Chimlin' had phoned me. There were no missed calls from Chimlin—and Boonsri tells me she'd sighed with relief. She'd taken quite a liking to me, and was secretly hoping that maybe something would develop between us. At the same time, though, Boonsri had known from the other night—when I'd drunkenly shared my innermost feelings with her, that Chimlin was someone important in my life.

Boonsri would later admit that she'd seen it in my eyes when I'd spoken about Chimlin. Call it women's intuition, I guess, but she'd known I had special feelings for Chimlin.

Little did Boonsri know, though, that I'd never given Chimlin the number to my latest private cell phone. No one had the number to this cell phone, actually—it was part of my disappearing act. I hadn't wanted contact with anyone. I'd just wanted to drown my sorrows and make the nightmare I'd been living disappear by drinking copious amounts of alcohol every day.

Boonsri had gathered a bag from the wardrobe and quickly packed a couple of changes of clothes for me. Whilst she was doing this, my phone had apparently rung another two times. She'd ignored the ringing of the phone and continued packing.

Just as she was looking around the small, basic hotel room to make sure she hadn't forgotten anything—literally zipping the bag closed at that moment—Boonsri had realized she'd left the phone on the table. As she'd picked it up to place it in the bag,

Boonsri had glanced at the two most-recent calls. Both were from Pat Gabriel again.

Boy, that man must be impatient, she told me she'd thought at the time. Fifteen missed calls in just over an hour?

Boonsri told me she'd picked the phone up to place it in the bag when it had rung again. Once again, it was Pat Gabriel. Instinct had got the better of her— and Boonsri had answered the phone.

"Hello—Billy Houston's phone. Can I help you?"

"Billy, is that you? Who is this?" The voice at the other end was screaming.

"My name is Boonsri. I'm a friend of Billy's."

"Where's Billy? I need to speak to him urgently!"

Boonsri says she'd hesitated—not sure that she should tell my best friend what had happened.

"Billy's not here," she'd lied. "He's gone away for a few days."

"I don't know who you are," Pat had told her, "but I'm Billy's best friend. I've known the guy since he was fourteen. We grew up together in the States. I've been trying to contact Billy for months on end on his other phone. I leave message after message—and I never hear back from him. I've contacted everybody I know in Bangkok and no one knows where Billy is. The message on his other phone simply says: *"I've gone away for a few months of solitude and I'll be back in contact later.""*

Pat had scoffed: "Can you believe that? "Solitude"?" He'd told Boonsri: "An old friend of ours, Griff Peters, said he'd bumped into Billy in a bar in Bangkok the night before last. He'd finally got this cell phone number. Griff phoned me just over an hour ago.

I'm not sure what your relationship is with Billy, Boonsri—but Griff told me Billy looked horrible. Unshaven, long hair, lost weight, pale. He looked like death warmed up. Griff thought Billy wouldn't last another six months if he kept going the way he's been going."

Boonsri says she'd been silent after hearing that— not uttering a word until Pat had demanded: "Are you still there, Boonsri?"

She'd been silently contemplating whether or not to tell Pat what had happened to me.

"Are you there, Boonsri?"

"I'm here, Pat," Boonsri had finally responded. "I'm here. I'm just listening to what you're saying. Are you in America?"

"Yes, I live in Los Angeles. Why do you ask?"

"How long does it take to fly from America to Bangkok?"

"It's a long flight. Takes about twenty hours or so, depending where I stop on the way. Why?"

Boonsri had sighed and taken a deep breath— unsure whether I'd approve of her telling Pat about the previous night. But she later told me she'd cared about me—and knew I wasn't in a good place right then. Boonsri had thought about what I'd told her about my nightmares, and the guilt I felt about what had happened to Mandy, and the woman who Boonsri had correctly guessed was more than 'just a friend'— Chimlin.

After having seen me wake up in the night, scream-ing from a nightmare, Boonsri told me she'd made an instinctive decision: Pat Gabriel needed to know the truth.

"Billy hasn't gone away," Boonsri had told him. "Billy got mugged last night. He's now in the hospital in Bangkok."

"He got mugged? Is he going to be all right?"

"He got hit from behind by some Russian thugs last night. He's okay—but he'll be recovering in the hospital for the next few days."

"What sort of injuries has he got?"

"He's had stiches to the back of his head and stiches to his lips. His nose is fractured. They did an MRI to make sure he had no brain damage. The x-rays were clear, but they're keeping Billy in the hospital for a few days just to make sure there are no adverse effects from the head injuries. The doctors said he's lucky to be alive. Another few centimeters to the right and he might have suffered severe brain damage."

"Fucking hell!" Pat had breathed. "That man has been through so much shit over the last six months. How come you have his phone, Boonsri? Are you his girlfriend?"

"No, I'm not his girlfriend," she says she'd felt awkward saying that. "I just met Billy two days ago. He was very drunk and very lonely, and he shared with me some of the things that have happened to him recently. I've been at the hospital with him for the last few hours. He gave me the key to his hotel room to get his phone and some clothes. I was just here packing some clothes for him when I heard his phone ring. He'd told me about you, Pat—how you're his best friend. He'd put your number in his phone. I saw all the missed calls from you, and when you rung again, I thought I should answer the call. I'm not sure if Billy would want me to answer his phone. Please don't tell him I've spoken to you."

Pat had responded: "Don't worry, I won't. In Billy's state of mind—over the last few months—he probably wouldn't want you to answer his phone, or to fill me in with what's been happening. Billy's gone to great extremes to leave all his old friends behind. It's as though he'd dropped off the face of the Earth."

Boonsri had told Pat: "I don't want to cause Billy any trouble. I shouldn't have spoken to you. Please, forget this conversation. Please, please?"

"Boonsri," Pat had fired back, "I don't know you—and I probably shouldn't be telling you this—but I'm a million miles away, and I have to accept what you tell me as the truth about your friendship with Billy." Pat had sighed. "Billy isn't well. He's ill, and he needs help. He's been through an incredible emotional roller coaster and he blames himself for everything that happened to his friends. It's been horrible—and, by all accounts, he's hit the bottle pretty hard, and is a shell of the man he once was."

Boonsri hadn't argued with any of those assumptions.

"I knew Billy was in a bad place," Pat continued. "I knew he was hitting the grog pretty hard—but from the message he'd left on his other phone, I'd just thought he needed time to himself to process things. Time heals all wounds, right? And the Billy I've known for the last forty years has always been a strong man. He's dealt with a lot of shit in his life. We all do."

Pat had paused.

"But he's always been full of zest, before—very positive. In the past, Billy hasn't let any setbacks bring him down. From my conversation with Griff Peters, though—just over an hour ago—I'm worried Billy's had a breakdown. You've met him. How would you describe his current mental state?"

Boonsri had admitted: "I don't know him well, Pat—but he seems troubled and, yes, he drinks a *lot*. He has blackouts and forgets what happens to him."

Boonsri would later tell me she'd been reluctant to tell Pat how she'd ended up in my bed. She'd worried that if she told Pat that I'd only wanted her to hold me—and even if she was adamant that, in my drunken state, I'd not wanted sex—Pat wouldn't have believed her.

"So, what happens now, Pat?" She'd asked instead. "Billy needs your help."

"I'm going to hop on a plane and come over to Bangkok. I'm going to contact Billy's other best friend—my best friend as well, Chook Burns—and get him to come with me to Bangkok too. What's the time in Bangkok now?"

"It's 08:30am here."

"It's 05:30pm here, on Thursday. I'm going to try and book a flight for me and Chook later tonight, or early tomorrow morning. Hopefully, we'll be there by tomorrow night. We'll head straight to the hospital from the airport. What's the address of the hospital?"

Boonsri had given Pat the details of how to get to the hospital.

"Boonsri," Pat had warned, "please don't tell Billy that we've spoken. Given how Billy has tried to hide himself from everyone, I don't want him knowing we're coming. He might discharge himself from the hospital to avoid us. Can I trust you not to tell him, Boonsri?"

"Yes," she'd promised Pat. "You can trust me."

"This is important, Boonsri. He needs help. If he doesn't get help, Billy might well die the way he's currently been living."

"I won't tell him, Pat."

Pat had paused, before asking: "Boonsri?"

"Yes? What?"

"You need to delete this call from his phone. You also need to delete all my missed calls to Billy's phone. I don't want Billy knowing that I've got his phone number. If he knows I've got his number, he'll probably think that I'm coming to see him. Okay?"

"Yes, I understand," Boonsri had said. She'd been crying.

"Hey, there's no need to cry," Pat had reassured her. "We're both here to help Billy—to help him get well. You've done the right thing, Boonsri. I'm just so glad you answered the phone. I was scared if Billy answered, he'd immediately hang up and I would never have had the chance to see him. We're here to save him, Boonsri."

"It's okay, I understand."

"What's your cell phone number?"

Boonsri had given Pat her number, and he'd entered it into his cell phone—repeating it back to her once again to ensure he'd entered the number correctly.

"I'll call you tomorrow when we get to the airport. See you tomorrow, Boonsri."

"See you tomorrow," Boonsri had repeated.

CHAPTER 23

I AWOKE AND my head was throbbing. I had a splitting headache—and this time, it wasn't entirely as a result of drinking.

I glanced at my imitation Rolex to check the time. *Only 5:00pm,* I muttered to myself.

I was expecting Boonsri to drop in here about 6:00pm with my clothes and my cheap cell phone, on her way to open the bar she managed.

Boy, I thought to myself. *I'd love a cold beer right now.* Better still, I'd love twenty cold beers right now—followed by a few whiskey chasers. My mind drifted back to the events of the early morning. I couldn't believe I got 'king hit' from behind by some thug. I counted my blessings that I was still alive. The doctors had told me if I'd been hit a few centimeters to the right, I might have ended up with brain damage—or worse. I could have died.

I shivered. I've read countless stories about people being 'king hit' from behind, cracking their heads on the pavement and never waking up.

Yep—while I was definitely in the wrong place at the wrong time, I was nevertheless lucky to be alive. I exhaled a big sigh and reflected on what the doctors had told me earlier this afternoon. Because of the massive headaches I was experiencing, they wanted to keep me in the hospital for the next five days. I'd originally been hoping to change my clothes when Boonsri came in and then discharge myself from the hospital for good that afternoon. That apparently wasn't going to happen— not after the earlier visit from the doctors.

I thought about my two best mates, Pat and Chook. I wondered what they were up to. As I lay there, I imagined Chook driving his pick-up truck around LA, nice and tanned, mowing lawns. He'd probably already been out for an early morning surf at Malibu. Not a worry in the world, had Chook.

Pat, no doubt, was already in the office at Future Wealth, steering the financial planning conglomerate as chairman—a steady pair of hands at the helm. I hadn't spoken to either of them for months, nor anyone else— including my own kids, who I usually Skyped with each week. I'd sent the kids a text to advise I'd be uncontactable for a few months—but nothing after that.

My mind wandered back to my childhood in Santa Monica—to all the fun times I'd had with Pat, Chook, and Rodger the Dodger. We'd hung out at the beach, chased girls, surfed, and smoked too much dope. It all seemed so long ago. Then, I chuckled to myself. It only seemed so long ago because it *was* a bloody long time ago—forty years or more!

I reflected on the fun and success Pat and I had enjoyed, building the Tax Refund Shop across America—one of the largest tax and accounting franchises in America. I also reflected on my time building a global surf clothing label—and then, of course, Future Wealth; the company Pat and I had listed on Wall Street. There were good times associated with those businesses.

Then I thought about the corporate crooks we'd met along the way—Tom Carroll and the late Steve Roberts, and their equally crooked cohorts. Nothing but grubs of the worst kind: Liars, cheats, and utter scum.

I thought about my three ex-wives, and wondered how they were all doing. I hadn't spoken to my first wife for over fifteen years. I had some contact with my second wife—but only when it required a discussion about the kids. She'd remarried some IT whiz-kid, ten years younger than her, who was a leading light in Silicon Valley. He'd done extremely well for himself.

Our kids lived with them both, but they visited me every year for a few weeks and stayed at my house in Choeng Mon. My oldest boy was eighteen now—and had plans to follow me into business—whilst the youngest two, I assumed, would end up working for their step-dad in his IT business, since both of them displayed a passion for everything involving technology.

My third ex-wife and I still got on well. We'd phone each other every couple of months, and when I was last in California two years ago, we'd caught up for a nice dinner. She'd also spent a few days with me in Thailand at my house in Choeng Mon, four years earlier.

It's funny, the life we weave—some good times, some fun times, and some bad times. If the good times and fun times outweigh the bad times, I guess you could count yourself lucky and pat yourself on the back; saying what a great life you've had. Up until twelve months ago, the good times and fun times had far outweighed the bad times in my own life—but I reckon the bad times had caught up over the last six months. Hell, I reckon the bad times had leapfrogged in front of the good times and fun times by a county mile during these last six months.

But then, I thought to myself: Only one person can change my current circumstances, and that's me. I needed to get off the grog. I needed to get fit and healthy again. I needed to clean up my act. *Boy, I'm dying for a beer,* I thought. But then, reality set in—and I thought to myself: If I'm going to beat this alcohol addiction, I need to go cold turkey, no matter how hard that might be.

I thought of Chimlin and how differently my life might have turned out if I'd taken her up on her offer six years ago and moved to Bangkok to live with her as a couple. Yep, I wouldn't have been out by myself last night, drunk in a bar at 03:00am, and getting beaten up.

I probably wouldn't have hired Martin Spinkle in the first place. Chimlin had great intuition—she could instantly work out the good people from the bad. She'd probably have told me that Spinkle couldn't be trusted.

If I hadn't hired then fired Spinkle, the extortion attempt would never have taken place. Those criminals would never have known about me. I'd have flown under their radar; and Mandy and Sean would still be alive.

I wondered how Chimlin was doing. I knew she'd have been frantically trying to contact me on my other cell phone. She'd have got my message that I'd gone away for a few months, and she'd have been very upset with me. She'd then have been confused—and, by now, given that I hadn't phoned her back, probably very bitter toward me.

My other cell phone was at home in Choeng Mon, and I had no idea when I might return there. It was no doubt full of lots of messages from many, many people—all of which had gone unanswered. All those who'd left messages would have been bewildered by my sudden disappearance—claiming to be seeking some solitude.

I lay in that hospital bed feeling sorry for myself, reflecting on my past life events. I realized that that I was suffering a breakdown—a major breakdown. I was simply running away from the past and all my perceived problems. While the alcohol numbed the senses and pain, when I sobered up, it only added to my feelings of depression and helplessness.

I reflected on the time I'd resigned as chairman of Future Wealth. It had been as though my brain was fried. This time, though, it had been far, far worse—since I blamed myself for the murder of Mandy, the suicide of Sean, and—of course—the kidnapping of Chimlin.

Back during my first breakdown, I'd sought the assistance of Dr. Sam Draper—a clinical psychologist based in Los Angeles.

Perhaps I needed to get back to California for a while and spend some time with Dr. Draper, to help overcome the issues I was currently experiencing.

THE SOUND OF a zipper woke me up. I opened my eyes and there was the lovely, smiling face of Boonsri, unzipping a bag.

"Hi, Billy. How are you feeling?"

"I'm good," I lied—before admitting: "Well, actually, I'm not too good. I've got these splitting headaches. The doctors tell me I'm going to be here for another five days, so they can monitor my head injuries."

"You've had a major blow to the head, Billy," Boonsri warned. "You're lucky to be alive. Five days of rest in the hospital will do you a world of good."

"Yep. I'm going to get off the grog, Boonsri."

"That will be good for you, Billy."

"I'm a pretty determined person when I have to be. Did you get my clothes and cell phone?"

"Yes, all here, Billy." Boonsri picked up my overnight bag and rested it on the bed in front of me. "Here's your cell phone, too."

I grabbed the cell phone and quickly searched for any missed phone calls. I was concerned that I'd inadvertently given my cell phone to Griffith Peters when I'd met him in the bar the night before. I was hoping he hadn't given my number to Pat Gabriel.

I breathed a sigh of relieve when I saw no missed calls. Griff can't have given my number to Pat. Thank God—I didn't want anyone to know where I was, or to see me in my current state.

I'd been kicking myself for the last 24-hours for my lapse in judgement, giving my cell number to Griff.

Boonsri asked: "What do you plan to do when you get out of here, Billy?"

"I don't know," I shrugged. "I might go back down to Choeng Mon and face my demons." I chuckled. After thinking about Dr. Draper, I'd made my mind up in a matter of seconds to get across to California and seek his help. Boonsri didn't need to know about that.

A thought suddenly crossed my mind.

"Boonsri, have you ever been to Choeng Mon?"

"No, never. Why?"

"Perhaps you should come with me for a couple of days. I have a separate self-contained guest room where you can stay. It'd be my way of thanking you for your help. We don't know each other very well, but you've certainly helped me over the last few days. I'll pay for the airfare—you'll just need to pack a case and bring your bathers. There's a beautiful, white sandy beach with crystal clear water at Choeng Mon. I'll teach you to stand-up paddle board. There are half a dozen restaurants on the beach we can dine at—just no alcohol. Water only."

"Sounds fantastic, Billy. When are you thinking of heading back down there?"

"As soon as I get out of here. It's time for me to grab my life back."

"Okay," Boonsri smiled her beautiful smile. "I'll check with the owner of the bar to see if I can get five days off starting next Saturday. It shouldn't be a problem. I haven't had a holiday for over twelve months."

CHAPTER 24

I'D HAD A sleepless night in the hospital—maybe catching an hour or so of sleep, then waking up covered in perspiration. This process repeated itself throughout the night. I think it was a combination of my injuries, coupled with the withdrawal symptoms of quitting alcohol. The headaches, while still there, had reduced in severity—no doubt as a result of the painkillers the nurses had prescribed me.

I'd just finished my dinner and was about to doze back off when I heard the most familiar voice I'd ever known:

"Billy Houston? What the fuck has happened to you? You look terrible! Terrible, mate! I wouldn't have recognized you with all those bandages and the bruising on your face—not unless the nurses had assured me that it was you lying in this hospital bed."

I was dumbfounded when I looked up and saw my best mate, Pat Gabriel, standing there in front of me. I had to pinch myself to ensure it wasn't a dream.

After a few seconds, realizing this was no dream, I muttered: "Let me guess, Pat. Griffith Peters gave you my number?"

"Yes, he did, Billy." Pat nodded. "He tried to phone me immediately after he saw you. I was away at the time, but he finally managed to get a hold of me. He told me you looked like death warmed up—hardly recognizable as the guy he did business with fifteen years ago. He suggested I get over here and try and save you, because he didn't think you'd have long to live if you kept living life the way you have been."

"But, how did you find me here?" I was confused.

"I phoned you at least fifteen times, Billy," Pat explained. "After I got your number from Griff—but you didn't answer any of my calls."

"I don't take my phone out with me. I'm sick of getting drunk and losing phones."

I then realized how Pat had found me here. "Boonsri!"

"Correct, Billy—Boonsri. That Thai woman happened to answer one of my many phone calls. She was reluctant to give me any details about where you were, but after some gentle persuasion from yours truly, she finally divulged what had happened the other night. I told her not to tell you I'd phoned up, and to delete all my missed calls from your cell phone. I was concerned you might try and leave before I'd had a chance to get to Bangkok and see you."

Pat looked me up and down.

"Oh, Billy—what the fuck have you been doing to yourself, mate? You've lost so much weight! You look like skin and bones lying on that bed."

As I sat up and hugged Pat, I started to weep—and, for the next thirty minutes, I cried as I shared with Pat my journey over the last three or four months: A journey I called *Billy Houston's Fall from Grace*.

"SO, BILLY—WHY don't you come back to LA with me? I'll help you get back to the Billy Houston we all know and love. Plus, as you mentioned, it'd be a great idea to see Dr. Sam Draper again. I assume he's still practicing—and still alive, for that matter. You, me, and Chook can get the surfboards out and start catching some waves at Malibu, just like old times. It'll be fun. You can work out then whether you want to stay in California or come back to Thailand."

I'd been giving things a lot of thought while I'd spent the last two days lying in this hospital bed. Yep, I'd fucked up—fucked up badly, actually. But one thing I'd always been able to do was move fast once I'd decided on a plan of action. I was a quick thinker—and, most of the time, quite rational. Though, anyone who'd met me over the last few months probably wouldn't have thought that! I'd been acting like the most irrational person on the planet.

I put that down to the effects of the alcohol—simple traits of drug abuse.

I was about to tell Pat my plans—plans I'd articulated over the last 48-hours—but was stopped in my tracks by the sudden appearance of Boonsri, who'd popped in to see how I was doing.

"I believe you've already spoken to Pat," I introduced Pat and Boonsri to each other.

"Glad to meet you in person, Boonsri." Pat shook Boonsri's hand. While Pat was a happily married man, I could tell from his body language—and especially his eyes—that he was quite taken aback by Boonsri's beauty.

"Thank you so much for taking my call and keeping it all a secret from Billy," he held onto Boonsri's hand a few moments longer than necessary. "I'm here to help Billy get well again."

"We all are, Pat," she smiled. "We're all here to help him get back to his old self—though I never knew the old Billy." She admitted: "I have Googled you over the last few days, Billy. I also read your book yesterday. You're quite a man."

My cheeks heated a little, and Boonsri chuckled. Next, she asked Pat:

"Where's this other man you said was going to come with you from America?"

"You mean Chook Burns? His son's getting married in a few days," Pat explained. "He had to stay in California—but he'll be catching up with me and Billy as soon as we get back to America."

"Oh, you're not going to Choeng Mon then, Billy?" Boonsri turned to me with a confused expression on her beautiful face.

"No," I countered. "I *am* going to Choeng Mon—as soon as I get discharged from this hospital. Nothing's changed there. I was just about to fill Pat in on my plans."

Boonsri nodded.

"I'll go, Billy, and leave you and your friend to talk. I'll pop in to see you tomorrow before work." She blew me a kiss—and, with a big smile on her face, waved to my friend: "Bye, Pat".

The moment she'd left, Pat turned to me and whistled.

"Wow, Billy—she's gorgeous. Absolutely stunning. You can certainly pick them, Billy. She's as beautiful as that other Thai girlfriend you had."

"You mean Chimlin?"

"Yes, Chimlin."

"Boonsri is beautiful," I nodded, "but, more importantly, she's got a heart of gold." I looked up at my friend. "Pat, I get out of here in four days. I'm going to head back to Choeng Mon for a couple of weeks. I've got to face my past demons. It's part of my healing process. I'll run into all my old friends in Choeng Mon—who'll all be asking how I am doing, where I've been, and if I'm okay. I'll deal with that. I'm also going to take Boonsri with me to Choeng Mon. It's just my way of thanking her for helping me over the last few days."

"So—you and her are a couple, Billy? Is she your girlfriend?"

"No, Pat! There's no romance between us at all. She's just never been to Choeng Mon, and I've offered to pay her airfare to come and spend a few days with me. She'll stay in the guest room."

"Come on, Billy," Pat grinned. "I know the old Billy Houston. You'd never let a pretty girl like that slip through your fingers."

"Actually, Pat, she slept in my bed a few days ago partially naked, and held me when I was in one of my drunken wipeouts. You'll find this hard to believe, but there was no sex."

"You're kidding me, Billy! A beautiful girl like that was in your bed and you didn't try to fuck her?"

"Correct, Pat."

Pat leaned closer, glancing toward the door, making certain no one was about to enter and overhear what he'd planned to say.

Then, Pat whispered in my left ear: "I'm happily married, Billy—but even I'd be tempted to fuck her if I had the chance. You're unbelievable, Billy Houston—unbelievable!"

I ignored his comment, and replied: "If I struggle to stay off the alcohol in Choeng Mon, then I'm going to check myself into a drug center in Phuket. There's a clinic in the jungle there, where they help people get off all sorts of drugs. Give me a month here in Thailand to get myself off the drink, then I'll return to LA and see Dr. Draper to get my mind back in shape."

"How are you for money, Billy?"

"Well, you know, Pat—I've given all my wealth away. My kids and Mandy's kids are set for life, but everything else has been given to charity—other than the annuity I receive from the money you've invested for me; in your name, I might add. So, for all intents and purposes to anyone in the outside world, I'm stone broke." I snorted. "But the hundred thousand I receive each year is more than enough for me to live a very comfortable life over here in Thailand."

"If you come and live in America, I can give you a few million, Billy. Without your vision and hard work, I'd have never made the money I've got. I've enough saved up for me to live a life of wealth ten times over."

"Thanks, Pat, but I don't need your money. I'm comfortable with what I've got."

"You're only fifty-five, Billy! What do you plan to do with the rest of your life? Wait, before you answer that question, I assume there are no more businesses you plan to start?"

"Yep, there are no more businesses I plan to start, Pat. I'm over starting up businesses."

When I uttered those words, a strong flush came over me. My heart fluttered for a moment. It was as though my inner body sensed I was telling an outright lie to my best mate—even though he was standing right next to me. In four years, I'd recount the strange feeling I experienced when I uttered those words.

"You okay, Billy?" Pat asked. "You're sweating all of a sudden, and your face is all red."

"Just had a little turn," I gestured dismissively. "I'm fine. Now, where was I? That's right." I looked up at my friend. "I don't know what I'll do, Pat. I'll wait until I meet with Dr. Draper and get his words of wisdom and, of course, help."

The words I'd uttered to Pat about being over starting up businesses weren't exactly a lie—but I did have a good inkling about what I might do for the next six months or so. The words of Dr. Draper came rushing back to me: "*Given everything you've told me so far about your life, perhaps you should write a book.*

Writing a book about your life might be part of your healing process."

This time, it wasn't a book I was going to write: It was something completely different. Something no one in their wildest dreams would've ever imagined.

CHAPTER 25

BOONSRI AND I disembarked from the plane, and I said: "Welcome to Koh Samui airport. It's my favourite airport in the world." I gestured ahead. "See those thatched huts over there? That's the airport terminal. So different than most other airport terminals."

We quickly grabbed our luggage and hopped into a taxi to travel to my beachside villa at Choeng Mon.

After we'd arrived, I paid the cab driver—and, as I did so, I heard the familiar voice of Tom, my gardener: "Mr. Billy! Mr. Billy, you're back! I've been so worried about you."

Tom quickly rushed up to me and grabbed both my hands, clearly pleased to see me.

He grabbed our luggage and walked down the pathway ahead of us, excitedly talking to me. I introduced him to Boonsri, and they immediately started talking in fluent Thai. While I'd lived in

Thailand for over six years, I was far from fluent in the language—in fact, I only spoke a few words. If I concentrated hard, I could decipher *some* Thai words, but I didn't have any idea what Tom and Boonsri were chatting about. With my dyslexia, I found English a struggle as it was, let alone learning a new foreign language like Thai!

Boonsri and I entered my villa. Nothing had changed since I'd left, over three months earlier. The Bangkok Post was resting on my coffee table in the same place I left it. I rushed into my office, quickly opened the draw on my desk, and there was my cell phone.

I punched in my code. Nothing happened. The battery was flat after lying dormant for three months. I found my spare charger and plugged the phone in. I'd have to wait thirty minutes or so for the phone to charge before I could even retrieve my messages. I was eager to see what had been left during my long absence.

I walked back to the lounge and Boonsri was standing out on the balcony, staring out at the ocean across Choeng Mon bay.

She turned to face me.

"Billy, it's so beautiful—absolutely gorgeous. I can see why you like Choeng Mon."

I grabbed her hand and we walked down from my balcony to the white, glistening sand.

"Dip your toes in and feel the water," I suggested.

As she did so, Boonsri smiled happily. "It's warm, Billy."

"Constant temperature all year round," I told her. "Always between 23 and 26 Celsius—or, in my language, about 75 degrees Fahrenheit." I gestured back towards the villa. "Let's unpack the luggage and we'll go for a swim. Ever been on a stand-up paddle board?"

"No, never."

"It's easy. Get your bathers on and I'll teach you."

I WAS SITTING in my office, scrolling through my messages. There were lots and lots of messages, and even more missed calls. I quickly scrolled through the countless texts, looking for one name in particular among them.

Chimlin.

As it was, there were dozens and dozens of messages from her—both voice and text. I listened to all the voice messages and read all the texts. The last one was perhaps the most pertinent:

> *"Billy. You've broken my heart twice now—there'll be no third time. I've phoned you countless times, but you've never answered or bothered to return any of my calls. I've left message after message for you, but you've never bothered to return any of those, either. You say you've gone away for a few months to find solitude? What a cop out, Billy. I know you're getting these messages because you never go anywhere without your phone. I've been trying to help you overcome your nightmare. Believe me, Billy—I've been going through my own nightmare after the kidnapping, but I've come out the other side. I've been getting professional help from a psychologist. I've told him all about you. I've told him all about*

how I've been trying to contact you, and how you refuse to contact me back. His professional advice is that I need to move on from you—to refresh my life. Goodbye, Billy. Please don't contact me. Kind regards, Chimlin."

I contemplated her last message. It wasn't what I wanted. Why did it take me so long to realize what I wanted?

All the bloodshed. All the turmoil. I guess sometimes, we don't know what we want until we've lost it—until it's gone forever. It looked like I'd lost the opportunity to ever be with Chimlin again. There was no point trying to contact her. Her last and final message was quite blunt.

Boonsri knocked on my office door and peered around the corner. "Billy, do you want to come and sit on the balcony and watch the sunset?"

"Just need another fifteen minutes to go through the last of these messages. There are literally hundreds of them."

There were missed calls from Pat, Chook, my kids, Ivan Cameron, two of my ex-wives, not to mention lots of people from Future Wealth and 21st Century Fitness. It was going to take me most of tomorrow, and perhaps the day after, to go through them all and respond to each one.

I quickly drafted a message to send to a dozen people very close to me—and simply copied the message to each recipient:

"Hi. I'm safe and sound and now back at my villa at Choeng Mon, enjoying the sunshine and ocean.

I've been on an adventure the last few months re-appraising where I'm at in my life, given recent events—and how I want to spend the rest of it. I'll give you a call in a couple of days to say hi - Love Billy. P.S. Thanks for caring and taking the time to contact me and check how I'm going. I really do appreciate it."

There was a separate message, which I'd rather not share, that I sent to each of my children. I was going to spend some quality time with each of them when I returned to LA to catch up with Dr. Draper.

I'd phoned Dr. Draper's office while I was in the hospital and, much to my delight, he was still alive and still practicing. We had a long chat and I shared with him what I'd been through over the last few years since the last time we'd met—which had been just over six years earlier.

Dr. Draper didn't let on whether he'd read about what had happened to me, although I assumed he was aware of it. I thought any professional therapist would take an interest in what had happened to a recent patient—and I knew what had happened to me was quite big news in my home town of LA, because Pat had shared that little piece of information with me.

Fortunately, Dr. Draper had said he could help me—and my first appointment was booked for five weeks' time in LA. In the meantime, I had plans of getting fit and healthy again here in Choeng Mon. Tomorrow, I was going to start my daily walks, daily paddles and relax in the sunshine, followed by a nice dinner in one of the many beachfront restaurants—

with, of course, no alcohol. It was going to be water only for me for the foreseeable future.

SOON, IT WAS the last night here in Choeng Mon for Boonsri. She was booked to fly back to Bangkok early the next morning. She'd spent four beautiful days living by the beach—and we'd enjoyed early morning walks across the sand together, and she'd become quite competent on the stand-up paddle board.

Boonsri would even head out by herself on the board for a few hours while I locked myself away in the study, returning lots of phone calls to those who'd left messages during the preceding months.

No intimate relationship had developed between Boonsri and I. We slept in separate rooms, although I'd sensed that if I'd have given Boonsri the opportunity, she'd have quite eagerly hopped into bed with me.

I was tempted, but I didn't want to make my life any more complicated than it already was for either of us. Plus, I'd already had three failed marriages and one failed relationship with Chimlin. I was no good in this relationship caper—even with somebody as lovely as Boonsri.

On our last night together, I'd planned for us to have dinner at my favorite restaurant in Choeng Mon. It was a beautiful little establishment on the beach, and I'd reserved the best table in the house. It was my first time eating back there since I'd left Choeng Mon three months ago.

That night, I was sitting on my villa balcony waiting for Boonsri so we could walk along the beach to the restaurant. I glanced up and there she was—looking stunning.

She was wearing a full length, low-cut, tight-fitting dress in a crisp white. With her dark hair, deep brown skin, and large eyes, Boonsri looked beautiful. I was quite taken aback.

Hand-in-hand, we walked together along the beach for the ten minutes it took us to get to the restaurant. The sun hadn't set yet and there were still quite a few people on the beach. Boonsri certainly got the attention of every male—and many females, for that matter—as we walked along the beach, chatting idly.

I thought to myself how all these people were probably wondering how an old guy like me got to have such a lovely-looking girlfriend. They, of course, didn't know she wasn't my girlfriend—only a close friend who'd helped me when I'd needed it most.

We arrived at the restaurant. There, Herman and Gertrude—the two European owners—were waiting at the front to greet all the guests like they always did. They were so pleased to see me again—not to mention with a glamourous lady, no doubt thinking I'd found the love of my life yet again. Gertrude had always been mocking me about never settling down with Chimlin.

"Billy," Boonsri sighed, as we sat down for dinner, "this is the most magical place I've ever been to. It's a world away from managing that bar in Bangkok."

"To Choeng Mon." I raised my glass of water, while Boonsri raised her glass of wine.

"To Choeng Mon."

For the next two hours, Boonsri and I relived how we'd met, the state she'd found me in, and how much

I'd improved both physically and mentally since I'd stopped drinking and returned to Choeng Mon.

We held hands during the walk back to my Villa. Just before we reached my home, Boonsri stopped and turned around. She reached up on tiptoes and started to kiss me passionately on the lips. I was taken aback—it wasn't what I expected.

I quickly stopped her, grabbing her hands. I looked into Boonsri's eyes and breathed: "Boonsri, I can't. My life is already complicated enough. I can't be with you. Friends only. Okay?"

"Oh, Billy. I feel something here for you." Boonsri pointed to her heart. "I don't want to go home. I want to stay here with you."

"It can't happen, Boonsri."

"It's Chimlin, isn't it? You want her. Am I right?"

"No, it's not Chimlin," I shook my head. "She doesn't want anything to do with me. I showed you the message she sent me. It's just... I need to get well. I've told you and no one else about my plans—and what I plan to do once I return to America, after my sessions with Dr. Draper. I need to focus on that. You and I will be friends for life, Boonsri—and I'll always be grateful for how you've helped me. My life is all the much better for meeting you."

I laughed bitterly.

"Without you, I might still be sitting in some bar in Bangkok—getting drunk, getting beaten up, and within six months, perhaps dropping dead from the abuse I'd be inflicting on my body."

"What about I share your bed, Billy? Just for tonight?" Her cheeks flushed. "I love sex, Billy—and

I've been told I'm pretty good at it. Right now, Billy, I'm feeling horny. I *want you*, Billy—I want you inside me. I'm wearing no underwear, Billy—and, feel this… No bra." She grabbed my hand and placed it on her erect nipple.

"Come, Billy," Boonsri purred. "Come with me."

Boonsri grabbed my hand and led me up the steps to my villa.

THE NEXT MORNING, I awoke with a sudden jolt, recollecting what had happened between Boonsri and I the night before. Reality quickly set in, and I realized we'd actually gone to separate bedrooms last night—without any romantic entanglement.

I looked at my watch. It was six in the morning. I put on my shorts, quickly washed my face, and went to wake up Boonsri for our final walk on the beach—the last one before she grabbed a taxi to the airport.

Her bedroom door was shut. I knocked on the door, but there was no answer. I knocked again, but still no answer.

Slowly, I opened her door. There was no sign of Boonsri inside.

Her sheets had been pulled off the bed, no doubt placed in the washing machine. Her luggage had disappeared from her room.

On the dining room table, I found her handwritten note:

"Hi, Billy. Thank you for a lovely few days staying at your villa. I'm sorry about last night. I have

feelings for you, Billy—but you obviously don't have the same feelings for me. I thought it best that I was gone before you woke up. I didn't want to see you and feel embarrassed by my actions last night. Please stay off the alcohol. You look so much better now than the man I met in the bar a few weeks ago. Please take care. Forever your friend, Boonsri.

P.S. - I'll tell no one about your plans once you return to America. Good luck with that.

XXXX"

I slumped in the lounge room chair, clutching Boonsri's handwritten note in my hand. Perhaps I shouldn't have turned her away. Perhaps Boonsri and I were meant to be together. She was smart, caring, gorgeous—what more could a man want? I vowed to give her a call next week and ensure we keep in touch.

But now it was time to go for a walk along the beach—to clear my head and put in place the next stage of my plan. It was a plan that I'd been thinking about repeatedly over the last few days.

I hadn't encouraged the romantic relationship with Boonsri because of these plans. I knew what I wanted— I just had to work out a way to get it, knowing I had only one chance to make this work.

If I stuffed this up, there'd be no second chance.

CHAPTER 26

I GOT BACK to my villa covered in sweat after my morning walk.

I checked the GPS watch on my wrist—eight miles walked. I'd been in a zone and blocked everything out of my mind other than the plan I'd been working on. I'd finally worked out my strategy.

After I'd had a shower, I was going to head into the village for a coffee, followed by some bacon and eggs while I read yesterday's Bangkok Post. Once I got back to my villa, I'd put my plan into action.

I PULLED THE chair up to the outdoor table on the balcony and grabbed my cell phone. Before I dialed it, I looked out across the ocean—and thought to myself how lucky I was living here, living the life I did.

My mind flashed back to Mandy Jones and her husband, Sean—but I quickly managed to block them out of my mind. I'd developed a process to block those types of thoughts from my head. Whenever they sprang up, I'd simply focused on the words both Pat Gabriel and Johnny Kean had said to me: "*Billy, none of this is your fault. You did what you were told to do by the experts.*"

The experts were, of course, Ivan Cameron and his assistants. I'd simply followed their instructions—instructions that, unfortunately, had led to everything going pear-shaped.

Anyway, enough thinking about that. Now it was time to send this message—and put my little plan into action.

I grabbed my cell phone and searched for Chimlin's number, which I knew off by heart. I started typing away.

> "*Dear Chimlin. I got your message. I wasn't avoiding you—I simply didn't have my cell phone with me. I left it at my villa while I traveled for three months, trying to escape my demons.*
>
> *I've now realized I need professional help—which I should have sought much earlier. I'm heading back to the States in four weeks to see Dr. Draper, the psychologist I told you about who'd helped me six years ago, when I'd had my breakdown after dealing with those crooks who'd tried to steal my business.*
>
> *I've been on a bender the last few months, dealing—in my own way—with the things that happened to me: Mandy's death, Sean's suicide, and, of course, your kidnapping.*

I drowned myself in alcohol, which numbed the pain while I was drinking—but only made my problems much worse the next day when I woke up. I got beaten up and had thirty-five stitches in my head and another twenty or so stitches in my lips and mouth. I only got out of the hospital last week.

It's a long story—but a couple of things happened that perhaps helped save my life.

After I see Dr. Draper, I have a plan that will keep me in the States for a couple of months. This is something I need to do. It's part of my healing process—much like when I wrote that book after listing Future Wealth on Wall Street, and my subsequent breakdown. This plan doesn't involve writing another book, though.

I've had time to reflect on many things while lying in the hospital. You've never been far from my thoughts throughout the last few months. I've done lots of reflecting about you and me, and what could have been. I won't share those thoughts with you in this message. I'd rather do that face-to-face—if you can forgive me, and agree to meet me.

I'm now back at my villa in Choeng Mon. I've been off the alcohol for twelve days and plan to stay off it completely for the next twelve months. I'm back walking eight miles a day and taking the stand-up paddle board out every morning.

I'm going to head off in two days' time to Phuket. There's a drug rehabilitation centre in the jungle there that I want to check out. Not for me, as I've managed to escape the demons of the grog quite easily, and have no cravings for alcohol as I'm getting my body back into good shape. No, I want to help the people in Phuket help others fight their drug dependence.

I'm staying at a five-star resort called Andara for six days. It's on the headland at a beautiful little beach called Kamala. I've never been there before, but it certainly looks pretty. There's a tennis court and gym, and there are heaps of beachfront restaurants to choose from. I'd like you to come and stay with me. I want us to sort things out and discuss plans. My plans involve you, Chimlin—subject to you wanting me as part of your future. That's your call.

I'll text you in two days when I get to Andara and let you know which room I'm in. It would be great if you flew down to Phuket and joined me at Andara, so I can right the many wrongs I've done to you—and our past relationship.

Always yours,
Love,
Billy
XXXX"

I sat in the chair for the next hour, gazing out across the ocean. Every time my cell phone buzzed, I quickly checked it, hoping it was Chimlin responding.

There were messages from Pat, Chook Burns, and my kids—all checking how I was doing. There was a lengthy message from Ivan Cameron advising me that the Mr. X operation appeared to have shut itself down. The gang had apparently disappeared off the face of the earth. Ivan suggested the massive publicity generated by what had happened must have forced them all underground. He assured me that while surveillance of Mr. X had ceased, the file would always remain open in the hope that they'd one day catch the crooks who'd kidnapped me and murdered Mandy.

There was no message from Chimlin.

I spent the rest of the day walking, swimming, and just lying on the beach. Tomorrow, I was going to catch up with my good friend Lars for coffee. He'd suggested drinks at our favorite bar, but I'd told Lars that, for now, my drinking days were over—and coffee suited me far better, anyway. I didn't want to risk the temptation of drinks in a bar.

The day after, I was booked on a 10:00am flight from Koh Samui to Phuket—or, more particularly, Kamala Beach on the island of Phuket.

I OPENED THE shutters to the balcony. There, in front of me as far as the eyes could see, was the magical blue ocean of the Andaman Sea, glistening in all its beauty.

To the right of the ocean was the small, seaside village of Kamala Beach. I'd check the village out later this afternoon—but I intended to spend the first few hours in my villa waiting, and hoping, that Chimlin would contact me.

She'd failed to respond to my initial message two days ago. I couldn't tell whether she'd even opened the message or not. I had a sick feeling in my stomach that the next six days at Andara were going to be spent alone.

That meant there was one more message I had to send—the final message to Chimlin:

'Hi, Chimlin. I haven't heard from you, so I'm not sure whether you're coming to stay with me at Andare or not. I did say in my last message that I'd send you details of where I'm staying. It's Room 212.

The hotel is located on a road they call "Millionaires' Road". I'm sure the taxi driver will know where it is.

It's a special villa I've rented—high on the side of the headland, with magical views of the ocean as far as you can see. Plus, the villa has its own private plunge pool with a spa. It's a great pool to sit back in with a glass of champagne, naked, overlooking the Andaman Sea. Champagne for you, I mean. Sparkling mineral water for me.

Love,
Billy
XXXX"

I hit the send button, but I wasn't confident I'd get any response. I thought about how I'd fucked up my relationship with Chimlin. The one time I'd actually decided I wanted to be with her, she apparently didn't want to be with me—but I only had myself to blame. She'd given me plenty of opportunities to be with her, and I'd knocked back each opportunity as soon as it came my way.

Yep, I was no good at this relationship caper, I thought to myself.

CHAPTER 27

IT WAS LATE afternoon. I'd spent the last few hours lying on the sun lounge on my balcony, enjoying the view of the beautiful, blue ocean. There'd been no messages or phone calls from Chimlin. I now assumed there was no chance she was coming to stay with me.

I headed off down "Millionaires Road" for a stroll along the beach—and afterward, I planned to find a nice little beachside restaurant for dinner. I had my phone with me, fully charged, just in case I received a message.

The beach was over a mile long. The tide was out, and it revealed a beautiful expanse of gleaming, white sand. It was a great beach for walking on, and a great beach for me to get into that zone and be creative. Yep, a few days of walking on this beach and I'd be able to nut out an even more detailed plan for my next little conquest once I returned to the States—albeit after I'd finished my consultations with Dr. Draper.

I finally reached the far end of the beach, where a couple of young Thai guys were surfing on longboards. I thought about how nice this place was. Beautiful beach, waves to surf, and twenty or so restaurants on the boardwalk.

I turned and looked back toward the headland I was staying on. It was a magical sight—the large hill covered in lush, dense jungle intermixed with the rooftops of the villas of the resort. This place had a certain appeal to me. Perhaps I should move here— move away from the memories of the extortion that I'd now forever associate with my life at Choeng Mon. I'd raise that idea with Dr. Draper and get his professional opinion on whether a change of location might be good for my healing process. I'd even noticed there was a house on the beach that had a 'For Rent' sign out front. It might be worthwhile for me to explore that option while I was here. It couldn't hurt to at least have a look…

My stomach was churning with worry about Chimlin—or, more correctly, about the fact she hadn't called or messaged me. Worrying about Chimlin made me feel slightly nauseous—and while I didn't feel like food, I knew I had to get some dinner in me as I hadn't eaten since I'd left Choeng Mon that morning.

I decided to check out the menus from the restaurants I'd previously walked past, on the edge of the beach. I was feeling tired and I hoped—even with my worry about Chimlin—that I'd be able to sleep tonight.

I'D LEFT THE curtains open the previous night, so I was now awoken by the blinding sun flooding my room. I glanced at the bedside clock. It was 6:30am. I grabbed my cell phone—but there was still no message from Chimlin.

I sighed. I thought to myself: I could either mope around all day feeling sorry for myself, or return the old Billy Houston to the driving seat and jump out of bed—thanking my lucky stars I was still alive and make the most of the day in gratitude.

Yep, the old Billy Houston appealed to me far more, so I jumped out of bed, pulled on my board shorts and runners—along with my GPS watch—and thought to myself that I'd walk ten miles that morning, then grab a coffee somewhere.

I quickly grabbed a thousand Thai baht and off I went, down "Millionaires Road" toward the beach.

There were already other people walking on the beach, even at that hour—a mixture of local Thais and holidaymakers, all getting some early morning exercise. I saw a group of a dozen ladies, who all appeared to be Thai, doing one of my exercise programs on the hard sand at the edge of the beach. They were all wearing the 21st Century Fitness clothing. If only they realized that I was the founder of the company!

I guess they probably wouldn't have believed me even if I'd told them. I always got a bit of a thrill when I saw people in public doing our exercises, or people wearing our fitness apparel. It was a bit like a proud father watching one of his children achieve something special in their life, I guess.

A guy with a dog on a leash was walking toward me. He stopped and introduced himself.

"I'm Allan. I'm the onsite property manager at Andara. I look after the sales of the villas.

I see you're staying at Andara."

"Yes, I am." I offered Allan my hand. "I'm Billy— Billy Houston. Pleased to meet you. Your accent— South African?"

"Yes," Allan laughed. "South African. I've been with Andara for the last eight years. And you're American?"

"Yep, American. This is my first time here in Kamala. A beautiful beach."

"It's a beautiful town! Not too busy, but big enough to stop you from getting bored. Some great restaurants and, if you like a surf, you'll often get a small wave on the point up there."

"If I may ask, Allan, what do villas at Andara sell for?"

"The type of villa you're staying in? Anywhere between $10 million to $12 million."

"Wow, that's a lot of money."

"A lot of Chinese money here. Eighty percent of my sales are to the Chinese."

"Great to meet you, Allan. I better go—I've got to get to ten miles this morning." I pointed to my watch, then patted his dog as I waved goodbye.

$10 million to $12 million. That was a lot of money—way beyond my current yearly income of $100,000. Twelve months ago, I could have bought thirty of those villas and paid for each of them in cash. Not now, though. I had no assets left.

I walked and walked along the beach, and then through the township—deep in thought about many things. The bell on my watch rung, signifying I'd hit the ten-mile distance mark. I was less than five hundred yards from the villa. I decided to head back, have a shower, and then head down to the buffet for a nice breakfast.

I GLANCED AT my watch. It was 12:15pm. Perhaps I'd go for a swim, and then find a nice little beachside restaurant for lunch.

The doorbell rang. I assumed it was room service. I walked over and opened the door…

…and there she stood, in all her beauty.

The long, dark flowing hair. The large, wide-open brown eyes. The dark, olive skin and petite, slim body.

Chimlin.

We embraced immediately, kissing passionately, my foot holding the door open. Chimlin was still standing partly in the outside hallway, partly in the entranceway to my room, and fully in my arms.

"Chimlin!" I pulled my lips from hers. "Oh, God—I didn't expect you to turn up! I've been feeling sick to my stomach. Come in, come in!" I grabbed her overnight bag and guided her onto the balcony. "Look at that view, Chimlin."

"Sensational, Billy." She turned to me. "Oh, I've missed you, Billy. Don't tell me what's been happening yet, that can wait for later. It's been so long, Billy, since we had sex. Put the "Do Not Disturb" sign up and come to bed with me."

As she spoke, Chimlin undid her dress, took off her bra, and waited for me to peel off her white, lace G-string.

The last person I'd had sex with was Chimlin, and that had been six years ago. I'm not sure if she'd been with anyone else since—and now wasn't the time to ask.

We were like two sixteen-year-olds making love for the first time—exploring different positions, entwined in many and varied passionate embraces. After what seemed like an eternity, we both lay on top of the sheets, covered in each other's perspiration, both exhausted. My arm was around Chimlin's shoulders.

"Billy, you're breathing heavily."

"I've been a bit out of shape over the last few months," I admitted. "I really punished my body—drinking far too much alcohol, not eating properly, sometimes going for days without food and only surviving on a liquid diet." I sighed. "I've been in a bad place."

"Your head, Billy. There's a big lump—scar tissue."

"Yep. I'll tell you about that later, too." I turned to her. "I didn't think you were coming. I thought you were going to be true to your last message and never want anything to do with me ever again."

"Billy, I wasn't going to come. I only changed my mind at 02:30am this morning. My psychologist said I need to move on from you—that I had to get you out of my life. But ever since I got your first text, I haven't been able to sleep—arguing with myself about whether

I should follow my psychologist's advice, or my instincts."

She rolled over to face me.

"You've told me many times to always go with your gut feeling. You always said the gut feeling is always the one to follow. I couldn't sleep because I was worried I might never see you again. I thought: *This is crazy. I'll disobey my psychologist's advice and go with my gut.*" So, at 2:30am this morning, I got up and booked a flight online—and here I am."

Her wide eyes stared into mine.

"I had to drop Kiah off at my mum's at 06:30am this morning. Crazy! But here I am with you, Billy Houston."

Little did I know about the bombshell Chimlin would drop in five days' time.

THE NEXT FEW days and nights whizzed past with Chimlin, and I enjoyed countless walks on the beach with her, swimming together in the ocean, relaxing in the spa, and—of course—lots of sex and fun.

There was something different about Chimlin this time, I just couldn't put my finger on exactly what it was—but it *was* something. Just a slight, worried look on her face at times when she didn't think I was looking at her. A couple of times, I'd caught her just staring off into space—and when I asked what she was thinking about, Chimlin had simply replied: "It's nothing."

Plus, she'd stopped drinking. The Chimlin of old had always loved a glass of white wine over dinner. I assumed she'd stopped drinking because of me—

thinking that if she drank in front of me, it might tempt me to have some alcohol too.

Chimlin laid the ground rules on day one: She didn't want to discuss her kidnapping—or anything else about the extortion, and that whole sordid turn of events. It was something she'd said her psychologist had told her to do—part of her way of healing by blocking it from her mind.

Yesterday morning, I'd been out to the Drug Rehabilitation Centre in the jungle. I'd had a good two-hour meeting with the General Manager there, and one of the owners. They were fully supportive of my plans once I returned to America—with my goal being to assist their organization. In their words: *"Any assistance you can give to help us do what we do even better will always be most appreciated."*

Unknown to Chimlin, I'd also met the owner of the beachfront house in Kamala. I was getting to like this little village more and more each day. When I inspected the three-bedroom, three-bathroom house, I realized then and there that this was the place I wanted to escape to. This was where I wanted to spend the next few years.

Within an hour of meeting the owner, we managed to agree on terms and shook hands to cement our deal. He was going to email me agreements—and, subject to my lawyer in Bangkok approving, we'd sign the lease before I departed in two days' time.

I planned to share this news with Chimlin over dinner on our last evening together. I was sure she'd be as rapt and excited as I was about calling Kamala home. It would even be an opportunity for me to get back into surfing, once I returned from my next little venture in America—which would hopefully only take a few months.

In the space of five days, we'd established which of the many restaurants was our favorite—and tonight, on our final night in Kamala, I'd secured the best table in the house, situated right on the water's edge.

We were both drinking mineral water, watching the sun set across the ocean. Now was the time for me to share the good news about the house with Chimlin. My lawyer had perused the agreements and advised me they were fine to sign. Tomorrow, before we left for the airport, I planned to meet the owner on site and sign the agreement. That meant, before we left, I'd be able to show Chimlin my—or, more correctly, *our* new home.

"Chimlin, I have some exciting news. You know that house we walk past every day? The one available for rent?"

"Yes," Chimlin looked at me coolly. "You remind me every day that it's for rent, Billy."

"Well, not any more it's not. It's mine. I mean, it's *ours*. I've agreed to terms with the owner. I have a three-year lease, with a second three-year option if I want it. Plus, I have the option to buy the property if we like it."

Chimlin's eyes widened.

"But you have no money, Billy. How would you buy it?"

"Well, it doesn't cost much. I'm sure Pat would give or lend me the money, given that I've made the guy very wealthy."

There was silence from Chimlin. She looked away, then turned back to face me. She was smiling, but it was a smile that didn't seem quite real. There were a few seconds of lingering silence, which made this an unusually awkward moment.

I had that feeling once again that there was something different about Chimlin. I'd expected her to be ecstatic about the news.

"Billy," Chimlin eventually said, followed by a big sigh and a further pause. "Oh, Billy—I'm so, so sorry."

"Sorry about what?"

Tears started to stream down Chimlin's cheeks. I grabbed a napkin to pass to her.

I didn't want to attract the attention of the other guests to Chimlin's state, so I whispered: "What's wrong? What's wrong, Chimlin? I thought you'd be over the moon about this new house."

"I'm pregnant, Billy."

I was choked for words.

I felt a sudden lump in my throat as I repeated what Chimlin had just said: "Pregnant?"

We'd only been having sex for the last six days, so I knew immediately that I wasn't the father. A sick feeling came over me. I felt dizzy. I was suddenly perspiring. I pushed my plate of food away.

"Who's the father?" I battled to get the words out of my mouth.

"It's my psychologist."

I was silent for what seemed like eternity.

"You're kidding me. That's a blatant breach of professional duties."

"It takes two to tango, Billy. When I couldn't get a hold of you on your phone, and you didn't return my calls or messages, I confided in my psychologist about how sad I was—how emotionally distraught this had all made me. I was feeling worthless. He was there. He comforted me. I hadn't had sex with anyone since you—years earlier. It just happened, and it happened so quickly."

"Let me guess, on the shrink's couch?" I was shocked at how sarcastic I sounded.

"Yes, on his couch," Chimlin replied coldly.

"You're kidding me. Fucking unbelievable! And not safe sex, obviously."

As I said this, I thought about us—how we'd been having unprotected sex repeatedly over the last six days. We must have made love upwards of twenty times.

Chimlin must have sensed what I was thinking. She reassured me: "I had myself checked out. I haven't picked up any diseases."

There was stunned silence between us both. I turned and peered out across the sea, gathering my thoughts. I felt the cold, hard stare of Chimlin's eyes on my face. She reached over and grabbed my hand, whispering: "I'm so sorry, Billy. I only wanted to be with you. I don't see the man. I actually stopped seeing him immediately after it happened."

"It only happened once?" I asked.

"Yes, only once. I wish it didn't happen at all, but I can't change the past, Billy."

"How many months pregnant are you?"

"Two."

"What are you going to do?" I asked, not wanting to mention the word abortion.

Tears were still running down Chimlin's face as she spoke:

"I initially thought about an abortion, but I can't do that. It's against my faith. I'll have the baby and raise it alone. He doesn't want anything to do with me or the baby."

"So, he *knows* you're pregnant?"

"Ah, yes," Chimlin nodded. "He knows. I'm weighing up whether to inform his professional body or not. I was a wreck, Billy. I wasn't dealing with the kidnapping well, and then I thought you'd just dumped me because you weren't returning my calls or texts."

"I wanted us to be together, Chimlin. Together forever."

"Billy, until yesterday, I was still trying to convince myself to have an abortion—thinking that if I did, we could be together." She took a deep breath. "But I can't bring myself to have an abortion."

"We could still be together, Chimlin. You could have the baby and we could raise it together."

"No, Billy. You want to live here. I can't leave Bangkok, just like I couldn't leave Bangkok six years ago to live in Choeng Mon like you wanted. We're in the same circumstances we were six years ago. The only difference being that I'll have two children, to two different men, both of whom I don't love."

"What a fuck up," I whispered to myself.

"What did you say, Billy?"

"I said what a fuck up. An absolute fuck up."

"Billy, I don't think karma has ever been kind to us. I don't think the gods ever wanted us to be together for the long-term."

"Why don't we give it a go, Chimlin? See if we can make it work?"

"Billy, you'll forever be thinking that this baby isn't yours. You'll have remorse, I know you will. It will always be in the back of your mind—and that's not good for a relationship. I made a mistake, Billy—and, unfortunately for me, I've got to pay the price for that mistake."

If only I'd had my cell phone with me and returned Chimlin's calls. She'd never have been feeling the way she had—and she'd never have let herself be taken advantage of by her psychologist.

Some doctor he was! A complete lack of ethics and morals, taking advantage of an emotionally fragile and distraught patient. Yep, a grub—a complete grub, who couldn't keep his dick in his trousers.

CHAPTER 28

I WAS SITTING on the couch opposite Dr. Draper. Over the last month, I'd had twelve sessions with the good doctor, trying to clear my mind from all the 'rubble' surrounding the events of the extortion and kidnapping. Given Chimlin's recent, shattering news, I also needed his assistance in moving on from that relationship.

After Chimlin had left Kamala Beach, the morning after our eventful dinner, I'd seen the owner of the beach front house and signed the lease agreement. That was where I intended to set up my base for the next six years, once I completed this unfinished business in the States. The beach front house had three double bedrooms, three bathrooms, and a beautiful balcony leading to a small patch of grass. Beyond that was the glistening blue of the Andaman ocean. It would be a great place for my kids to come and stay with me when they were on vacation.

The day after signing the lease, I'd hopped onto a plane to Koh Samui—and within two days, packed up my villa and all of my possessions. I told Tom, my gardener, that I'd be away indefinitely and to check on the villa each week in my absence. I said I might have an old friend and his wife staying in the villa while I was away—and told Tom to treat my guests well.

He'd asked me how long I'd intended to be away this time, and I'd told him six years. He didn't blink an eyelid, as he was now used to my frequent comings and goings.

On my last day in Choeng Mon, I caught up with Lars and Dao for coffee at my villa. I was still off the alcohol—and though I was tempted to hit it again, and perhaps hit it hard given the recent news from Chimlin, I realized that would only lead me back into a downward spiral that I might never get out of this time.

I didn't want to go back there. One of my strengths has always been that, when I set my mind to something, I can normally achieve it. Getting off the alcohol was no different. It was something I was determined to do.

"Mr. Billy! My long-lost friend. How are you?"

"I'm good, Lars." I shook my Norwegian friend's hand and gave Dao, his wife, a warm hug as they entered my villa.

After some discussion about how I was doing, I awkwardly shared the news about what had transpired between Chimlin and I. The news completely dumfounded them both—especially given that Dao was one of Chimlin's best friends, and yet she knew nothing about Chimlin's pregnancy. Then, it was finally time to move on to the real reason I'd invited them both to my villa.

"You've both always told me how much you like this villa."

"Billy, you have the best villa in Choeng Mon," Lars grinned. "I love coming here and sitting on this beautiful balcony."

Dao squeezed her husband's hand.

"I keep on telling Lars that it's always been my dream to wake up in the morning, draw the curtains, and have the blue, sparkling ocean right in front of my eyes." She sighed. "I know you've worked hard, Billy—but you're still a lucky man, having this right at your doorstep. You simply walk off your balcony, right onto the white, sandy beach."

I smiled. That's exactly what I'd wanted to hear.

"Well," I told them, "I'd like you both to move into my villa—for the next six years, rent free. You'd look after it for me."

Lars and Dao glanced at each other, then glanced towards me. There was silence for a spell, before Lars finally said: "I don't understand what you're saying, Billy. Where are you going?"

"I need to leave Choeng Mon, Lars. It has too many bad memories for me right now—memories of the extortion attempt and, of course, memories of me and Chimlin. I need to get away—get this out of my system. It's part of my healing process."

"But, where will you go?" asked Dao.

"I've found somewhere else to live. I've just signed a six-year lease on a stunning beach front house in a little village called Kamala, on the island of Phuket."

"Yes, we've been there, Billy," Lars nodded. "A very beautiful place."

"Well, I know you don't like where you're currently living, what with the noisy neighbors and a landlord who doesn't seem to give a damn about the complaints you make. So, now you can have all this." I waved my arm across the table, out towards the blue water that stretched as far as the eye could see.

With that agreed upon—and some further talk about the finer details of Lars and Dao moving in—I finally advised them that I was heading off to LA, via Bangkok, tomorrow morning. Rather than hanging around Choeng Mon for a few more weeks, moping about and feeling sorry for myself given Chimlin's recent revelation, I'd decided to get back to LA as soon as possible and start my sessions with Dr. Draper.

I'd phoned Dr. Draper's office the same morning Chimlin had flown back to Bangkok, and I'd managed to bring my appointments forward. I'd be back in LA that Friday—and sitting in the good doctor's office at 9:30am the following Monday. We'd agreed on four weeks of counselling. I was looking forward to it.

I was going to spend the weekend in LA catching up with Pat and Chook, but I didn't want to see them again until I'd finished the sessions with Dr. Draper and got myself back in shape physically as well as mentally. I wanted them to see the "before" and "after" versions of me.

Pat, of course, had seen me when I was down and out in the hospital a few weeks ago. In six more weeks, he wouldn't recognize me.

"TODAY IS OUR last session, Billy. Now you start your new venture in the States. Tell me—how's that going?"

"Well, it's not actually a venture, so to speak. It's just something I need to do. I have a meeting with the organizers this afternoon—and it looks like both New York and Seattle are already booked out. I'm going to hang out at Chook Burns' pad at Malibu for the next two weeks, as he's gone away for a few weeks. Just catch a couple of waves and spend some quality time with my kids." I snorted bitterly. "I've probably neglected them over the last few years."

"Tell me how you're feeling, Billy."

"I'm good, Doc. I'm feeling strong. I jump out of bed each day excited at what lies ahead. I'm still off the grog, and I don't miss it. I won't stay off it forever. I think I'm back to the old Billy Houston—the Billy Houston full of energy and excitement."

"Do you have flashbacks to those recent events?"

"For sure, I think about it—but those first two weeks, back with you, when I first poured out my emotions about the torture and the death of Mandy, and Sean's suicide, and, of course, the kidnapping of the person I truly loved... That helped me. You've cemented in my mind—just like Pat, Chook, and Johnny Kean did to a lesser extent—that none of this is my fault. I did what I was told to do by the experts: Ivan Cameron, and his fellow Interpol agents. I've stopped thinking about all the 'what if' scenarios, because I know—thanks to you—that it gets me nowhere. I feel good I've helped Mandy and Sean's children, and they show no signs of blaming me for what happened."

"And you got rid of Sean's suicide note?"

"Yes—I burned that. I don't carry it around anymore. You've helped me there as well—to understand the mind of someone who's suffering from acute depression. I thank you for that."

"And Chimlin?" Doctor Draper asked. "Have you accepted that you must move on from her? That you need to get her out of your mind?"

"Yes, I've accepted that. You're right—she was too young for me, and it would have been impossible at my age to attempt to raise two young children—especially to two different fathers. As you quite rightly pointed out, I would have forever been bitter about the fact that Chimlin had two children, to two different men, and I'd always question why Chimlin and I never had children together."

"You've come a long way over the last month," the Doctor nodded. "I know from our past sessions, six years or so ago, that you're a strong man, Billy. I see it in your eyes—the excitement, the get-up-and-go attitude, the energy. I see the old Billy Houston back. I see the passion about your next little venture." He laughed: "Or perhaps a better term for it is: Your next little way to help other people."

I felt a swell of pride. "Yes, I'm excited about that."

"Billy, what happens after that? Where will you live? And what do you plan to do?"

I pursed my lips.

"Yes—that's something I also ponder, Doc. I've thought of staying here in LA, where my roots are, but that's not right for me. I love Thailand. I love the way of life over there. From an outsider's viewpoint, looking in, it might seem like chaos—but it's chaos that seems to magically work. I love the warmth of the people, their kindness, how they care for their families and their elderly. I think it's the place I want to call home for the rest of my life. Of course, I have the house on the beach at Kamala, where I can swim and surf. There's a gym at the end of the beach, where I can work out a couple of times a week—and there's a tennis court where I can play a couple of times a week. It has everything I need. Most importantly, it has that little village feel—kind of like Choeng Mon. One day, I'll probably return to my villa at Choeng Mon—just not yet."

"And what about business, Billy? Any plans to start another business? You're an entrepreneur, after all—always thinking of ideas. I don't think it's the money that motivates you, Billy. I think it's the sense of accomplishment. Am I correct?"

I nodded. "Yep, the money's not important to me. It's the sense of starting something—nurturing it, growing it, building a team of like-minded individuals, and achieving goals. It just gives me great satisfaction. I've been going for walks along the beach at Malibu. The beach is always where I think of ideas. It's my creative time. I thrive on it—it gives me a buzz."

"But you haven't fully answered my question. What about starting another business?"

I looked up at Doctor Draper thoughtfully.

"Doc, if I was ten years younger, perhaps—but I'm fifty-five. I'm going to go back to how I started out in my late teens. I'm going to become a beach bum at fifty-five. Perhaps I'll even grow my hair long, just like I used to have it in my teenage years."

The doctor laughed, but there wasn't much humor to it.

"Billy, you need to do *something*. Your mind gets fueled by new challenges. It loves the reward of achieving those challenges—it loves the sense of success. If you stop, it might well kill you."

"So, you're saying I should get back into business?"

"Perhaps not your own business, Billy. What about being a mentor to others? Teach other budding entrepreneurs what it takes to be successful? Why don't you share your knowledge—your failures, as well as your successes?"

"I don't know, Doc. I'm not sure if I have the patience for that—plus, I'm not sure I could do that while living in Kamala. I don't want to spend every week traveling across the country like I used to." But I didn't say no. "Let me sleep on it."

The Doctor nodded, shuffling his papers. "Well, Billy—I think we're done. I think you're ready to go back into the world. I think the old Billy Houston is back in the land of the living. One last word—don't drown your sorrows in alcohol again. You'll never find the answer in the bottom of a glass."

"I know, Doc." I shook my head. "I know only too well."

Chapter 29

Four weeks earlier

"It must be five years since we last met face-to-face like this, Billy—just the two of us, sharing a drink."

"Five years and six months to be exact, Cynthia. Remember, I never forget dates and times." I looked across at my former publisher. "Our last meeting was at my favorite little bar in Choeng Mon. We were drinking margaritas, and it was your first time in Koh Samui. I told you about the new business venture I was about to embark on in the fitness industry."

"That's right," Cynthia smiled. "I remember now, Billy. Then, four years to the day after that meeting, you phoned me and asked me to attend the celebrations as you entered the Chinese market with 21st Century Fitness."

"Yep, and here we are—eighteen months after those celebrations, and my life has changed in a way both of us could never have imagined."

"Billy, I'm so sorry for what happened to you after those celebrations." Cynthia shook her head, unable to make eye contact with me.

"No need to be sorry, Cynthia," I reassured her. "It's happened—and I can't change what's happened, no matter how hard I try. No one can change the past." For a moment we were both silent, until I murmured: "But that's not why I asked you to come and see me."

I glanced at my watch.

"You've set aside three hours for this meeting, right, Cynthia?"

"Yep, I'm all ears until five o'clock."

"Good. I'm going to share with you, in a macro view, the story of 21St Century Fitness Group—and the tragic circumstances of what transpired over the past eighteen months. It isn't a happy story, Cynthia," I warned, placing a box of tissues in front of her.

There was a look of confusion on Cynthia's face, so I explained: "You might need those as I share the story—all factual—with you. My doctor, Dr. Draper, certainly needed tissues when I told it to him—and so did my two best mates, Pat and Chook." I laughed sadly. "And they only heard the condensed version, not the full story like I'm about to share with you." I paused, meeting her gaze. "Are you ready?"

"As ready as I'll ever be, Billy."

For the next two and a half hours, I shared my story with Cynthia—the story of the rise and fall of 21st

Century Fitness, and the story I'd aptly named *Billy Houston's Fall from Grace*.

Toward the end of my tale, I had to stop several times to allow Cynthia to regain composure and get her tears under control. By the end, she was a rambling mess.

As for me? Well, I'd told this story several times over the last few weeks. The first time was to Dr. Draper, and I'd certainly been as much of a mess as Cynthia was now. By this stage, though, I could tell the story without shedding too many tears—but it still took a physical toll on me. I'd be covered in sweat and quite pale by the end of the tale.

"WOW, BILLY—I never realized what you'd been through. I mean, I was aware of the headlines—about the murder of Mandy Jones, and her husband committing suicide, and the kidnapping of that Thai woman—but the rest? I had no idea."

Cynthia asked me the question I'd been expecting ever since we'd sat down together.

"So—you want to write a book about it? A follow-up to your first book? I think you have another bestseller on your hands, Billy. I think it'll sell more copies than the first book—and that was in the top-ten sellers in America when it was released."

"No, Cynthia," I laughed, holding up my hand. "I don't want to write a book. I want to tell my story in six cities across America—with all proceeds going to a drug rehabilitation centre in Phuket, Thailand." I slid two typed pages across the table toward her. "Here's my proposal. I'll grab some water while you read it."

It didn't take Cynthia long to go through what I'd prepared.

"This is great, Billy. Have you thought about turning this into a movie?"

"No," I laughed, shaking my head. "I don't want a movie. I just want to tell my story in six cities: New York, Seattle, Washington, Chicago, Boston, and Philadelphia—and in that order. Do you think people will pay $795 to hear my story over three hours?"

"Billy, it's an incredible story—you're going to have people in tears. They'll be on the edge of their seats the whole time. You'll have no trouble at all selling the tickets. But, why not LA as well?"

"LA's my home. It's too emotionally disturbing to tell the story here, to people I know. Plus, my kids live here, and I don't want them to hear the story 'warts and all' yet. I'll tell them in a few years' time, when they're a bit older."

"So, you've got the venues already worked out?"

"I've actually got the venues already *booked*." I handed Cynthia the dates and times for each session.

She stared at the list of event dates.

"In that case, why am I even here, Billy? Especially if you don't intend to turn this story into a book."

"Cynthia, you have lots of contacts in the press. I want you to donate your time—or, more accurately, your company's time, free of charge—to get the promotion happening. We need to move quickly, as the first talk is booked in New York in just six weeks' time."

"That's a tight timeline, Billy—nearly impossible, perhaps."

"Cynthia, if they can put a man on the moon over forty years ago, I'm sure we can get these speaking engagements up and running in just six weeks. Once we've done one, we'll simply roll out the same process for the next one. There'll be no props, there's no fanfare—it's simply you introducing me, and then me telling the story for the next three hours, just like I've done this afternoon."

Cynthia said nothing. She stared at me for long moments before she finally spoke again:

"Why are you doing this, Billy?"

"Because I need to give something back to those less fortunate than me. Those in trouble. Those who need help."

"Haven't you already given enough back? You've given away all of your wealth—hundreds of millions of dollars—and you've also set up the Future Wealth Foundation in America. One can only imagine how much money that's raised in the last six years."

"I developed an addiction to a drug," I explained. "My drug was alcohol—and it took control over my life for many months. It was a quick fall into oblivion. I managed to make myself fall off the face of the Earth. I was uncontactable. If it hadn't been for a chance encounter with Griff Peters, in some bar in Bangkok— if he hadn't phoned Pat straight away, telling him he needed to get over to Thailand to help me—I'd be dead."

I leaned back in my seat.

"I did some research on what I went through, and how common it is in society. It's happening every minute of every day, Cynthia. People are getting overwhelmed by stress, they're suffering from depression, and they're walking away from everything. Some use alcohol to escape their demons, some prefer cocaine, some ice—meth—or whichever other drugs they can get their hands on."

"I get that, Billy—but why the drug rehabilitation centre in Phuket?"

"I searched for organizations helping people with drug dependence. There are literally hundreds and hundreds of such organizations, all throughout the world. Most are very expensive, and some are only accessible to the rich and famous. But I came across this place, in the jungles of Phuket, where they're helping everyday people overcome their drug dependence. Predominantly, people without much money. I went there a few weeks ago and met the owner and the general manager. There were young Americans there, plus Australians, Germans, Thai—people of all nationalities. The place operates on a shoestring budget. They need help—and I can give it to them. If we have six thousand people attend my talk, across the six venues, we'll gross about $4.8 million. I've managed to get the venues to reduce their rental to half-price, and offer catering at-cost price, as long as all funds raised go to charity."

I pointed to one of the lines on the printed document I'd handed Cynthia.

"I need to keep expenses at no more than eight-hundred-thousand, so I can give a check for $4 million to the drug rehabilitation centre. That's why I need you, Cynthia—to get as much free promotion as you can and keep all other advertising at-cost; since all funds raised are going to this charity."

Cynthia nodded, then asked: "Are you charging a fee for your time, Billy?"

"No, Cynthia. My time is all free."

"A very noble cause, Billy." She smiled. "Of course, I'll help—or, more precisely, World Focus Publishing will help. But six weeks, Billy—that's a tight timeframe, but we'll make it happen. I still reckon we should turn your story into a movie, though. Think of the money you'd raise for the drug centre if *that* happened!" Cynthia raised her eyebrows.

I laughed. "No, Cynthia—I don't want any more publicity. After this, I'm going to escape back to Kamala and live a happy, quiet life as a beach bum. It's how I started my life."

AND THAT'S HOW I came to be in Seattle that night— to give my second speech, with Pat Gabriel and Chook Burns in attendance.

CHAPTER 30

I STOOD ON stage, gazing out across the packed auditorium—where over a thousand people were in attendance. Some were young, some were old, and there was a mixture of men and women, some dressed in suits, others more casually. It was a typical cross section of America.

I was covered in perspiration after standing beneath the bright lights of the stage for so long, delivering the second of the six, planned speeches.

I paused my talk and glanced at my watch. I'd been speaking for two hours, fifty-seven minutes. I had the final three minutes left to add my final words of wisdom. I could hear people in the audience crying, overcome with emotion.

When the lights in the auditorium had been dimmed, I'd been able to clearly see the people in the first three or four rows, sitting right in front of the stage.

Just about everyone in those rows was wiping tears from their eyes during the section in which I reflected on the torture and ultimate death of Mandy Jones, and the resultant suicide of her loving husband—along with the kidnapping and ultimate rescue of Chimlin.

I began to wrap up my speech:

"So, if you're wondering how 21st Century Fitness is going, I can tell you the business now has over sixty-five million users of its fitness apps—each paying twenty cents a week. If you've got your cell phone handy, do the calculations. Add in the yoga programs, plus the dietary foods, supplements, and clothing, and 21st Century Fitness is a very profitable and valuable company. I'm also proud to say that five percent of all profits go to local charities in the same markets the company operates in, all across Southeast Asia. I've always been a big believer in giving back to those less fortunate."

The audience was silent as they listened to me finish.

"Ladies and gentlemen—thank you for your attendance this evening, and thank you for giving me, Billy Houston, the chance to tell my story. Everything I've told you is fact. It all happened—and the last few months of it were a living nightmare."

I lowered my voice:

"I'm often asked: *"What would you do differently, if you had a second chance?"* The answer is quite simple: I'd have given those criminals the $20 million straight away. Would that have saved the life of Mandy Jones? Who knows? It might have simply meant the crooks thought I was an easy target, and they'd have come back—threatening me again, and demanding more money. Would I have given them money a second time around? Probably not. I probably would have followed the advice of the experts, and not given into their demands a second time—which, of course, might have meant I simply delayed the inevitable torture and murder of someone very close to me."

There was a solemn silence from the audience.

"I call my story *Billy Houston's Fall from Grace*," I told the assembled crowd. "I'll let *you* decide what you call it yourselves. Thank you all—and God bless America."

With that, I walked off the stage to thunderous applause. Cynthia smiled at me as she crossed paths with me, approaching the lectern to formally close the night's presentation.

"Ladies and gentlemen," she quieted the applause, "you've heard a truly remarkable story of success, failure, lies, treachery, abuse and—unfortunately, in the end—torture and death. I think you'd all agree with me that Billy Houston is one of America's greatest entrepreneurs: A man with vision, drive, and passion, who has never feared failure. The evolution of 21st Century Fitness into the world's leading fitness business was all started by one man: Billy Houston."

There was more applause, until Cynthia gestured for quiet.

"I've known Billy Houston for nearly six years," she told the crowd. "I first read about the man and his exploits in building two businesses—both of which are now household names across America: The Tax Refund Shop, and Future Wealth. I took the time to meet him, and then undertook some research to see if his life was worthy of being told in a book. A year after that, Billy's book about his life—*Billy Houston Rags to Riches*—was published by my company, World Focus Publishing; and became one of the top-selling books in America. It's now being made into a movie."

She smiled proudly.

"Tonight, from ticket sales alone, we've raised over $800,000 dollars for the Phuket Drug Rehabilitation Centre—a group based in the jungles of Phuket who are helping people fight drug dependence—whether it be prescription drugs, alcohol, cocaine, heroin, meth or other addictive substances. Only last week, Billy was appointed to the board of that organization. The idea behind tonight's event was all Billy's. Given the alcohol issues he faced—and thankfully appears to have overcome—Billy wanted to reach out and help others, who might have faced similar demons as he did. Billy spoke in New York last week, Seattle tonight, and then he'll be speaking in Philadelphia, Chicago, Boston and Washington."

Cynthia raised her arms.

"Our goal is to raise over $4 million to help people around the world fight and beat drug dependence. If you'd like to make any personal donations, the details are on the screen behind me. Once again—let's show our gratitude to Billy Houston for sharing with us his story this evening, warts and all."

With that, I was pushed back on stage. Cynthia grabbed my hand and raised my arm skyward. The audience were now all standing, giving me a standing ovation—with many people still crying, tissues in their hands, wiping their faces.

"GREAT STUFF, BILLY," Pat slapped me on the shoulder.

"Empowering, Billy," Chook added. "I never realized the shit you've gone through. We were both up in the back, shedding a few tears."

"You want to come out with me and Chook," Pat asked. "Grab a bite to eat?"

"No thanks, guys," I appreciated their offer. "These talks take it out of me, both emotionally and physically. After the talk in New York last week, I hit the sack and slept for ten hours straight—which is unheard of for me."

Chook and Pat stayed back in my dressing room for twenty more minutes or so, as we reminisced about the old times. Neither were game to ask me what I had planned for the future. I *did* have a plan—but was in no hurry to tell anyone about it. Not yet anyway. I planned to get the next four talks out of the way, then perhaps I'd return to LA for a few days to catch up with my kids, Pat and Chook, and say a final goodbye as I entered the next chapter of my life.

There was one question I hadn't expected, though.

"Billy—do you know who Mr. X is?" Pat asked.

"Come on, Pat," Chook rolled his eyes. "You shouldn't ask him stuff about all that crap that went on. Billy told us all he knows tonight. We don't want him to relive it again, not here in this dressing room."

There was an awkward silence as I considered how I should respond. I could sense both Pat and Chook's unease at my silence.

Finally, I responded:

"Yes."

They both looked at me sharply.

"Yes," I repeated. "I think I do know who Mr. X is."

There was stunned silence. I leaned over and whispered to both Pat and Chook, so no one else in the room could hear what we were talking about.

"Pat—can you please do something for me?"

"Of course, Billy," Pat nodded. "You know I'll do anything for you."

"I want you to go and see your wife's cousin—that FBI agent, Fred. I want you to ask him if the FBI actually had you, Chook, and my kids under 24-hour surveillance when these crooks were trying to extort the money from me. They were threatening to kidnap and torture those closest to me if I didn't obey their demands, remember."

"Yes, sure thing, Billy—but who do you think Mr. X is?"

"I'll tell you when you get that piece of information to me," I said quietly. "I suggest you see your wife's cousin in person, rather than phone him. I also suggest you meet him in a public place—where there's less chance of your conversation being overheard or, for that matter, bugged."

Pat's face was pale. "Of course, Billy. I'll do that. I'll call you in the next day or so."

CHAPTER 31

"BILLY?" IT WAS Pat, calling me on my cell phone. "Like you asked me to, I met with Fred over coffee. I've just finished our meeting. He said he wasn't aware of any FBI surveillance on me, Chook, or your kids. He's going to check the official records when's he's back in the office today—which is probably illegal—but he'll call me this afternoon to confirm."

"Thanks, Pat," I said quietly. "Call me as soon as you know. I've just landed in Philadelphia for my next talk, tomorrow night." I paused. "Before you go, Pat—I have one more question for you. Did Ivan ever contact you? Wanting my private cell phone number? The number only you, Chook, my mum, and my kids had?"

Pat paused.

"Yeah," he finally answered. "Yeah, come to think of it, he did phone me wanting that number. It was just after you'd left a message on my phone saying you were off to Singapore for a while. It was when you actually went to Chiang Mai—before Mandy was kidnapped."

"Did he say why he wanted my private cell number?"

"He did. Said he'd been trying to call you on your business cell, but he'd got no answer. He had some important information he wanted to share with you, and he wanted to know if I had another number you could be contacted on. Because of who he was, I didn't think twice about giving him your private number." Pat paused. "Did he call you?"

"He didn't call personally," I breathed quietly, "but the criminals did. They phoned me on my private cell number. I've wondered for months how they got that number, given only a handful of people had it."

Pat's voice was low and serious. "Where's this leading, Billy?"

I murmured: "Wait till you get the information from Fred and I'll tell you where it's leading. Talk soon."

Two hours later

"BILLY?" IT WAS Pat again. "I just got off the phone with Fred. There's no record of any surveillance on any of us. He can guarantee there'd been no directive—from anyone, anywhere—to put any of us under FBI surveillance."

I was silent. This was exactly what I'd been afraid of.

"Billy, what does that mean?" Pat demanded. "Who is Mr. X, or 'Mr. Big'?"

I sighed heavily.

"It means, Pat, that Mr. X is Ivan Cameron."

Pat was as silent as I had been.

After a long, long interval, he breathed: "You're fucking *kidding me*? The guy from Interpol? Who came all the way over here to LA to interview me?"

"I'm not kidding you, Pat," I had a heavy heart. "I've played every day of my life over and over these last twelve months—every little event, in the back in my mind. I started to have my doubts about Ivan a month or so ago. Once I got off the grog, and my mind was functioning a little better without all that alcohol and stress, I got what you might call a 'gut' feeling, if you like. It had all been a bit weird, the way I'd met him and some of his team in the so-called Interpol office— which was unmarked, and apparently—in Ivan's own words—'off the grid'."

I lowered my voice.

"I've told no one this, Pat—not even Dr. Draper. When I first had these doubts about Ivan, I went back to the office where I'd first met him. Well, guess what, Pat? The whole floor of the so-called Interpol offices was vacant. All the furniture was gone—it was completely empty. I then went to the 'off the grid 'office. Same thing. The whole floor had been gutted. I reckon it was all just a set-up, Pat. Ivan was never part of Interpol. He's a fraud—it was a sting from day one."

Pat's voice was a croak.

"When did you last see Ivan?"

"He texted me about two months ago, to say they'd lost all trace of Mr. X and his thugs. He told me he was being transferred to another department, in another country, on a special engagement—that he'd be impossible to contact. He told me his team had been dismantled. I tried to phone him a few weeks ago—and guess what?"

"What, Billy?"

"His phone was disconnected. I still don't know how he hacked into my laptop, or how he found out about Code 8888, but hacking government computer systems—even with the most up-to-date firewalls—is a problem agencies face throughout the world. With enough money, anybody can buy their way in to the most secure systems and do anything. I'm sure with the right contacts, it's pretty easy to hack into any IT systems from anywhere in the world."

Pat exhaled loudly.

"Billy—you said he texted you to say his team had been dismantled. Maybe that's why the offices you'd met him at were closed."

"Nah, gut feeling, Pat. Ivan Cameron was an imposter. He was *pretending* to be an Interpol agent, and I fell for it. That's why he made certain the police were never involved in chasing down those thugs." I sighed. "Didn't you think it was strange, Pat, that he never had the police looking for Mandy? That he never got the police involved in the case at all?"

Pat admitted: "Yeah, that is strange. But how did he know my wife's cousin, Fred? He's a real FBI agent. It doesn't make sense, Billy."

"Google your name, Pat," I snorted bitterly. "There's an article about you—about the work you were doing with the FBI to clean up corporate America after the experience we'd both had with Roberts and

Carroll. There's a picture of you and three FBI agents. The article mentions that the person to your left, Fred Redpath, is your wife's cousin, and had been part of the FBI team working with you. Ivan pretended to be an Interpol agent and befriended Fred to give him credibility with me. It enabled me to become his puppet without me ever realizing it at the time."

Pat was silent for a second, before muttering: "But if Ivan's Mr. X, why wouldn't he have just told you to pay the thugs the $20 million? Why would he risk all that bloodshed by telling you not to give in to their demands?"

"I was puzzled about that too—until I did a little research into extortion and kidnapping cases in different countries throughout the world. Ninety-nine percent of the time, Pat, the authorities don't give into the demands of the criminals. They don't pay the money. Instead, they try and capture the thugs. To maintain his credibility, Ivan had to do what the authorities always do in extortion attempts—knowing full well he'd eventually get his twenty million."

"Holly shit," Pat breathed. "What do you plan to do now you know this, Billy?"

I sighed bitterly.

"Nothing, Pat—absolutely nothing. This whole series of events just about killed me. I don't want to relive it all over again."

"Why don't you go to the authorities and tell them everything you now know?"

"Pat—there's just so much corruption in this world. We saw it first-hand at Future Wealth, with Carroll and Roberts. Unfortunately, it's getting harder and harder to tell the good guys from the bad guys these days." I sighed. "I'm going to let sleeping dogs lie."

"I'll tell Fred. We can get the FBI onto Cameron."

"Pat, there hasn't been any crime committed on American soil. It's all outside their jurisdiction—and they're already under-resourced as it is, following up what they have to do in America. They don't have the jurisdiction or bandwidth to start worrying about something that happened in a foreign country, across the other side of the world, more than a year ago."

"Christ," Pat breathed. "Who'd have thought it… Ivan Cameron."

"Ivan Cameron is one very smart man," I reluctantly admitted. "Also, a very *dangerous* man." I glanced at my watch. "I've got to go, Pat. I need to get set up for tonight. Talk soon."

After I'd hung up, I reflected on my gut feeling—a feeling that had now been confirmed. Mr. X had been Ivan Cameron all along—the very same man who'd befriended me, and who'd told me to leave everything in his capable hands. He'd had me like a puppet on strings—with complete control of what I did, because he was playing both the good guy and the bad guy at the same time. As I've said before: Hindsight's a wonderful thing.

Whilst sitting in the back of the taxi, driving through the streets of Philadelphia, I thought about the advice Dr. Draper had recently given me. He'd told me I needed to find love—someone to care for me. Someone to cherish me. I had to stop running away from relationships.

I thought of Boonsri. That stunning, gorgeous, intelligent woman. I reckoned she might like living on the beach at Kamala. I smiled, looking down at my phone and thought about sending her a text message.

CHAPTER 32

Two years later

"AH, BILLY! IT'S after midnight here in LA. Why are you ringing me at this hour? What do you want?"

"Pat," I laughed. "Have I got a deal for us—a deal that's going to make us both lots and lots of money. Do you know, Pat, the next big thing in the world is going to be AI?"

"Billy, what the fuck is AI?"

"Artificial intelligence, Pat. You even went to a seminar in the States about it a few years ago. It's the next boom in the global economy—and I've worked out how you and I can be pioneers in the market and make a killing. An absolute *killing*, mate."

There was silence on the other end of the phone.

"Pat, are you there?" I demanded. "Are you there, mate? Have you hung up on me?

ABOUT THE AUTHOR

I was born and raised in Melbourne, Australia, and later moved to Noosa, Queensland, Australia, where I've lived for the past 28 years.

I commenced university in Melbourne, but after a horrific car accident—then being tied up at gunpoint by a man wielding a sawn-off shotgun—decided there was more to life than finishing my university degree.

I spent a few years travelling, doing odd jobs and I guess like many young people at the time, searching for the meaning of life.

At 27-years-old, I finally returned to university in Melbourne to complete my degree and commence a career in the accounting profession.

When I was 35, I opened an accounting firm in Noosa, Australia. I was the sole employee and started the firm with three clients. Fifteen years later, my accounting firm was listed by BRW magazine as one of the top 100 accounting firms in Australia by revenue and one of the top 10 fastest-growing accounting firms in Australia.

Whilst running the accounting firm, I established a surf clothing company with clothing retailers in Australia, New Zealand, Japan, and the United States of America stocking my clothing label. After operating for three years, with the global financial crisis upon us, I closed this business at considerable cost to myself and other investors.

I then commenced one of Australia's first franchised insurance businesses for insurance advisors. This business then morphed into an Australian Financial Services Licensee. With a lot of hard work, this business grew substantially over a six-year period to include over 300 licensed advisors and accountants throughout Australia.

The business won many national awards and was acknowledged as one of Australia's leading independently owned financial services licensees. In growing this business, I spent a lot of time living in hotel rooms, Monday to Friday, while traveling all across Australia, recruiting new advisors and accountants.

In June 2017, as the largest shareholder, the business was sold for $20 million AUS to a company listed on the Australian Stock Exchange.

In October 2017, I officially retired from corporate life.

I'm known in business circles as a successful entrepreneur. Most of my business ideas have come to me on my daily walks, when home, along Noosa Main Beach. I find the feel of sand under my feet, along with the sound of the ocean, aids my creative thought process.

I've always had an imagination, I'm full of ideas, and decided to write my first novel, *Billy Houston Rags to Riches* which was published in November 2018.

My second novel, *Billy Houston Fall from Grace* is the sequel to my first novel. Next year, I'll complete the third and final novel in the Billy Houston trilogy. The story line for this book came from my daily walks along the beaches of Noosa, Australia, and Koh Samui and Phuket, Thailand. It's a work of fiction—and all characters are products of my imagination.

It's a story of persistence, failure, greed, corruption, and lies—with murder and torture intermixed with mystery, success and, at times, laughter.

I now spend half my life in Noosa and the other half in Thailand, where I have a beautiful house on the beach in a small, lovely Thai community. A relaxed, stress-free, idyllic lifestyle.

People ask me what more can possibly happen to Billy Houston in the third book? Hasn't Billy endured enough? Well the plot for the third book is already ticking away in my mind. A few more walks along the beaches of Noosa and Phuket and I'll have the outline ready to go.

Between now and then, I've got a bit on my plate—as I head to Bangkok to build an online fitness, yoga and diet app designed for South East Asia - *à la* Billy Houston. Yep, perhaps there is a bit of Billy Houston in me.

No matter where you may be in life's journey, I hope you find Billy Houston an inspiration.

I hope you enjoy reading *Billy Houston Fall from Grace* as much as I enjoyed writing it.